Gamelord

Judge Vincent Hartington, finalizing his controversial report into the future of the football industry, is lured to a mysterious rendezvous at the Balham United ground and murderously assaulted. Attacked with him is DCI Taff Roberts, recently returned to the Yard to investigate Met corruption. The bedside plea from Isabel Hartington is for Taff to avenge her husband's injuries, which may well prove fatal.

The trail leads from United's manager, players and supporters, to the club's Gamelord chairman and his captivating mistress. With the help of an ex-girlfriend, TV Crime Reporter Kate Lewis, Taff's investigation widens to include a giant distilling company, a Cabinet-level politician and Special Branch. All too soon, the detective finds himself in the dog-eat-bloodhound John Stalker dilemma of being investigated by the Met.

Thanks to Kate, a vital witness is found, the action moving to a Munich international match for the first of several arrests, each leading Taff back to the formidable Gamelord. Yet, twist on twist, the dramatic climax to the investigation is radically different from the detective's expectations.

by the same author

AN ABUSE OF JUSTICE
RIOT
————————

THE FOURTH MONKEY

ROGER PARKES

Gamelord

COLLINS, 8 GRAFTON STREET, LONDON W1

William Collins Sons & Co. Ltd
London · Glasgow · Sydney · Auckland
Toronto · Johannesburg

First published 1990
© Roger Parkes 1990

British Library Cataloguing in Publication Data

Parkes, Roger, *1933–*
    Gamelord.—(Crime Club)
    I. Title
    823.914[F]

ISBN 0 00 232311 7

Photoset in Linotron Baskerville by
Rowland Phototypesetting Ltd
Bury St Edmunds, Suffolk
Printed in Great Britain by
William Collins Sons & Co. Ltd, Glasgow

To John Williams and Patrick Murphy
Also to Simon Inglis
with many thanks for
their abundant help

CHAPTER 1

Club chairman Ted Oxted bounded forward in the directors' box, his chant echoing the thousands of Balham United supporters massed below on the terraces and stands of the Bullring. 'Bully-Bully-BULL!!'

The winger's chip flicked over the Preston defence with cool precision to find striker Kennie Kent rising dolphin-like from his marker to head the ball into the top corner of the net. 'Bully-Bully-BULL!'

The Chairman swung back, thumbs aloft and laughing, while the kop-end errupted with howls and Kent disappeared beneath the embraces of his elated team-mates. Still laughing, Oxted goosed Patsy Craine, the tall blonde who for three years now had been his lady, then returned with a gesture of wry satisfaction to his guest.

'You get what you pay for,' he quipped. Kennie Kent had cost the club the season's highest transfer fee. 'His fifth in three games.'

'It was the winger's goal.'

'Aye, well, Len didn't come cheap neither. I've not built up the strongest attack in the League without a price-tag.'

His guest, a Queen's Bench judge called Vincent Hartington, nodded in silent irony, well aware of the Chairman's notorious extravagance with non-existent club funds, running United ever deeper into debt for the purchase of high-priced, selfish prima donnas like Kent. More, the Judge also knew what Chairman Oxted was *really* aiming for—that the club's crippling efforts to buy its way out of relegation down to the third division were merely strategic steps towards the ground's ultimate destiny as a hypermart and housing development. Well, time would tell on that count; battle would soon be joined over the Bullring's future.

'The survival of the game,' he remarked over the equally pricey champagne during half-time, 'must depend on a shift in attitude.'

'Oh yes?' Oxted snorted. 'A community sport appropriate to the Leisure Age, right? Well, I'm here to tell you, soccer's essentially a win-win macho sport. Kill the combat and the spirit of the terraces, and you'll kill off the game along with it.'

'Change its character, perhaps, but—'

'With respect, Your Honour, if that's what you're recommending in your inquiry report, you'll waste your time and effort.'

'In your view.'

'Happen I'm closer to Cabinet opinion than what you are.' The eyes had hardened in Oxted's deceptively boyish face. 'Cosmetics—that's all this inquiry of yours is about.' He snorted again. 'Be a miracle if you even get a change of face powder.'

'They should have half the divisional force here for a Littlewoods Cup match like this,' Detective Chief Inspector David Roberts remarked in the seating area directly below the directors' box. Involved as a rookie in policing numerous Swansea Town matches, Taff Roberts's attention was habitually drawn from the game to the state of the terraces. And in his view those Balham yobbos packing the lower-end kop merited maximum policing levels. One copper to every hundred fans simply wasn't enough.

'It's costing the club more than they can afford as it is,' Jack Walsh grunted, nodding at the ranks of coppers massed in their luminous-yellow traffic jackets around the terraces. 'When I was a woodentop, the line was thin, cheap and blue; now it's swollen like a sickly great banana butty.'

'It's swollen a whole lot more since the Hillsborough disaster,' Taff Roberts pointed out.

'And that hi-tech toy up there?' The retired Chief Super nodded up at the police helicopter hovering above the pitch. 'What the hell use is that thing?'

'PACE is the short answer to that,' Taff retorted, referring to the Police and Criminal Evidence Act. 'If you'd had all the evidence hassle we get in court these days, Guv'nor, you'd never have got away with half of those famous convictions of yours. That chopper's up there with a very powerful camera—same as these others mounted in the stands, only bigger. They're information-gathering, of course, but also for evidence-gathering.'

Foxy Walsh pulled a face, shaking his head in rejection. 'I still reckon they could do without the banana butty.'

'No way, Guv'nor. It just needs Preston to score and they'll be bulling all over the pitch.'

'Preston won't.'

'Could if they break through. The Herd's all attack and no defence.'

'Know why, don't you?' Walsh chuckled, his gaunt face creasing with irony. 'Teddy Oxted knows it's goals that make the best television. That's what the game's all about these days, so he's been paying out a fortune for scorers at the expense of the Herd's defence. Cunning sod.'

'It takes one to know one.' Taff Roberts grinned. In the years before Foxy Walsh's retirement from the Yard, he had shown Taff what career survival was all about. He had also taught him some less creditable tricks about corner-cutting and evidence-stacking; also, more valuably, he had schooled Taff in solid, painstaking detection, a vanishing craft among today's Yard yuppies.

'So what brings you back from your Thames Valley rustication?' Foxy asked with mock casualness. 'It couldn't possibly be linked to your sudden interest in the sport of plebs, could it?'

Blast, is there nothing escapes him, Taff thought. Sitting there in his fat security job in the City, his computer links stretching out like the scanes of a spider's web, prying and probing and plotting. 'Since you obviously know already, Guv'nor . . .'

'On my life, Taff boyo, nothing more than idle gossip how you and Chiefie Briggs are wearing Sox and snooping on the hooligan-snoops.' Then as Taff scowled in resentment: 'Seems to me you've taken on a distinctly thankless task, what with the collapse of all those high-cost prosecutions and recent appeals.'

Taff was saved further taunting on Operation Sox by

a roar from the upper-end kop reserved for the Preston supporters as the break indeed came, their winger gathering a loose ball for a wild run. He was chased to level with the box, then slipped it inside to the striker, who dodged the defence for what looked like a certainty—only to be grabbed and swung off balance as he went for the kill.

Preston's roar of rage was soon drowned by the Bully thunder of the Balham fans as their goalie crouched to face the penalty. Simultaneously a dozen of their fans directly behind the home goal started to swarm up the perimeter fence. Seeing them, Preston's striker paused to point in apparent objection before suddenly doing the business with a swinging drive, low and hard into the far corner of the net.

In seconds, Taff's prediction proved correct. The Bully fans scrambled en masse over the top of the perimeter fence to race on to the pitch in a raging tide, egged on by the deafening Bully chant from all sides. The massed police presence was quick to respond, mounted officers leading the force from the mid-field, while the television cameras swung as one to catch the ritualized rampage. Meanwhile, up in the directors' box, Chairman Oxted put on a show of embarrassed apology for his judicial guest while secretly glorying in the spectacle of his Bully lads once again brazenly 'steaming in'.

The Judge sighed as the 'phone intruded for the third time in an hour. He put down his pen and moved to where the instrument sat incongruously atop a splendid Louis Quinze bureau. 'Vincent Hartington speaking.'

There was a brief pause and then an indistinct mumble. 'Kindly speak up. It's a rather poor line.'

'Me again, sir . . . about the Bulls.' Although distinguishable, the words were oddly rushed and muffled. 'Photo evidence . . . an NF link.'

'Really?' Given the strength of the previous stuff he'd got from the informant, whoever he was, it could well be valid. 'Are you all right?'

'No, sir, not really. You'll have to collect it. The Bullring, soon as poss.'

'Hang it, man, you know I—' Hartington checked as the fellow rang off, frowning as he replaced the receiver.

'Not the mysterious Deep Throat again?' his wife asked from the study doorway. Isabel Hartington was tall and imposing and indefatigably academic: Bachelor of Arts, OU tutor, lay justice, viola-player, daughter of a law lord. Born out of her time. 'What's wrong?'

'For once he wants to meet.'

'Where?'

'At the ground. He sounded, well, scared, I suppose. Certainly rather odd, Tibs.' The Judge had searched out a phone number and now started to dial. 'He said he'd got hold of photographic evidence on the Front, though why he couldn't post it like before, I don't know.'

'The National Front? My goodness.' She shook her head. 'Vincent, don't go.'

'Not alone, that's for sure.' He made the connection and asked for extension 208, only to draw a blank.

'Sorry, sir, the CI asked for all calls to be stacked. Can I get him to call you back?'

The Judge gave his number, then rang off and moved to get his coat. 'I promise, no heroics,' he said, anticipating his wife's objection. 'Tell young Roberts I'll park outside the multi-storey near the club and wait for him to find me. Perhaps you'd confirm with me on the car phone once he's on his way. All right, Tibs?'

Isabel Hartington knew better than to argue. The combination of an Oxford rugby Blue and active service in the Guards had fuelled his confidence well into his sixties. He was still as decisive and self-assured as he was slim and agile.

Taff Roberts stared at the nervous young constable seated at the opposite side of the interview table, suspecting he was probably just another prat-brained victim of the Met. The biggest, richest force in the country, yet lurching from one hot-potato botch-up to the next, often induced by its chronic

11

PR paranoia. The pressures to boost their clear-up and conviction rates, Taff reflected, reduced them to the level of the Balham Bulls pulling endless tricks and professional fouls to fulfil Oxted's win-win imperative.

'You're not under caution, Smith, nor is this room wired. At this stage you may safely disregard the fact that my chief and I have power, under the terms of our internal inquiry, to initiate disciplinary and even criminal proceedings. Understood?'

'Sir.'

'Right, then.' Having established the mailed fist in the kid glove, Taff allowed DC Smith a thin smile. 'Informal, then.'

'Sir.' He was a burly, thick-necked, East Ender skinhead; a National Front clone and, as such, a dead ringer to infiltrate tough crews in the more notorious supporters clubs.

Taff paused, opening a file to consult case papers before launching in. 'The witness, an Old Bailey juror at an affray trial a few years ago, has testified how he was collared by two club supporters in a public-house toilet during a lunch-time adjournment. He claims they threatened him and his family with violence unless he voted to acquit all six defendants. Well?'

'Mind if I smoke, sir?'

'Not unless you want me to sue for exposure to pollution.'

'Sorry, sir.'

'In the event, the juror confided in his colleagues, several of whom promptly admitted to receiving similar threats. These were reported to the Judge, who, after suspending the trial in its twenty-fourth day, eventually decided it would be safe and proper to continue. In his summing-up, he explained to the jury how there was no evidence the threats had been made by people known to any of the six defendants and therefore they were totally irrelevant to any considerations of guilt or innocence. Pious hope. Not surprisingly, the jury convicted on all counts. Heavy sentences all round. A rare success among the numerous cases abandoned by the Crown Prosecution Service, which had just cleared some one hundred and twenty alleged football hooligans. Well?'

'Right, sir,' Smith nodded vigorously. 'Right.'

'What is?'

'Like, as you'll know, I was undercover on one of those cases the CPS threw out—that bloody no-no where we'd nailed three Arsenal crews.'

'And were doubtless left deeply embittered over it. All that risk and effort only to have the Crown refuse to prosecute.' Taff paused, staring dourly at the constable. 'Hence those threats in the case which succeeded, eh?'

'Sir?'

'The juror identified your mugshot, Smith, as one of the two men who threatened him in the pub toilet.'

Heavy pause. PC Smith must have known to expect it; even a rookie would have seen it coming. Yet he managed a creditable show of bewilderment.

'Several years ago and all but forgotten, eh, Smith? Just another dodge in the line of duty.' Pause. 'None of those jurors will have forgotten. Them and their families threatened with violence. You knew it was a pretence, but *they* didn't. Scared stiff by footsteps in a lonely street, or lying in bed at nights waiting for the firebomb through the window . . .'

'Only two, sir.' The lad was sweating now and sitting bolt upright, Taff noticed, like he was skewered end-on with a broomstick. 'We didn't have words with the other couple. Not with the two women jurors.'

It surprised Taff. He had assumed the stunt had been jacked up by one of the detective-sergeants on the affray case; yet, if so, the sergeant would have been careful to limit personal involvement to Smith and his partner. So who was it who'd threatened the two women jurors?

Smith shook his cropped head, reading the CI's surprise. 'See, Guv, we'd been on jury watch. We knew their yobby mates would likely try it on—try and nobble some of the jury. But then, after three weeks of watching the blokes in the jury, we figured maybe they'd targeted the birds instead.' He nodded, gesturing in solemn satisfaction. 'Sure enough, soon as we put the frighteners on the two Henrys in the pub toilet

13

and one of them coughed, a couple of the birds sung up and all.'

'So your actions were prompted by expediency,' Taff murmured in irony. 'Counter-insurgency to redress the balance of justice, eh?'

'Right, sir.' Smith nodded earnestly. 'Right.'

But no, not necessarily, Taff thought, because if I'd been into loading up the verdict like young Smithie here, I'd have cooked up precisely this same counter-nobbling yarn. The more years you serve and the more tricks you learn from the likes of old Chiefie Walsh, the harder it gets to believe any damned thing.

'It's the road to hell, Constable. The answer to *nothing*.'

'Just let 'em screw the system, sir?' Smith's jaw jutted in defiance. 'Just let 'em wave two fingers at justice?'

'Two fouls don't make a score, son.' Taff was speaking from bitter personal experience, too often waking in a cold sweat lately in grim recollection of the stunts he'd pulled in his last major case to try and nail a vile sex offender. 'All right, Constable, so you swung the jury to convict on that occasion, but now it's come back to haunt you.'

'Informal, you said!'

'Sure. But the fact is, I've got that juror's ID over you. Whatever way I choose to use it, it's still going to haunt you.'

He would have liked to tell Smith the circuitous route which had led to his haunting dilemma: the wily trial judge, suspecting police involvement behind the jury-nobbling ploy, had recounted his suspicions to a brother silk, Vincent Hartington, at an Inner Temple dinner. Hartington had referred it, along with several similar cases, to the Sox team to reopen the file. DCI Roberts had not, of course, told the juror witness that many of the mugshots he was showing him were undercover DCs deployed to infiltrate notorious supporter crews; moreover, when the witness cautiously identified Smith, Taff had reassured him there would be no risk of his having to swear to it in open court. The information and the ghost it raised for Smith were sufficient for now, thank you very much.

*

14

The telephone message was barely a quarter-hour old when Taff checked with the switchboard for calls. Before he could dial Hartington's number, however, his chief bustled in for a run-down on the session with DC Smith.

Chiefie Briggs had the heavy-set posture and bull neck of a rugby forward, the voice of a sergeant-major and the smile of a traffic warden. Taff was ambivalent about the man, suspecting that any misgivings about snooping on his fellow officers were outweighed by the recent promotion it had earned him.

'Well? Did Smith cough?'

'Not significantly, no, Guv'nor. Tacit admission only and with no names or backing.' Then, heading off his chief's comment: 'Best used solely as a lever to prise open rather bigger oysters.'

'Nobbling Bailey witnesses isn't big?'

'Counter-nobbling.' Taff shrugged. 'Redressing the balance of justice was how he saw it.'

'Damn it, Roberts, just because you were in the Met yourself, that's no call to condone jury-rigging.'

'I do *not* condone it—sir.' Taff could get Welsh-touchy over digs about his spell in the Met. 'But in view of the weakness of the evidence, our best deal is definitely to wait and use Smith later.'

'Deal, deal, deal! Met talk again. And don't you scowl at me, Roberts. We've been seconded for this inquiry to root out precisely the sort of sleazy, wheeler-dealer tactics you keep using! I know, I know: expediency for results, the *quid pro quo* and all that.' He shook his squat, shaggy head in rejection. 'We have to be above reproach, you and me, or we'll undermine our own integrity.'

'Sir, can we come back to this another time? I have to make an urgent call to our master.'

'You what?'

'To Judge Hartington.'

Curious the effect the old bloke had on him, Taff reflected, drumming impatiently on the steering-wheel in the inevitable traffic snarl-up round Westminster. His first im-

15

pression had definitely been that Hartington was a bit stiff and remote—not an easy man to chat to, no time for pleasantries, certainly not one for trading pints down the boozer. Yet now, after a month or so of liaising with him, Taff felt he was not so much aloof as shy—odd as that seemed in a man once notorious as a defence counsel and latterly imposing his authority day to day in court.

Nor, although this was the QC's first appointment to conduct a major judicial inquiry, was he cowed by the unusual task. On the contrary, from some of his remarks to Taff about his forthcoming report, he seemed about to emerge as something of a maverick. *Community, Roberts, that's the key word; the national game should relate to people, not market forces.*

The significant thing for Taff, however, was the way his contact with the Judge had resurrected his own onetime desire to study law. It was by no means unknown for police officers to read for the Bar, least of all officers of Welsh background; damn it, his own dad had attempted it before urging young David to become articled rather than joining the force. That Officer Roberts had later studied only sufficient law to get through his promotion exams had in fact been due less to work pressure than to cynicism: Taff's court experiences had disillusioned him over the extent of materialism and sharp practice, of fee-running and hypocrisy, among a legal fraternity pledged to uphold the principles of fair play. Yet the example of Vincent Hartington QC—his genuine concern for truth and justice, his independence from the Establishment despite his origins within it, his evident commitment to egalitarianism—were all prompting his Welsh protégé to think again.

At first, driving past the United's ground and its adjacent multi-storey car park, Taff feared the Judge had given up waiting. But then, driving back along the street, he located the man's grey Volvo estate discreetly parked at the top end.

'My apologies for whistling you out like this, Roberts.' The smile lighting his deep-set eyes belied the rather formal

16

tone of voice. 'In fact, it's more for my wife's peace of mind than my own.'

'No sweat, Your Honour.' Taff got in beside him, noticing from his tweed jacket and twills that he must have been working at home. Now that the evidence-gathering stage of his inquiry was complete, the Judge was into the final stage of drafting the report itself. 'What's the form?'

The QC started up and drove towards the multi-storey as he explained about the unusual request to come and collect photographic evidence.

'The fellow rang off before I could question him, but it sounds like evidence linking some of the Bulls' supporters and the National Front.' He gave a brief cackle. 'All rather cloak-and-dagger, ha.'

'But you've heard from this informant before?'

'Indeed, yes.' He repeated the laugh. 'My wife and I refer to him as Deep Throat. He's leaked me a lot of background on Oxted's more venal ambitions for the club. The ugly face of Capitalism again, I fear.'

Everything seemed very quiet as they turned in over the ramps. From the racy style of the dozen or so motors parked around the lower storey, Taff judged there must be a late first-team practice session underway. He pointed to a vacant bay near the lifts, then asked: 'Any idea who your Deep Throat really is?'

'We've never met before, as I say, but from the extent of the information he's sent me, he's privy to a lot of Oxted's secrets.'

'Also, from this latest call today, tuned in to supporters-club secrets.'

'So it would seem.' The Judge released his seat-belt, chuckling once again as he opened the driver's door. 'Right then, Roberts, you're in command now. How do we proceed?'

Taff started to tell him to wait while he had a quick scout around, but then he glimpsed a sudden movement to his left. As he turned round to check, he heard a strangled gasp beside him. Swinging back, he was shocked to see the Judge being dragged bodily out by a couple of masked figures. He made a futile grab to pull him back inside, then flung himself out of the passenger door to head round the further side.

They were waiting for him behind an adjacent concrete pillar—three burly figures, their faces similarly concealed in stocking-masks, and all apparently adept at the martial arts. Taff was floored in seconds. In falling, he managed to grab one of them by the leg, using it as a pivot to swing himself across and underneath the Volvo. Frantically he writhed across to roll out the further side. He managed to tackle one of the Judge's assailants, by chance hammering into the man's crutch. He heard the yell of agony a split second before the heavy Doc Marten boot crashed blindingly into his face.

Taff was only dimly aware of events after that—of movement and heavy thumps and of doggedly hanging on—until darkness finally engulfed his senses.

CHAPTER 2

News of the assault reached the ITN news room within an hour, details of both victims and of their injuries. The news editor punched up their respective library files on screen, then promptly sent for Crime Reporter Lewis.

'Special for you, Katie. Very special, assuming it's the same David Roberts you were snuggled up with a few years ago.'

He gave her the brief facts as supplied by their contact in the hospital's casualty department, noting her involuntary shudder and nodding in sympathy. 'It all sounds pretty savage, doesn't it. Sorry. How long since you were last in, er, contact?'

'With Taff? Well, he remembered my birthday—sent some flowers.' She sat down. 'He's been with the Thames Valley Force down at Marlbury since—well, ever since we broke up.'

'So you've no notion what he might have been doing here in town with Judge Hartington?'

18

'None. He was on indecency the last I heard. Nailed that bastard Snow, the Marlbury Menace, remember?'

'Of course, yes. That's a long way from football hooliganism.' Then, seeing her surprise, he added: 'That's what the worthy Judge is, or was, due to report on shortly. Since they were together, it could be that your Taffy's tied in with Hartington's inquiry. Assuming, of course, it's the same Roberts. Did you know he'd made it to chief inspector?'

'No, but it's on the cards. Taff's a high flier.' She stood up, restless now to get busy. 'I'll get at it.'

'I've scheduled a slot for the second part of Ten.'

The reporter paused a little way from the big circular news desk, head cocked as she eyed the editor. 'Knowing Taff, he'll thank us to keep his name out of it. OK?'

'Depends on whether the Beeb mention him.'

'Fair enough. But if they don't, neither do we, right?'

The news editor gave her a wry shrug, suspecting that, for all her professionalism, she was capable of blowing away the story for this particular fella. 'Katie, just so long as we get the *quid pro quo* from Romeo later on, OK?'

'Naturally, Lawrence, and screw you, too!'

She was on the move again now, merely nodding as he called after her: 'In any event, we'll run a piece on the Judge. Apparently, it's doubtful he'll come through surgery.'

'Just what exactly were you and His Honour doing down the Bullring together, Mr Roberts?'

Taff groaned and shook his head, avoiding eye contact with the local officer. It was a disquieting experience to be on the receiving end of an assault inquiry, let alone one being run by the Met. He decided to play for time—injury time, in fact, since he was still very much under treatment: awaiting various lab and X-ray results, and also mildly sedated for concussion.

'Listen, mate, I don't like hassling you like this, but any leads you can give us, the quicker we can get after them.'

Taff glanced around the casualty cubicle and wished they'd left him his clothes. He closed his eyes as another

19

wave of nausea surged inside him, wondering how much blood he'd lost on the car park floor. He opened his mouth, wincing at the stab of pain in his jaw. 'How—er, how is the old guy?'

'Still in surgery, but it's bad. Ruptured insides, they reckoned. So stop pissing about, will you.'

'They—all I can remember, they were geared up: stocking masks, bother boots, knuckle-dusters.'

'Wearing?'

'Denims, jeans, one in camouflage stuff, the usual kids' stuff.' The effort started him coughing again. He examined his sputum for blood and was relieved to find it clear.

'So they knew to expect you?'

Taff shrugged, then groaned again, his head lowered. He was reluctant to let on what little he knew, aware that it was anyway unlikely to lead to quick arrests. It was a relief to see the casualty officer lift the cubicle curtain, papers in his hand, his expression clouded with disapproval.

'We're nearly through, Doc.' The Met officer leaned closer, his voice lowered. 'Just tell me what you're doing off your patch, OK. You're a bloody long way from Marlbury.'

'DCS Briggs. Yard extension 8534. Now piss off and collar those animals.'

She was sitting bolt upright in the waiting area, a technical journal held high like a musical score in front of her. She wore gilt-framed bifocals and had her coat buttoned up to her throat as though to repel germs in the stuffy hospital air. Taff knew she must be Isabel Hartington because there was no one else around who would have been right for the old bloke. Yet she was not what he had expected from the voice on the phone: slimmer and less matronly. She looked younger, too; still in her fifties, he decided, and of a quite striking appearance: strong-featured, her fine eyes emphasized by high cheekbones and well-balanced chin.

Taff eased painfully down on to the seat beside her and waited for her to look up. Then he noticed the journal was upside down and, glancing at her eyes, saw their puffiness magnified by her glasses.

20

'Mr Roberts?' she asked, registering his glance, only to react in shock as she saw the ugly swelling and inflammation disfiguring his face. 'Dear God, their savagery.'

'It looks worse than it feels—at least at the moment.' He had his clothes back on now and the medic's reading of the X-rays still warm in his ears: no visible jaw or facebone fractures; we'd prefer to avoid strapping up those broken ribs, but if you insist on playing action man we've no alternative; keep a close eye on your stools, urine and sputum; ideally, you should have been off work for at least a week, so don't say you haven't been warned, Mr Lucky.

'I wish to God your husband had fared so lightly.'

'Yes, well, it can't be much longer before we know the score.' She managed to keep her voice controlled and steady, like the journal still held there for effect. 'Not much longer.'

'I—Mrs Hartington, I'm extremely sorry.'

'What on earth for? I'm sure you did your best.'

'Not best enough, though, was it.' Then, heading off her retort: 'Like, if I'd thought to warn him, told him to keep the driver's door locked . . . It was just, damn it to hell, all so bloody unexpected!' He shook his head, reaction and shock starting to penetrate the sedation. 'I'm sorry. Damned sorry.'

She touched him lightly on the hand, shaking her head in rejection. 'How much did he tell you?'

'Beforehand? Not a lot. Had this call from an informant to collect something to do with the National Front. Anything you can add to that?'

She shook her head, frowning in forced recollection. 'Only that Vincent said the man, Deep Throat he used to call him, sounded pretty scared.' Then, abruptly bitter: 'Typical of him! Typical. Reckless idiot!'

Taff shook his head but was spared finding a reply by the arrival of the surgeon, gown and skullcap still on, face-mask pulled down below his mouth, his chubby face furrowed with concern.

'They've just taken him along to intensive care, Mrs Hartington. You'll be able to take a look at him shortly.'

21

She was standing now, tall and erect, braced in anticipation as she stared at him. 'Go on, please.'

'You see, a lot will depend on whether his condition stabilizes . . . also, the extent of the damage to his liver— whether there's impaired function beyond what we found in theatre. Also . . .'

'Well?'

'He took a massive blow on the head. Skull fracture would seem inevitable. You see, in a man of his years, well, it's . . .'

'It's what, please?'

'One shouldn't be too optimistic, Mrs Hartington.'

'Impaired brain function, you mean?' Her voice had a flatness of tone like words repeated over and over in a dream. 'Disablement?'

'That—yes, one has to concede that possibility.' Then, his hands raised: 'Possible, not probable. But further than that, I simply cannot predict.' He glanced round as a theatre sister whisked up to murmur a cryptic message, then turned in apology. 'Time, Mrs Hartington, time will tell. At least he's alive.'

'The question,' she whispered, her eyes on the surgeon as he hurried back to the casualty theatre, 'is whether it's what *he*'d call living.'

'An endorsement,' she remarked after a long silence, her eyes fixed on the mass of tubes and leads connecting her husband to the monitors, 'that's what they're looking for in this report of his: confirmation of Cabinet policy, approval for their Draconian efforts to curb hooliganism, approval of saturation-policing methods, support for the *status quo* and all those ugly market forces they keep on about.'

'But no such luck, I gather.' Taff had the uneasy feeling she was leading up to some sort of a pledge. 'His Honour's refusing to play ball.'

'He told you that?' Then, when Taff nodded: 'I wonder who else he told.' She pointed at the wavering oscilloscope registering her husband's frail hold on life. 'Maybe we wouldn't be watching that blessed line now if he'd just kept it to himself.'

'Hey now, hang on . . .'

'You, Chief Inspector. It's got to be your investigation.'

'*Mine?*'

'The Met—' She shook her head. 'No, not just the Met; it's the whole police hierarchy. They'll resist his proposals to the bitter end. You know that. You've done match duty; you know the thrill of it. He said you'd mentioned that to him. But of course, it's far, far more than just the excitement; it's status, it's manning levels and overtime, it's the whole power ethos, it's—'

'You're suggesting,' he cut in, 'that they'd prejudice the assault investigation out of misgivings about what's in his report? Come on, now.'

'What I'm saying is that the chances of impartiality are, to say the least, slender.' Then, over-riding Taff's protest: 'That's the reason I told that local DCI nothing about why you and Vincent were there at the ground. And it's why I shall continue to tell him nothing.'

'Mrs Hartington . . .'

'It's got to be you! For God's sake, you heard that blessed surgeon: Vincent's virtually dead! It's *de facto* murder!' Then, increasingly shrill as she pointed at him: 'Just now you apologized. Very well, this is your chance to make amends—to purge whatever it is you're feeling guilty about!'

The control was still there, Taff reflected. However influenced by grief and hysteria, her mind remained needle-sharp—unlike his own increasingly befuddled, throbbing skull.

'Mrs Hartington, there's no way on this earth they'd ever approve it.'

'I have influence . . .'

'Not even if you were the Lord Chancellor's daughter and sister to the Attorney General. No chance.'

It was still no more than mid-evening when Taff found a phone in the hospital and contacted Chiefie Briggs at his lodgings. It came as little surprise that the man already knew.

23

'I've had some pushy DCI called Lawley on from O Division asking chapter and verse.'

'Sorry, Guv'nor. How much did you tell him?'

'No more than the usual. Enough to confirm your *bona fides* but no more. Why?'

'What about my liaising with the Judge?'

'I hedged on that.' He cleared his throat. 'Well, not being in full possession of the facts, it seemed prudent.'

Taff grinned. Cagey old Briggs. 'Thanks, Guv.'

'Don't thank me, just tell me what the hell's going on!'

'I wish I knew.'

'Listen, Roberts, that DCI was in a mood to pull rank. If I get the brass on to me tomorrow, I'll have to cough up some answers. Now let's have it.'

Taff told him the bare facts—the Judge contacted by his mystery informant, then their vicious welcome in the multi-storey and the resulting fears for the Judge's survival.

'So it could turn into a murder job.'

'Likely, yes, but until it does . . .'

'What, Roberts? Bloody what?'

'There's more to it, you see. Background stuff from his wife. It's too sensitive to explain right now. All I'm asking is that you stall the brass till I've seen you in the morning. OK?'

There was a pause, Briggs's chesty breathing clearly audible before: 'Naturally, you can justify this request in respect of Operation Sox?'

'Naturally, sir.' The nausea was surging up again. He groaned, doubling forward to keep from fainting before at last muttering an apology. 'The aggro's catching up with me a bit, Guv'nor.'

'That DCI said you were in pretty poor shape. Be off sick for a while, he reckoned.'

'In an ideal world, yes, sir. I'll see you in the morning.'

Taff Roberts found the address off Kensington High Street in one of those modern blocks of flats designed for modern people—no frills, no distinctive features, no character—as bland as the young woman who eventually let him in. She

24

had kept the door on the chain as she peeped out in answer to his knock. Seeing his mutilated face, she had at first slammed the door closed again, only reluctantly reopening it enough for him to slide in his warrant card.

This call had been Taff's one concession to Isabel Hartington's plea that he investigate. She had given him the address of Vincent's secretary, urging him there on his way home from the hospital so as to be sure of getting copies of the Judge's notes and half-drafted report.

Taff had met Virginia Cohen once before at Hartington's chambers, registering her as somewhat dressed-up and plummy-voiced. But here at home, with her hair in curlers, wearing a housecoat and minus the fancy spectacles, she looked about as different as Taff now did with his face job.

'You look in a fearful state. Can I get you anything? Come and sit down.'

'Sorry, Miss Cohen, I should have phoned to forewarn you.'

'What's happened? What's it all about? Something to do with the Judge, is it?'

'I'm afraid so, yes. He's in Balham Infirmary grievously ill.'

He was watching for a reaction, of course, but hadn't expected quite such extreme shock, the colour draining from her face as she tottered back on to a chair, hands clasped over her mouth to stare at him in muted anguish. Surely, he thought, glancing round at the chintzy furnishings and yuppy colour scheme—surely old Vincent wasn't into a ding-dong on the quiet? Maybe the young woman simply had a fixation about her boss, adoring him as an austere but dependable father-figure.

Virginia continued to stare as he crossed to pour her a glass of mineral water from the sideboard, meanwhile explaining about the surprise assault in the car park. He refrained from giving details of the rendezvous.

'Why, Chief Inspector? Why would anyone . . .?'

'I was hoping you might have some suggestions.'

'Me?' She gulped the water, her colour if anything even paler. 'Why should I?'

25

'Working so closely with him, I thought you might know if he had enemies.' Then, when she stared, shaking her head in bemusement: 'Someone set him up for this assault, Miss Cohen. Someone with a pretty heavy motive.'

The secretary was still shaking her head, but now in denial. 'Not unless it's revenge from the past.' She grimaced in rejection. 'That's an awful cliché, I know: some villain he'd once sentenced to life and now coming after him.'

'Given the place and circumstances, Miss Cohen, I think we can assume it's related to this football inquiry of his.' It was definitely not what she wanted to hear. 'You, being as familiar with the work as anyone, might be able to come up with some clue. Think on it, at least.' He nodded, eyeing the bottle of malt whisky beside the mineral water and wishing the casualty doctor hadn't vetoed alcohol. 'Meanwhile, I'd be obliged if you could let me have copies of all your notes and all records relating to the inquiry.'

'I've nothing here.' It was stated quite sharply, almost like a denial of guilt. 'Nothing. It's all at chambers.'

'Fair enough. First thing in the morning.'

'It'll take quite a lot of copying.'

'Then the earlier you can start the better. I'll call in about nine-thirty.'

'Eleven would be more realistic.'

'Nine-thirty,' Taff repeated, anxious to stay ahead of DCI Lawley. 'With an assault of this savagery, anything's realistic.'

In the early days of Sox, because he regarded their liaison with the Judge as highly irregular, Chiefie Briggs had ordered Taff to wear a wire to record their meetings. In the event, it had proved unnecessary because at the outset Vincent Hartington had suggested they record what was said on tape. Years of elaborate note-taking in court, he claimed, had undermined his memory faculties—an excuse Taff came increasingly to doubt since the old silk seemed to have total recall.

Now, returning to the high-priced box advertised as a most desirable, centrally-situated, self-contained Edward-ian bed-sit, Taff sorted through the tapes, checking them against his own brief notes until he found the one where he and the Judge had touched on politics, discussing the so-called Yob Society, the reputed rampages of the lager louts and the explosion of Saturday-night violence in the shire towns.

He took the tape-player into the cupboard-like bathroom, switching it on while he stripped off and then, careful to keep his chest-strapping dry, lowered himself gingerly into the bath.

'Is it real, Roberts?' the Judge's voice asked gently in his ear. 'Is there really an epidemic of drunkenness and yob violence?'

'There's no shortage of coppers who'll show you real bruises received in the line of Saturday-night duties.'

'No doubt, no doubt. But are there really that many more bruises, *pro rata*, than before? Surely there's always been a yob element ready to have a go once they're—what's the mod phrase?—once they're tanked up? Youth's natural aggression finding an outlet and so on. Dash it, I remember times as an undergraduate when our behaviour was severely wanting. You, too, I dare say. All right, I acknowledge today's youngsters often tend to have more cash to throw away on drink than hitherto. Moreover, in relative terms, the blasted stuff's far cheaper and more accessible now than before. I dare say both those factors may make for rather less restrained drinking than before. But is it really this "explosion of yob violence" we're being told is happening? I just wonder about that.'

'The statistics would seem to verify it, sir.'

'Ah, but look where those statistics originate. From you chaps, Roberts, from the police. Charging rates, prosecutions. But I can't help wondering how much those statistics might be influenced from on high. The word goes out from the Home Office mandarins to the Chief Constables to crack down on the lager louts. You've been given the powers under this latest Public Order Act; now then, set to and use those powers. Add to that an escalation of tension stimulated by the media—sensationalist television and press coverage focusing on drunken disorders everywhere from the football terraces to the Wokingham market-place—and naturally the arrest and prosecution rates shoot up in response. Instant statistics, Roberts, to verify the myth.'

'You—er—you think the media are party to it? Letting themselves be used as part of a deliberate hype?'

'Hype. Now there's a mod word to play with. Well, I'll tell you, one of the television producers my wife works with from time to time was vocal on just that issue. She said there was nothing official, of course: the word passed quietly along from the politicians' aides to the programme policy-makers, the current-affairs producers and so on. And suddenly, lo and behold, the evolution of the Yob Society, along with handy supporting statistics from the forces of law and order.'

'But why, Your Honour? Where's the political gain? The present government campaigned on a law-and-order ticket, so surely the lager-lout disorders in the shire towns represent failure.'

'None the less, Roberts, the impression of a divided society will carry far more clout at the next election. The Scare Vote. Vicious black muggers running riot on the underground, Scargill's miners and the Wappingites on the rampage, thicky lager-louts bringing anarchy to the High Streets, football hooligans terrorizing whole trains and ferries and shaming the Flag in Europe. Vote for the party that will flood the streets with police, build more prisons, crack down on riotous assembly, meet the challenge of rampant disorder and . . .'

Taff switched off the tape, grunting in irritation as persistent ringing of the door-bell penetrated the bathroom. He hauled himself up, leaning over to yell across the sitting-room.

'Just a second! In the bath!'

'Great.' The answering female voice was light with laughter and disconcertingly familiar. 'Stay naked, why not?'

The recognition of her voice hit him with no less force than the pounding he'd taken just a few hours before in the car park.

'Which is it then,' he called out as he limped across, tying the bath-wrap prior to opening the door, 'Kathy or Kate?'

It had been the difference between the two which had forced their split three years earlier—Kathy, the warm and human and latently maternal, versus Kate, the shrewd and talented and ruthless. Both dwelt inside her behind the lean, pointed face and slanting feline eyes; yet it had taken her affair with Taff Roberts to lure Kathy briefly to prominence. And, ironically, it had taken an unforeseen pregnancy to force her away again. The pregnancy had been soon terminated, yet the hurt of it lingered still.

She chose not to answer his question, knowing he'd prefer her to be Kathy. And then, by the time he'd got the door open and she saw the ghastly trademark they'd stamped across his face—normally so dishy with that shy, self-effacing smile guaranteed to charm even the robustly independent Kate—by then she could manage no more than a shocked gasp.

'Hey now, come on. It's still your old Taff behind the mask.' He squeezed her hand but refrained from the kiss he'd have preferred. Although he watched her regularly enough on the Box, it was far more of a turn-on to see her for real. 'You're like a fine wine, you know, girl, improving with the years.'

'Well, thankee kindly, sir, said she, her blush as ripe as haw-berry.'

Laughing together, it was almost as if the harsh words of three years back might be unsaid; yet the trauma of the abortion hung like a remorseless shadow between them. For Taff, it had seemed a rather fitting irony that, seeking refuge in the Thames Valley Force, he had been landed with running the indecency unit in Marlbury. Intimate witness of new-town sexual perversions had served effectively to put on ice any desires Inspector David Roberts might have had to establish intimate relations elsewhere. Three shell-shocked years of celibacy for the Monk of Marlbury!

'So what's the prognosis, Taff? It can't be as dire as it looks, seeing as the medics let you home.'

He contrived a lop-sided grin, pouring her a drink as he

explained how the doctor had wanted to keep him in for observation and, worse, that he'd have to miss out on bar-sports and aerobics for the rest of the month. 'Light duties only for the while; no paramilitary ops or grade-one interrogations.'

'Is that what you're doing back with the Met?' she asked, knowing it was no use tiptoeing around. 'Paramilitary body-guard duty on Queen's Bench judges?'

'If so, I'd hardly have earned a medal this evening.' He shook his head, regretting the bitterness. 'How come you people found out so quickly anyway?'

'Us people have bugs in every casualty department in town.'

'Really?' He eyed her, wondering at just what level of trust they were going to resume relations. 'Must be very well-paid bugs to risk supplying patients' bed-sit addresses.'

'You pay rent for this?' she laughed. 'I thought it must be a squat.'

'Don't duck the question, Kate Lewis.' Given the covert status of Sox, he kept this address largely secret, having indeed concealed it earlier from the hospital people. 'How come you managed to find me?'

She grinned, meeting what was visible of his eyes above the swollen cheeks. 'Have a guess.'

'I don't believe it—not Foxy Walsh!'

'Lover, I cannot tell a lie,' she confirmed, nodding in irony.

'Talk about an unholy alliance.' Her acquaintance with Walsh had been forged in the flames of contempt such as only an old-guard Yard chiefie could have for a brazen press hound; yet here she was now worming Taff's secret address out of him. 'Amazing how being in filthy Commerce corrupts people.'

'Nonsense, Taff, he's just a chronic romantic.'

Which, oddly enough, Taff thought, could well be truer than she realized, given his own improbable father–son relationship with the man.

'Of course, I know better than to ask how it was you and the Judge came to be pulverized together.' She paused, unsure whether the distortion of his swollen face was grin or grimace. 'However, just to start building up a *quid* fund, I persuaded Lawrence to exclude you from the piece on tonight's News. Fortunately for you, the Beeb don't appear to share our casualty bug. So for the time being, your incognito's safe in my frail hands.'

It came both as a relief and a surprise—a *quid* not to be disregarded. 'Thanks, Kate. Did you by any chance speak to a certain cocky DCI Lawley on the assault investigation?'

'No such luck. The divisional press office wouldn't even give out his name. They're playing it all very close to the chest as yet.'

'Right.' He nodded. 'Which means they haven't got any worthwhile leads yet.'

'Does that surprise you?'

'Stop fishing, girl.'

She spread her hands in exaggerated denial, laughing in self-mockery. 'Innocent, Officer, on my life!' Then, in a final attempt, she asked: 'Come on, Taff, you weren't there by chance this evening, so what's the score?'

He leaned across to give her cheek a teasing pat. 'Same deal as we had on the prison-riot story, OK? Mutual trust and mutual aid; you'll get the exclusive, but on my terms. OK?'

'You're on.' She grinned, taking his hand and placing it back on her cheek as she asked: 'What about the other part of that deal?'

The gesture got to him. For all the bruised and broken state of his body, it sent a tingle of desire pulsing through him, damn and blast her.

'You're a witch, you know that.' He handed her the glass to finish, then moved to open the door for her to leave as he added: 'I was only a spit away from intensive care this evening. Give me some rest and then we'll see about resumption of normal services.'

The brief report on *News at Ten* had brought a spate of calls to the hospital, mostly from news reporters, others from close acquaintances of the Judge. The receptionist logged each one, noting name and particulars before then reading out the prepared bulletin on Hartington's condition.

There was one exception, which the receptionist eventually put on hold while she contacted the intensive-care sister. 'A Mrs Patricia Johns claims she's the patient's daughter. She sounds genuinely distressed.'

'Put her through, then.' Pause. 'Hello, Mrs Johns, I'm afraid we persuaded your mother to get some rest.'

'I just—' there was no doubting the depth of anxiety— 'my mother wouldn't have known where to contact me. The TV report said severely injured—surgery and intensive care. How bad is he, in fact? I mean, how serious?'

'There really is nothing I can add to what the receptionist has already told you, Mrs Johns. I'm sorry. If you leave your number I'll give it to your mother when she wakes up.'

'Just—just tell her I'll be at home, thank you.'

The sister rang off, puzzled that although Mrs Hartington had earlier phoned some members of the family, she had omitted the daughter. It could, of course, have been a reporter trying it on, yet if so, the pretence of distress had been most convincingly done.

CHAPTER 3

'It's vital that officers of your calibre, Roberts, no matter how isolated or even disillusioned you may feel, should none the less remain in the Force.'

Taff had the tape running in the car now, this time creeping his way towards the Temple and his 9.30 appointment with Miss Cohen.

'Disillusioned, Your Honour?'

'For one thing, seeing the Force increasingly suborned as an arm of Government policy. No, no—don't comment, please. Undiplomatic of me to expect you to answer that on tape. However, the way I see it, the combination of the Police and Criminal Evidence Act and the Public Order

Act was a tacit sell-out by the police hierarchy. Legislate us the powers and we'll see that your policies are enforced. Scargill and Wapping, the Scare Vote hype, any number of discreet enforcement favours. Not pleasant for clear-sighted democrats like yourself, Roberts, to feel you may be serving the wrong master—answering less and less to the People and increasingly to the Party.'

'Diplomacy, as you say, sir.' Yet Taff well remembered the nod and the wink he'd added in agreement while saying that.

'But the cost, the cost to society as well as to the Force. Loss of public confidence, loss of the Bobby image; seen instead as faceless riot-control officers. Juggling statistics and clear-up rates the way executives juggle their tax returns and fiddle their expenses. Meanwhile everyone sinking into the have-have, grab-grab, greed-driven society. And no wonder, eh, the example we're being set from the top. But the point, Roberts, the crucial point is that if men of integrity and good faith like yourself decide you can't stomach it and throw in your hands, well then, God help us all. Then the politicos will have won and the rest of us will be immeasurably the losers.'

Longish pause on the tape, during which Taff could recall his discomfort in face of the Judge's expectant gaze. Finally: 'Assuming you were right about my deciding to stay on, sir, don't forget the promotion factor. The brass who've sold out to get to the top aren't the types to wish senior promotion on officers of, as you put it, integrity and good faith. It's unfortunate but surely it's a case of Sod's Law: If you can't join it, quit it.'

Not that Taff had given the issue of quitting a great deal of thought until that particular conversation. It was only afterwards that the force of the Judge's misgivings had fermented in his mind—along with Hartington's subsequent retort: 'Of course, Chief Inspector, promotion to the higher levels of the Force, commander and above, traditionally depends on Establishment patronage. Now I'm not saying the patronage of this particular Queen's Bench judge will carry that much weight, ha, not after

I've whacked in this rogue report of mine. But it's perhaps a credit for you to weigh against this, er, Sod's Law of yours, ha.'

Hartington's chambers were located up an arched-stone stairway in one of the older Inns. The oak panelling in the rooms all looked original, as did much of the period furniture. A shame they couldn't have found a walnut-veneered word processor to go on Virginia Cohen's desk.

The emotional strain was visible in her face despite her office make-up, fancy spectacles and executive outfit. She'd been at the office since well before eight, she explained, and precious little sleep during the night.

'You and me both, Miss Cohen.'

'Looking at the state of your face, you shouldn't be up and about at all.'

From all the aches and pains and delayed shock when trying to mobilize his strength first thing, Taff would heartily have agreed with her. Yet he had known of old that action was the best therapy. Time off to nurse a cold was the surest path to 'flu; resting merely stiffened the muscles and slowed the bowels.

'Did you manage the copying?'

She gave a tight smile, indicating a large envelope and a floppy disk. 'The confidentiality aspect worries me, I'm afraid.'

'How do you mean?'

'Much of this evidence is privileged. However, given that you've been liaising with His Honour, I suppose . . .' She trailed to silence in anticipation of his reassurance. He nodded, forcing the semblance of a smile, but then warned her that the same discretion might not apply to Chief Inspector Lawley. Not unnaturally, that confused her.

'I'm not suggesting you should be anything but co-operative with DCI Lawley. However, since he won't know about the existence of this privileged evidence, I think you can safely leave that side to me.'

'Yes. Good. Er, I'm sorry, Mr Roberts, but just which of you is investigating what?'

Taff wagged his head, aware he was walking a delicate line. 'You know about Sox. My interest lies in how the assault on the Judge and myself might be related to Sox.' He picked up the envelope and computer disk. 'Hence my need to check through these for any connection. DCI Lawley, assuming he questions you at all, is interested solely in collaring those vicious thugs who put in the boot last night. OK?'

Her nod was automatic rather than comprehending. It didn't make her any the happier when he added: 'As you know, Sox is a covert operation, involving the internal investigation of serving officers. So I'd be obliged if you'd extend the privileged status to this visit also. All right, Miss Cohen?'

'You mean, conceal it from him?'

Taff wagged his head, repeating his mangled smile. 'I wouldn't want to compromise you. All I'd suggest is that you don't mention anything about seeing me unless he asks.'

Deeper and deeper in, he thought, eyeing the envelope beside him on the passenger seat as he drove along the Embankment towards the inevitable set-to with his chief. You're letting yourself be drawn in like the proverbial moth. And why? Because you really believe all that spiel Madam gave you about police partiality over her husband's report? Or because of a hard core of tiresome old Welsh-Roberts guilt at having failed the old bloke? The latter was certainly there, gnawing away inside him just as painfully as the ache across his damaged chest and face. But the former? The misgivings that had long festered inside him about just how far to trust his brethren in the Met? Oh diawl!

The Sox offices, although linked to the Scotland Yard switchboard and computer network, were situated in one of the annexes off Caxton Street. Taff managed to reach his desk and get the disk up on his screen for long enough to establish that it was Hartington's largely completed report. He had barely started scrolling through the first file, however, when Briggs came bustling through from the inner office.

To his credit, his first concern was for his assistant's impaired state of health. 'Pointless to play the bloody hero, Roberts. Standing orders are fully clear on duty procedures regarding personal injury.'

'Appreciated, sir. None the less, it lies with me to interpret my own state of fitness.'

'Stubborn sod, aren't you. Well, just don't go filling yourself up with painkillers and driving off the bloody road.' He grunted in dismissal of Taff's reply, instead pointing at the screen. 'What's all this lot?'

His scowl deepened at Taff's explanation, the chief promptly snatching up the envelope and sifting through the copied evidence statements inside. He got even more twitchy when Taff outlined his advice to Virginia Cohen on how to deal with DCI Lawley.

'God in heaven, man, inciting obstruction! You suffering from acute concussion or what?'

'With respect, sir, I believe I'm acting well within the scope of our authority under Sox.' It wasn't going to be easy persuading the man, of course, but at least he'd had some time to rehearse his case in advance. He began by listing Isabel Hartington's misgivings about Met prejudice and her insistence on cooperating only with an investigation run by Sox. Next he stressed his own involvement and the fact that the Judge had already briefed him in advance of the assault. 'I can't prove that the two are linked, sir, but there's a clear circumstantial tie-up. So it follows it's legitimate under our Sox remit. And that in itself allows us discretion about just how openly or covertly we proceed.'

Taff could guess what was going through the Briggs brain during the ensuing pause: he was sniffing at it from all angles to see what if any career risk might be involved and what possible compromises he could find. And why not? He had a wife and teenagers and three cars to support.

'I suppose,' he grunted dourly, 'I can hardly forbid you from investigating an assault on yourself. But that doesn't give you the right to charge around obstructing that divisional DCI.'

36

'With respect, sir,' Taff repeated blandly, 'accepting that it's within the scope of Sox, then the same procedural freedom must apply. Covert if necessary.'

'It's your choice,' his chief snapped. 'Either you're on sick leave and it's unofficial, or you pursue it under Sox and you keep me fully informed of developments.' He bared his ursine teeth in a grin. 'Can't ask for fairer than that, can you, son?'

'I'll give it some thought, Guv'nor.'

'You do that.' He shuffled across to his office, then paused, just as Taff had expected he would, to add his insurance cover. 'If you choose the Sox option, I reckon I'll have to clear it upstairs. No, obviously I don't mean with the Yard. But certainly the Thames Valley nobs.'

The Judge's conclusions at the end of the inquiry report, although they were of little surprise to Taff, would certainly make sour reading to Cabinet hardliners hoping for an endorsement of government policy on football.

In the event, Hartington had started with the sugar on the pill with proposals to foster more women's teams, the use of women as club officials, touch judges and so forth, also a proper Women's League, akin to those in Germany, Scandinavia and, of all macho places, Italy.

Then, with all the meticulous clarity, fairness and balance of a trial summary, the old silk had laid out his case for what amounted to the partial nationalization—what he called 'socialization'—of the national game. The blame for all the worser ills of the sport—not just the rampant hooliganism but the insolvency and ageing stadiums, most of the mass fatal disasters and also the decline in on-pitch sportsmanship—were laid squarely at the door of club private-ownership. Conversely, the solution for all these ills—as exemplified in clubs such as Preston, Halifax, and even Millwall—lay in boardroom partnerships with local councils. By thus obliging clubs to open their doors to the local community in return for ratepayer funding, Hartington foresaw that the age-old traditions of macho, inter-tribal warfare and win-win aggression could at last be purged.

37

As community clubs with all-weather pitches, facilities would become available to all, young and old, rich and poor, male *and* female. This, he claimed, would break the exclusive cliquiness common to many clubs, replacing it with a spirit of openness and participation. This, as the experience of Preston and Halifax and to some extent Millwall had shown, would open the way to self-discipline and harmony on the terraces—through self-stewarding, removal of crowd barriers, huge cuts in policing levels and so on—in essence, the civilizing process so vital for the game's survival.

While conceding that this might be in conflict with the principles of private enterprise, the Judge pointed out that the sport was anyway heavily in violation of that since eighty-five per cent of all League clubs were already trading in insolvency. As such, their very existence was technically illegal. Moreover, the onset of the Leisure Age was arguably a social development destined to supersede the interests of market forces and League-club shareholders.

So much for the old chap's conclusions, Taff thought as he wiped them from the screen. But can the hundreds of pages of evidence and findings in the body of the report fully justify them?

By amazing good luck, at her third time of phoning the divisional station, the switchboard connected Kate Lewis straight through to DCI Lawley. The moment he realized she was the ITN Kate Lewis, however, her luck ran out with a curt referral to the press officer.

'One question first, Miss Lewis: exactly who was it gave you my name?'

'One question for you before I answer, OK? Is it true that the Judge wasn't alone? That he was accompanied by a police officer?'

'If that had been the case, miss, his assailants wouldn't have stood a prayer. Now you answer.'

'Only if you'll meet me down the nearest boozer.'

At which, surprise of the week, Lawley muttered a quaint Cockney epithet and hung up on her. Kate crossed his name off her list then dialled the number against the next name. 'Miss Virginia Cohen, please.'

'Speaking.'

Kate identified herself, then asked if they could possibly meet. Why? To discuss the Judge, of course, and also his impending report. Disconcertingly enough, the woman gave way to tears, gasping a mixture of apology and refusal through sobs before in turn hanging up.

Kate sighed, duly returning to the reference books and cuttings she was using to shape up on obit piece on Hartington. Eton to Balliol and first-class honours; National Service action as a subaltern with the Guards in Korea; joined father-in-law's chambers when called to the Bar; initially specialized in matrimonial but then switched to criminal work; juniored in the George Blake spy trial, the Moors Murders trial and the first Kray trial; took Silk and soon developed a name leading for the Crown in big-scale fraud prosecutions; rose with unusual rapidity from Recorder to Crown Court Judge, then to Queen's Bench, delivering largely uncontroversial judgements in generally unsensational trials. A man, so it seemed to Kate, of unwavering Establishment stripe who, if indeed he was possessed of any conceit or wittiness or flamboyance of character, had long succeeded in concealing it from the press. Maybe, she reflected wryly, that had been the reason for his rapid promotion, the legal establishment being traditionally wary of headline-grabbers such as the Yorkshire rebel, Judge Pickles.

'What progress?' Lawrence Cawley asked, for once coming to sit beside her desk instead of calling her to his. 'A somewhat dreary obituary by the looks of it.'

'Meaning that he doesn't believe in letting off rapists or child abusers or making wisecracks in court.'

'Ah-ha.' He shrugged. 'Which suggests he wasn't about to rock the Establishment boat with this football report of his.'

'Maybe not, Lawrence.'

'So what are you doing to find out about that?'

'I tried his secretary, but she threw a wobbly. Sounded genuine.'

'What about joy-boy Taffy?'

'Ex-joy-boy!' She eyed him askance, resenting the intrusion. 'From what the hospital said, I should imagine he's off sick.'

'You haven't found him yet? Come on, Lewis, get your act together. The Awards season's almost on us; can't have Kate Adie upstaging you yet again.'

Isabel Hartington, when they finally connected Taff Roberts's call through to the ward, sounded cautious and subdued. 'Reasonable news on Vincent in that he's no worse,' she explained. 'The old trooper's holding his own. Stabilizing, to quote the medics. And you, Mr Roberts? Are you fit enough to meet for a talk?'

'Certainly. The hospital?'

'No.' She cleared her throat. 'In view of what the surgeon said about the blow on his head, there seems little point in prolonging my vigil—not today, anyway.' Again she cleared her throat. 'Would it be possible for you to get out to Sunningdale?'

Taff had visited the Hartingtons' place only once before—on a raw afternoon of rain and wind. Today, seeing its flowers in sunlight, the full quality of the old place got to him: a Queen Anne farmhouse, its front corner clothed in a massive growth of wistaria, its red-clay bricks and tiles mellowed with lichen; adjacent timbered barn and stables, all set about with a walled English garden rich in roses and a fine herbaceous backing.

'What a show,' he remarked as she crossed with her two Labrador puppies to greet him at the car.

'Certainly a lot more presentable than your poor face. Lucky they breed you tough in the Welsh valleys.' She turned to follow the Labradors across to a border rich with late gladioli. 'It's a shared pleasure. Like so much in our life. The garden, the law—' she laughed—'we even agree in our viewing tastes. Singular compatibility.'

And that much more to lose from his impairment, Taff reflected, wondering how long she'd have to wait before she knew the bottom line on that. A bloody devastating ordeal.

For all her evident courage, she was going to need an exceptional fund of strength.

'Do you mind if we talk out here? The telephone's been going non-stop since I got home. Alternating between well-wishers and press people.' She paused to crouch down and pluck chickweed from among the rose-bushes, remaining among the plants as she asked: 'Well now, about my request of yesterday, what strings do you need me to pull?'

'None, for heaven's sake!' Given the sensitivity of senior-rank coppers, strings were best pulled only as a very last resort. Moreover, it was not in Taff's nature to reveal investigation details unless he absolutely had to. No matter how far he could trust Isabel Hartington, it was pointless to involve her in the groundwork. More, whereas Taff wasn't devious by nature, the covert work of detection had instilled the habit of discretion.

'There's something I feel you should know,' she remarked, misreading his response as reluctance. 'To do with my husband's opinion of you.'

'Madam?'

'All along, he's held you in the highest possible esteem.' She glanced searchingly up at him from the border. 'You won't have realized this, perhaps, but it was directly thanks to Vincent you were drafted on to the Sox team.'

Boom-boom! Yet, startling though it was, it provided answers to several things which had been puzzling Taff over the last few months—like the personality mismatch between himself and Briggs; like how come his prior service record with the Met hadn't disqualified him for the job. But, for all the answers, it threw up yet more questions.

'You'd made an impression on him way back,' she resumed. 'A City-fraud case he tried in Snaresbrook Crown Court.'

Taff nodded. He had been mutually impressed by the Judge's subtle handling of a grossly overblown defence. It came as a further satisfaction to the then Detective-Sergeant Roberts that the ensuing appeal, on the grounds of preju-dicial directions from the bench, had been speedily dis-missed.

41

'Then by chance,' she added, 'Vincent heard about your skilled handling of the Leonard Snow conviction.'

Boom-boom again—but this time in mystification and unease. For the case he had cranked up against the sex-pervert Snow, far from skilled, had been a dire botch-up which had largely come unstitched under tough cross-examination. That they had actually won in the end had been due solely to a crisis of conscience on the part of the defence solicitor and the tip-off he'd given Taff at the eleventh hour.

'Judge Hugh Wallace and Vincent are old sparring partners,' she said, flicking him a half-smile. 'They dined together not long after the case and Hugh gave him the—er—inside version.' Which, for sure, meant that Wallace had classified Taff as a Stitcher; which in turn meant that Hartington's phrase 'an officer of your integrity and good faith' had been a blunt and ironic misuse. Oh wow!

'It's a question of priorities,' she explained, her smile if anything even warmer. 'The courage of one's convictions. The courage to take the initiative, even at risk to one's own personal future. That's what Vincent respects most in a policeman, Mr Roberts.'

In other words, he thought ruefully, a lunatic chancer; pretty much the sort of idiot crusader she's asking me to carry on as right now!

'The gratifying thing,' she went on quietly, pulling secateurs from her coat and starting to cut the choicer gladioli blooms for her husband's bedside, 'is that, having arranged your secondment, his respect for you has continued to grow during your Sox liaison work together. Isn't that fortunate?' She handed him an armful of blooms to hold. 'In fact, typical of his sentimental streak, he's almost come to look on you as a son.'

'So far, I've only had time to read the conclusions to his report,' Taff remarked later, watching from beside the sink as Isabel Hartington trimmed and crushed the gladioli stems.

'Pretty radical stuff, didn't you think?'

42

'But does the evidence fully support it?'

She gave him a wry glance. 'Come now, Chief Inspector, knowing my husband, what would you expect?'

'Quite frankly, unless it's rock solid and irrefutable, I'd expect the politicians to bury it deeper than nuclear waste.'

She nodded in emphatic agreement. 'Obviously. Yes, agreed. Which is why he attaches so much weight to the appendix.'

'Er—appendix? There was none filed on the disk.'

'Ah.' She laid the flowers carefully aside, turning to look at him. 'Well now, yes, I suppose that is to be expected.'

'What is?'

'The fact that Virginia Cohen failed to give you what is probably the most vital and certainly the most sensitive portion of Vincent's evidence.' She beckoned him from the kitchen, leading the way through the exquisitely furnished house to the library. 'What did you make of Miss Cohen?'

'Efficient, concerned and probably . . .'

'Yes?'

'Probably very—' how to put it?—'very attached to your husband.'

'Attached? An ambiguous word to choose.'

'I mean, you know, the loyalty you'd expect of a secretary of many years working with a personality like your husband.'

'I see.'

'All I'm saying, look, is that she seemed deeply upset by the attack on him, that's all. It really knocked her back.'

'Ah.' Isabel had the manner, picked up either from father or husband or else perhaps from ajudicating as a magistrate, of implying doubt or denial without actually voicing the contradiction. 'Well now, for a start, Miss Cohen has worked for my husband for barely one year, employed specifically for the duration of his judicial inquiry. In fact, supplied by the Board because of her prior experience in such inquiries.'

Taff grunted, recalling how the secretary's suggestion of the attack being the settling of an old score had implied a long-term relationship.

'As for loyalty,' the Judge's wife continued, 'I fancy she holds a stronger allegiance to the government than to Vincent.' She paused, nodding in explanation. 'You see, from early in the summer, Vincent began to suspect her of reporting on the progress and direction of his inquiry. Eventually he fed her some misinformation as a trap which in due course, so to speak, came back to roost.'

'Confirmed her disloyalty?'

She nodded, moving to open a fine marquetry cabinet which turned out to conceal a sturdy combination safe. 'Hence, presumably, Miss Cohen's decision to withhold that particular evidence from you.'

She opened the safe, moved several stamp albums aside, then pulled out a folder. As she handed it to him, Taff saw it had *Deep Throat* written on the outside.

'This is to do with the club, yes? With Balham United?'

'To do with the man Vincent called Gamelord,' she confirmed, 'and his elaborate plans to destroy the club.'

'Gamelord?'

'One man with the motive to want Vincent stopped in his tracks.' She turned, her eyes suddenly hard behind the gold-rimmed spectacles. 'The club chairman, Edward Oxted.'

CHAPTER 4

There appeared to be no change in her husband's condition when she arrived the next day. He lay comatose among the drips and monitor leads, his face drained of colour save for the areas of abrasion, the wavering lines on the monitor screens the sole evidence of his battle to stave off infection and sustain the life-force within him.

The duty sister was courteous and non-committal, anxious to avoid the question of his chances, concerned instead to give Mrs Hartington the messages from the many well-wishers—so many, so anxious—a much-loved man.

'Also the night-shift sister left you a message. You were still asleep when she went off duty; then, when she rang later, you'd already left for home. It's about your daughter—simply to tell you she rang to ask after the Judge while you were asleep.'

'Ah.' She moved to stare at the monitors, her face averted. 'Did she say which daughter that might have been?'

'Mrs Patricia Johns.' Then, registering the woman's reaction, she added: 'Oh heck, I'm sorry. It's so hard to tell with some of the tricks reporters try on, you know, to find out about VIP patients like your husband.'

'Amazingly callous—if it really was a reporter.' She paused then added quietly: 'Perhaps, just in case she calls again—perhaps you'd ask the switchboard to connect this Mrs Patricia Johns to the ward so I can have a word.'

She waited until the sister had moved away and then went to start looking through the small jungle of flowers placed near the ward entrance. The largest bouquet, mainly of his favourite roses, was from his chambers; while, predictably enough, the showiest was from 10 Downing Street. However, to her astonishment, the costliest, with its orchids and hibiscus, was from the Bulls chairman, Edward Oxted, wishing His Honour a speedy recovery 'the sooner to resume the challenge of saving our national game'.

Whatever final reluctance Taff Roberts might have had about investigating the assault under the Sox umbrella was duly seen off by the Deep Throat folder. It made devastating reading, amounting to a blueprint for the rape, annihilation and dismembering of the famous old football club. Put in more commercial terms, it contained evidence which revealed a long-term plan by Chairman Oxted deliberately to strip Balham United of its fortunes to the point where its sole chance of survival lay in its amalgamation with one of the neighbouring League clubs such as Chelsea, Fulham or Wimbledon. There was also evidence—photostats of share registers, club balance sheets, architect's feasibility studies, boardroom minutes, listed diary entries and so forth—to show his motive: not solely an Oxted asset-stripping job but

45

a twofold development scheme involving first the replace-
ment of the Bullring with a hypermarket and housing
development, and secondly cornering the construction contract for Chelsea's proposed redevelopment of the stadium
at Stamford Bridge. Nor, it seemed, were Ken Bates and
his fellow Chelsea directors in a position to block Oxted
because, via a complex web of nominees, he effectively held
majority share-holdings in both clubs.

Whereas there was no shortage of irregularities and petty
bribes behind both his acquisition of these share-holdings
and also his gradual beggary of Balham United, there was
little specific crime involved. Nonetheless, once brought to
light as an appendix in Judge Hartington's report, the
Gamelord's joint development schemes could well be jeopar-
dized—at a massive cost both to his reputation and also to
his pocket.

'Motive for mutilating His Honour, is it?' Briggs grunted
as Taff dumped the Deep Throat file on his chief's desk.

'Depends on how many millions a millionaire like Oxted
can write off as a tax loss,' Taff replied. 'But he'll do as
number one suspect for now. One thing, though, Guv'nor,
whoever this Throat geezer is, he's gone to a great deal of
effort to screw Oxted.' He indicated the file on his chief's
desk. 'I'll tell you straight, when I was working with Fraud,
it would have taken us bloody hundreds of man-hours to
unearth a dossier this thick.'

Yet a good deal quicker and easier, Taff reflected as he
headed through the after-lunch traffic towards the Bullring,
for someone working on the inside as a trusted employee
. . . someone, as the Judge had said of Deep Throat, extremely close to the club and with access to Oxted's secrets.

The Bullring ground, although largely rebuilt after the
Hitler war, dated back to the United's earliest origins in the
previous century. Like other great London clubs, as it grew
to include reserve, junior and youth teams, a training ground
had been acquired out in the suburbs. However, the club's
business administration and its various other commercial
ventures—pools and lottery, sportswear marketing, travel

facilities and so on—were all run from the large office block built into the outer flank of the north stand.

Unlike the plushy directors' suite and facilities on the top floor, the team manager's accommodation was tucked away near the changing rooms on the ground floor. Taff stood for ten minutes looking at the inevitable team photos lining the walls of the reception area before Bryan Walton came out to welcome him into his office.

According to the sports writers, Walton's most notable achievement was his survival as the Bulls' team manager for ten hapless years which included their relegation to the Second Division nearly six years earlier. Now, grey-haired at forty, the man was referred to by the players as Boss Bryan more out of tradition than affection or respect.

Not that the team manager was unprepossessing: the physique and vitality which, in the mid 1970s, had carried him briefly into the first team (in fact in the high-point years as runners-up in first the League and then the FA Cup), that athleticism was still apparent, belying the chronic tendon injuries which had driven him instead on to the coach-cum-manager ladder. Still lithe and trim of build, there was an unassuming charm in his manner, enhanced by the Geordie burr in his soft voice.

Yet there was a lack of authority in the man's limp handshake and uncertain eyes, leaving Taff with the sense of a high-flyer who, for all his supposed prestige, knows it's no more than a sham. You're only as good as your last game, runs the manager's maxim. That being so, Taff thought, it was hard to understand Tycoon Oxted's decade of loyalty to the manager other than as a lethal clot in the club's terminal thrombosis.

'Sorry to keep you waiting, Mr Roberts. Landed from Ireland on the morning flight. Endless calls to reply to, not to mention this little lot.' He gestured at a stack of mail on one side of his desk. 'Any road, apart from letting the physio give you an embrocation rub for that face of yours, how can I help?'

Taff produced his warrant card, mentioning briefly how

he had special inquiry status into football matters before explaining about the assault on the Judge the previous evening.

'How badly hurt?' Walton interrupted before adding: 'Sorry, but the first I knew was from my secretary this morning. His Honour had been here some weeks ago, you know, taking statements for his inquiry.'

'He's in intensive care,' Taff confirmed, watching closely as he added a bit about the circumstances. 'It could yet turn into a murder investigation, Mr Walton. So you'll appreciate the need for frankness and collaboration.'

The man had turned very pale under his suntan, reaching to sip from a cold mug of coffee, shaking his head in regret. 'Appalling. And you know, this inquiry of his—it could affect the whole future of the game.'

'When did you leave for Ireland, sir?'

'Yesterday morning. With our chief scout. Our Irish agent had lined up half a dozen lads for us to look at, including a couple in last night's junior league match.' He spread his hands, repeating the headshake. 'What was the Judge doing here yesterday? I understood he'd finished taking evidence last month.'

'He had a rendezvous, Mr Walton. Someone had apparently set him up.'

'For the attack?'

'Those thugs were expecting him.'

'Dreadful.' There was no doubting his distress. 'Animals.'

'And lured here by someone at the heart of the club.'

'How do you know?' Then, shaking his head: 'Did he tell you who?'

Taff let him sweat on it through a longish pause, then moved to a chair. 'Suppose we keep this informal at this stage, Mr Walton.'

'What? Yes, fine.' He sat down then stood again to offer tea, duly moving to the door to call for a tray. 'Informal then, Chief. Shoot.'

Right, Taff thought, go for the penalty: shoot one deep down the throat! 'Just how would you characterize your relationship with the club chairman?'

'With . . .? Mr Oxted and I have, let's say, a working relationship.'

'Come on, this isn't a blessed press conference. Having stuck each other for ten years, obviously you have a working relationship. Now cut the flannel and tell me.'

The manager was sweating now, his face lowered in bitter irony as he wagged his head. 'OK, so maybe those bloody reporters aren't so way out about Puppy Bryan. It's obvious enough to see, I shouldn't wonder. Puppy jumps when Master calls.' He paused, gesturing in grim frustration.

'Go on.'

'Be frank, you said. OK then. Master decides the transfers, not me. I go to Ireland—for what? I devise a play strategy—for what? I try to impose discipline—I'm overruled. The Puppy barks, but Master decides whether to throw the ball. Resign then, why not? What worth is twenty years with the club if you're just a front man with no clout? Why stay on and take all this crap? Where's your dignity, Boss? But then, but then, where's the next job to come from? I've put out feelers. But who wants the boss who's drifted a great club like this down through one relegation and fast heading for the bloody Third Division?'

He broke off as the secretary came in, standing to take the tea-tray from her, then pouring them both cups as she left again. 'The one thing I'm good for these days is tea-boy. T for Twat. Team Twat. Boss, they call me, Boss Bryan. That's a laugh, eh? They all know. Everyone knows. And the swine of it is, a lot of them blame me for not standing up to him.'

He grunted, repeating the gesture of frustration. 'No chance. You know why? Because it doesn't happen that way, not any more. The days of Matt Busby are long over. Money rules now, not managers, by Christ. Leastways, it does with what are known as the Tycoon Clubs. We're just fronters and mouthpieces. Not sport or a game any more, just showbiz razzamatazz.'

'The Chairman owns a majority share-holding in the club?'

49

'Of course he does. Him and his puppet directors together. Easy. And why not, he'd say. Why shouldn't he use his money to buy his way into this business like any other commercial enterprise? No matter that it's supposed to be a sport. It's still a business, part of the free-enterprise system, just like bricks and mortar would be. To hell with the people and the traditions involved. Business is business, my son.' He broke off in renewed bitterness to gulp his tea, eyes averted.

'Bricks and mortar?' Taff asked quietly. 'You mean, he plans to dispose of the club and develop the ground as a building site? Is that it?'

'Nothing would surprise me with that bloke.'

'Come on, is it or not?'

'Of course it is! Why the hell else should he run the club into bankruptcy!'

'And naturally you'd resist that?'

Walton blinked, his eyes narrowing as he stared at him. 'There isn't a player or a supporter of this club who wouldn't resist it—not if they could see some way to do so. But how do you stop a man like that? He's got money on his side; he's within the law. Him and the club business affairs were all investigated a few years back but naught came of it.'

'Really?' Before coming to the Bullring, Taff had run Oxted and the club through both the CRO computer and the no-actions files but in vain. 'Investigated by who?'

'The tax people, of course. And the CID, looking for fraud.' He shook his head in frustration. 'A bullet's the only way, bang in his head. And even then it's on the cards some other gamelord would buy in just the way he did.'

'Earlier you said about the Judge's inquiry affecting the whole future of the game. How exactly?'

'The evidence me and other managers gave him—the Judge's questions weren't about hooliganism so much as about asset-stripping, profiteering, possible fraud dodges, all that. It was obvious he saw the business side as one of the main reasons for the crowd troubles and rioting—and equally obvious he was hoping to pull the game away from

50

being a big-money spinner and back into being a sport.' He paused, pointing at the detective for emphasis as he added: 'You want a motive for last night's attack, that's it. The last thing the gamelord tycoons want is to lose their hold on the football racket.'

'You're suggesting his rendezvous was with Oxted?'

'Why not?' He was red-faced now, his hands clamped tight in agitation. 'Why not? Whoever the Judge came here to meet must have been from this club. Obviously it could have been him!'

Too obviously, Taff reflected as he drove back to Scotland Yard; altogether too pat and convenient. Moreover, a man sly and crafty enough to become a multi-millionaire from nothing isn't going to set himself up as the prime instigator of a pre-planned, ruthless crime of violence.

Taff would have tackled the infamous Gamelord without further delay except, having now heard about the previous CID investigation, he had further checks to run.

Back in the office, he repeated the computer and file checks on Oxted just in case, then commenced a search of the CID duty rosters for the dates three years back which Bryan Walton had dug out for him. Nothing on the Fraud Squad or other Yard rosters, so he tried the divisional CIDs, starting with O Division in which the Bullring was situated. Bingo. Three coppers on it for three days—but headed by the one officer Taff most wanted to avoid, DCI Lawley, at that time still a detective-sergeant. It was no good Taff's asking him or any of the lads under him about their findings—nor about why there was no traceable record of their investigation which had gobbled up in excess of seventy manhours . . . not without prompting some unwanted questions in return.

He had just reported all this to Briggs and given him the tape he'd secretly wired of his meeting with team manager Walton when a call came through for him from Kate Lewis.

'For God's sake, Miss Lewis!'

'Wrong,' she snapped back, 'for my editor's sake. Any chance of a meet?'

'You're kidding!'

He rang off, pulled on his jacket and went outside to stroll up and down Caxton Street until he saw her red Polo turn in from Buckingham Gate.

'Poor Taff,' she said, touching his discoloured face as he got in beside her. 'Like the man in the iron mask.'

'Turn you on, does it, girl?'

'Ask me that somewhere less public than Caxton Street.'

'Will do.' He gave her a painful grin. Then, after hearing of her lack of progress both with DCI Lawley and the distraught Miss Cohen, he asked her if she could possibly raise him any ITN contacts inside the club.

'The players? The staff? The supporters?'

'Yes all round. Anything and everything.'

'I'll do what I can.' She grinned. 'Anything your end? Any crumbs to keep my editor quiet?'

He hesitated, as always torn over the degree of trust between them. 'Listen, all I can say now is just to hang in here because, if we finally crack it, you could land a very big story, OK? Not only big but worthwhile.'

'I've been in journalism too long to remember what that last word means.'

'Well, like airing certain issues about justice and commerce and sport which greatly matter to a certain old gentleman who—well, who happens to be rather special.'

'You're obviously talking about the Judge,' she said, intrigued. 'Unusual. Or is this your new Chief Inspector image? Rebel Roberts brought to heel at last?'

He gave her a wink as he got out of the car and slammed the door. Yet the thrust of her words hung in his mind as he headed back to the office. Was it the rank? Was it the invidious task of investigating his fellow officers? Or was it simply the discovery that his guru, for whom he'd built up a high fund of respect, had turned out to have a reciprocal respect for him? Everyone, no matter how self-assured, wants approval. To receive it from such a giant as Vincent Hartington was more than just a welcome boost to his self-esteem. It also amounted to an obligation, first to bring his assailants to book but, more crucially, to ensure publication of Hartington's report.

He found DC Smith waiting as arranged back in the office. Although nervous, the skinhead managed a wry thumbs-up at sight of the senior officer's injuries.

'I see someone done to you exactly what I felt like doing this time yesterday.'

'Right, Constable. Doc Marten special.' Taff gestured for him to sit down then surprised him by digging out a can of Foster's. 'OK, although it's sooner than we expected, it's time for the *quid*.'

'You what?'

'The chance for you to exorcise that ghost we found in your closet.' Taff waited while the lad popped the can for a hasty gulp of lager, then he confirmed that Smith was currently working late-shift on general duties and, as such, could make himself available for a bit of weekend overtime on the quiet.

'Like what, guv?'

'Much like you did before with the Arsenal supporters, but this time with Balham. Make your number with their heaviest crew, make a strong impression, win their confidence.'

Smith's snort of irony coincided with his taking another pull from the can so that he ended up choking on the amber liquid. 'You ain't bloody asking much, are you! How about I go in starkers with me dick painted in their club colours?'

'Do it however you like, Constable. You're the specialist.'

'Not at kamikaze, mate!' He guzzled down the remainder of the can, then buckled it in half. 'What's it about, anyway?'

Hooked you, Taff thought. And probably, if he'd made it sound any less challenging and hairy, the prat wouldn't have gone for it. Some blokes just have to have all the odds against them—win their spurs bareback, slaughter the lion empty-handed.

'It's to do with Judge Hartington's vicious reception at the Bullring last night, OK?'

'You and all, mate? That where you collected the face

53

job?' Then, seeing Taff's nod, the lad creased out a broad grin, wised up at last and full of understanding. 'So it's personal, eh, guv? You should of said before. Makes all the diff.' He reached for and opened a second can of Foster's, raising it in a mock toast. 'Any clues on who I'm looking for?'

Taff repeated what little he had been able to tell Lawley about the crew's being tooled up and masked. Then he got to the tricky part. 'This whole job's off the record, OK?'

The beercan came down fast at that, the DC eyeing him askance. 'No, Guv, not OK. Not after that Arsenal number. We all got our pills chewed off over that. We was none of us much more than woodentops. We was sent in green and told not to worry 'cos they'd guide us through it.' He groaned in recollection. 'Guided us into the shit, mate, that's where! Never no more, Stanley old son, I promised meself. Next time, you get it all writ down exactly where you stand. No more frigging around. You get it clear upfront.'

'Except, Constable Smith, you didn't hold to that. You let yourself be conned into that jury-nobbling caper and ended up sitting here in the hot seat!' He paused, holding the DC's resentful gaze until he finally glared him down. 'Right then, you want it upfront, here it is: Sox is an undercover operation, so you use this extension number as a last resort. You do the job in your own time, unpartnered, unpaid, unofficial. There's a divisional DCI who's investigating the assault. Avoid him, tell him nothing, report only to me. Stick to all that, and I'll stand by you. Deviate from it—by a whisker—and you're on your own. Savvy, Stanley old son? Now on your bike, and good frigging luck!'

Ted Oxted lived behind elaborate security gates in one of the more prominent mansions bordering Hampstead Heath. For Taff Roberts, the pseudo-Colonial styling of the place made a poor contrast with the Hartingtons' choice piece of English heritage. He also far preferred their Labrador pups to the fierce Rottweiler barking from the kennels beside Oxted's house.

A Spanish manservant about as daunting as the dog

ushered him through to the library, offered a sherry, then scowled when Taff requested tea.

'One teabag, lemon and no sugar, thanks. Also an aspirin if you can find me one.'

'Mr Oxted be with you soon,' the man retorted in a voice which implied he could stuff both his aspirin and his teabag.

Everything in the room, from the unread, tooled-leather books to the post-Impressionist paintings, was blatantly pricey. But just how much the silver-framed photograph on the mantelpiece had cost Oxted—pictured at a Mayfair reception handing over a cheque to Margaret Thatcher— only Tory Party records would show.

'I've already spoken with Chief Inspector Lawley about this ghastly business. What else can I tell you?'

The man had spoken from the doorway, typically getting straight to the point. Now, registering Taff's facial injuries, he grunted in a show of sympathy. 'God's sake, you must be the bloke what was with him. I thought they'd kept you in hospital.' He shook his head, crossing to shake hands. 'And if not, why not?'

'Because I'm a copper, Mr Oxted.' Taff nodded formally. 'Which means two things: first I know to get after the villains sharpish while the trail's still warm; secondly, it makes me obstinate, especially when the crime happens to be personal like this one.'

'Fair enough.' Oxted nodded, gesturing for Taff to sit down as he crossed to a drinks cabinet. 'Did that dago butler think to offer you a bracer?'

Taff explained about the tea and aspirin, surprised to find himself impressed by the stocky little tycoon. What didn't come across from the pictures and the press reports was his energy and ebullience, also the engaging way he held Taff's gaze as though searching out the inner person. The alertness and confidence one might expect of a self-made man; likewise the personal charm which can often characterize a king-sized ego. Yet there was no sign of the Attila-like ruthlessness capable of methodically destroying a one-hundred-year-old football club for personal profit.

'So what can I tell you over and above what I already

told your brother officer? The Judge is by way of being a mate of mine—well, in so far as he's accepted my hospitality at a couple of matches. We've exchanged views on the future of the game and the way it should or should not be run at League level. I happen to know he disagrees with me on that count, but that don't affect our personal friendship. Now, as to just what His Honour was doing at my club this time yesterday evening, I have not the faintest notion. No doubt, since you was there with him, you'll know more about that than the rest of us. But he certainly wasn't there to meet me.'

He paused, pouring himself a brandy and soda from which he took a hefty pull before resuming. 'Nor, since he was in Ireland at the time, was he there to meet that prat Bryan Walton whom I understand you already had words with, yes? But as for the bunch of animals who actually did meet the pair of you—what can I say? Everyone knows the reputation of a tiny minority of the Balham supporters. So-called supporters, I should say; they aren't real supporters, just apes using the club as an excuse for mindless violence. Two or three notorious crews engaged in infantile war games—leastways, that's how your people keep telling it to me.'

Evidently, Taff reflected, DCI Lawley had also informed Oxted what little Taff himself had revealed at the hospital, namely that it wasn't a random mugging but a prearranged reception mob.

'You have a liaison with the divisional force, sir?'

'Of course I have a liaison, Chief Inspector. Those bastards may be only a minority, but they cause no end of bloody trouble. The policing of home games—and of the area around the Bullring—is a subject of crucial importance to club function. If it surprises you to hear the club chairman personally involves himself with match security, then it shouldn't. You should know that I've repeatedly spoken out against this menace, including giving evidence first to the parliamentary select committee and now for the benefit of His Honour's judicial inquiry.'

What doubly fascinated Taff was the contrast between

the two men who, whether or not Oxted knew it, were pitted in direct conflict: the tall High Court judge, as reserved and courteous in manner as he was detached and just in his judgements, deeply concerned, despite his silver-spoon origins, with the rights and interests of the underprivileged— the ageing traditionalist versus this flamboyantly outgoing yet ruthless businessman who, having clawed his way up from among the underprivileged, was concerned exclusively with building his own empire.

The tycoon had crossed to ring a bell and now, as the butler came back, angrily demanded to know why he hadn't brought the tea and aspirins.

'I send out for some, sir.'

'Bollocks. Try my bathroom cabinet. Now get your finger out. Can't you see our guest's just survived a charity bout with Frank Bruno?'

He turned, hands spread in wry apology as the man-servant hurried out. 'Typical dago—anti-authority. Now where was we? Yes, yes, I was about to ask you a question. How come you're taking up costly police time to come here and ask me what Ted Lawley already belled me about? I mean, don't get me wrong: as your lads very well know, I'm for the fullest possible collaboration with inquiries. A strong law-and-order man, that's me. A sight stronger than what they dish out in the courts and all. Me and the Judge exchanged a few words on that front, I can tell you. They behave like animals, they should be treated like animals— that's what I told him. Eye for an eye, tooth for a tooth; bang 'em up and throw away the key. But of course, His Honour wouldn't wear that, oh no. Crime College, that's what he calls prison. "Send them in there, Oxted, they'll learn *real* crime." Well that may be so, my friend, but I'm here to tell you that once the word gets round about soft sentencing, that's it—unlimited bloody anarchy.' He nodded, pointing the message. 'Same as you and him found out down the club last evening. Poor old Vincent learned a lesson down there last night, right? Learned it the hard way.'

CHAPTER 5

'Kill the spirit of the terraces, that's what he'd do. Knacker the game—kill off the macho hype of winning. Emasculate it—chop the spirit of competition—same as what his ILEA brethren was after.'

'The Inner London Education Authority?' Since Taff was anxious to avoid identifying his Sox role, it seemed best simply to duck the issue of why he'd come to see Chairman Oxted. And how better to do that than to play on the Gamelord's intoxication with his own opinions? 'How do you tie Judge Hartington in with ILEA?'

'Only philosophically, you understand. All that Leftist cant about scrapping exams, right? Unfair on the underdog because for every winner there's got to be a loser and losing's bad for their frail little self-esteems, oh dear. Well, I'll tell you this, Mr CID-fella, it's all very well for the Honourable Vincent to suffer these twinges of upper-class conscience. But it's because he never had the chance to get beaten at nothing that he's able to entertain these fancy notions. Men like him and Wedgy Benn, they're all the same. If they'd experienced it—if they'd tasted failure and hardship—then they'd know the spur of it. It's all very well to rabbit on about the Caring Society. But that ain't going to do us a pisspot's worth of good in 1992. What's going to give this country the edge in Europe is Maggie's EEC—Everyman's Enterprise Culture.'

He gulped down the remains of his brandy and moved for a hefty refill. 'I know, I know. His Honour's talking about sport and not commerce. But my point is, it's an attitude of mind. It's having the grit and the bottle to go for it. And we won't have that as a nation if we let old Vincent and his ilk kill off the will to win and the spirit of the terraces, right?'

Taff nodded, having realized these queries were not invitations to comment so much as pauses for approval.

'Listen, you take that prat of a team manager you was with earlier. He had a good old whinge about me, I'll wager. Seldom slow to do that is Boss Bryan.' The normal Cockney accent on which Oxted evidently prided himself, was briefly replaced with a replica of Walton's Geordie burr. 'The original whinger is that one, poor sod. Well, I'll tell you about Boss Bryan. He's no more a sportsman than what I am. He's a technician. Given his way, he'd have a team of robots. Totally mechanical. And where's the entertainment value in that, eh? All technique and no art.'

He paused briefly to lubricate the run of his words with brandy before resuming. 'You go to any home match, you'll hear them chanting *Boss Out! Boss Out!* Well I dare say one reason's 'cos they know he's on the take, always looking for his cut, his bit of the action. But basically, they've just sussed him as a loser. Of course, he'll tell you the team's losing on account of I won't let him buy the expensive bloody defenders he wants. Not that you'll find a manager in the business what ain't singing that little song. As for team discipline, I mean, once a manager's lost the respect of his players—well, what the hell?'

Yet, despite seeing Walton as all wrong all round, Taff thought, this music-hall Mussolini will prolong his agony indefinitely because he fits his long-term game-plan finally to see off the club.

'Had the Judge shown you a draft of his report, sir?'

'Why should he do that? Just because we were friendly, that doesn't mean he'd compromise his position, no more than I'd ask him to. Never. Like I've said, we have our differences of opinion regarding the future of the game. But we've kept that separate from our personal friendship.'

'I imagined,' Taff resumed quietly, 'that in view of the appendix to his report citing the Balham Club as a classic of exploitive mismanagement, His Honour might have thought it fitting to allow you, let's say, a right of reply.'

The effect of this was one of instant hostility, Oxted thrusting out his hand as he crossed to confront him. 'I'll thank you to show me your warrant card, Chief Inspector.'

He took it and made a note of the particulars before returning it and then ringing the bell. 'You're attached to the Yard in what capacity?'

'That I'm not at liberty to reveal.'

'No more than what the hell you were doing at the Bullring last night with the Judge, or how it is you know so much about this unpublished report of his, eh?' He turned as the manservant opened the door. 'This police officer's no longer welcome. Show him out.'

On his way out through the reception hall, Taff glimpsed a leggy blonde staring down from the landing above. Although she eased back out of sight, Taff saw enough to be grudgingly impressed by the tycoon's taste in female company.

As he drove home to his desirable, centrally-situated box, Taff tried to decide if Oxted had already known. Surely, had news of the Judge's damning appendix come as a surprise, the tycoon's compulsive curiosity would have had him asking for the details. Equally, in view of its Deep Throat origins, Taff felt sure the Judge wouldn't have given Oxted prior sight of it. Which seemed to leave Virginia Cohen as the most probable source of leakage.

Briefly he considered driving to her Knightsbridge flat, but by now his headache was building to a blinder. Early bed for you, David boyo; put this residual concussion finally to rest.

Yet there was one last development still to deal with before he finally hit the sack. It emerged, oddly enough, from his telephoning the hospital for news on the Judge. It took him only a mild bit of rank-pulling to get connected to the ward extension and speak to Isabel Hartington.

'No change with Vincent,' she remarked tersely. 'No worse and no better. The traces all pulsing obediently away on the screens, but no flicker of consciousness. Did you happen to catch the news on the radio?'

'Not since this morning.'

'Somehow they've got hold of Vincent's report—if not the actual thing, at least a pretty accurate summary of his recommendations.'

'Lord!' Who from, for God's sake? 'Including the appendix?'

'They made no reference to it. So unless their lawyers advised them against naming Oxted, we can assume they didn't get hold of that.'

The same way I didn't get it from Virginia Cohen, Taff reflected as he rang off. Yet Miss Cohen keeping her political masters regularly informed of the report's progress was very different indeed from her now leaking the whole damned thing to the press, not least after her refusal even to meet Kate Lewis.

It was a view he found himself repeating in curtly defensive tones within a couple of minutes when he received a distinctly twitchy phone call from Kate herself.

'Wherever the Beeb got hold of it, Taff, ITN didn't! *I* didn't! OK, so it's nothing new to get egg on my face. But my editor knows me too well and he's refusing to believe I'm not in intimate touch with you!'

Taff groaned, cursing this new dimension and his persisting uncertainty over Kate, cursing his broken ribs and his aching head. Yet why not let her have a copy? Whether or not the BBC already had the full report, the Judge had got it mostly completed and was within a few weeks of distribution. Far better to be leaked prematurely, after all, than for it to be totally suppressed.

Yet just supposing the Judge, crafty old silk that he was, had been playing politics? Supposing he had gone way over the top with his first-draft recommendations, knowing Virginia Cohen would leak them to the politicos, knowing the Minister would come back to him for a compromise— and knowing he could then respond with a show of bitter reluctance, in the end agreeing to precisely what he'd really planned to recommend in the first place. A devious and laborious process, Roberts, but one engendered by the system.

Taff groaned again and rubbed at his forehead, only to wince from the bruising. Well, too bad, Vincent old sport, too bad: having hand-picked Stitcher Roberts for your team, you'll just have to live with his Welsh decisions. In fact, come to think of it, happen the old chap would be content merely to live!

'Fair enough then, Katie girl, you win the tablets of stone. Collection by red Polo, same place tomorrow morning, ten-thirty.'

The next morning started differently, however, a panic call from the Sox secretary warning Taff to get himself over to the office flaming pronto. He told her to alert Chiefie Briggs, then hung up without waiting to hear the details. Lawley was, after all, a problem he had known would catch up with him sooner or later; the only unknowns had been how soon and what level of brass would be blasting.

No time for breakfast or taking stock of his injuries; no time to divert and confront Miss Cohen on the way. His best charcoal-grey suit and Thames Valley tie on, shave in the car while hoping to catch the morning news bulletin . . . he did, and was relieved that there was no further mention of the Judge's report, an overnight air crash, a teachers' strike and an oil spillage having seen off yesterday's stories.

In the event the brass rank turned out to be an assistant commissioner crime, no less, a notorious plummy-voiced climber called Frank Blaize, known to Taff Roberts from his last case in the Met four years back. Sod's Law as usual, for the case had caused Blaize considerable humiliation over his mishandling of Taff's then governor, Chiefie Jack Walsh.

'Come in, Roberts. Your Sox outfit evidently enjoys irregular hours.'

'I was having a short lie-in, sir, as an alternative to sick leave.'

The ACC grunted, eyeing the bruising which, although less swollen, had now coloured to a grotesque face atlas of purple and yellow. 'Not so sick you couldn't tramp around quite a bit yesterday, hm? Perhaps trample would be the more fitting term in the light of the complaint lodged against you.'

'Before you proceed, sir, my chief is on his way over and—'

'It was you I sent for, not Mr Briggs.'

'None the less, sir, when working as a team within another force—'

'Then, as you very well know, it's out of order to start duplicating inquiries already under way within that force.'

'Accepted, sir.' The prudent way would have been to play it as laid-back as possible—Yes, sir, no, sir, three bags full, sir—ACCs being incapable of error and above correction. Yet Taff felt he simply had no alternative but to stall until his guv'nor arrived, if only to ensure that they kept their act together and both sang the same tune. 'However, sir, with respect, our terms of reference under Operation Sox allow us clearly defined parameters of discretion which, under the particular circumstances of the assault on His Honour Judge Hartington and myself, would appear to be fully—er—' He paused, trapped in the meshes of his fancy syntax.

'Fully what, Roberts?'

'Er, in order, sir.'

'It's in order to charge in on a prestigious and influential member of the public, making accusations of an intimidatory nature?'

'Sir?'

'Implications, then?'

'With respect, sir, might I hear the nature of these alleged implications?' Then, as the ACC glared, shaking his head at the junior officer's audacity: 'Moreover, sir, I'd like to know the exact route by which this, er, complaint has reached such senior rank as yourself.'

Audacity it was, Welsh Roberts never having been too hot on kowtowing to the exalted; yet Taff also had a wealth of cross-examination experience in court to draw on. Once one had developed the skill to counter the cut and thrust of a sharp defence barrister, then fencing with a pompous admin wallah like Frank Blaize was a dolly.

However, he was spared having to resort to these skills any further, because Chiefie Briggs at last came grunting in, all flushed and breathless and ominously defensive.

*

The question in Taff's mind was whether his chief's stance would prove entirely *self*-defensive or whether he would for once play it as a team. Briggs listened dourly as the ACC specified DCI Lawley's internal protest about a Thames Valley officer pursuing unapproved inquiries on his own initiative; these, moreover, culminating in Oxted's complaint of implied intimidation and harassment.

'Regarding the matter of approval, sir, David has kept me fully informed and has satisfied me that any duplication of DCI Lawley's investigation is within the scope of our Sox brief.'

Which had David breathing out in silent relief that he'd apparently underestimated his guv'nor. For his part, the ACC glared in renewed displeasure which, given the knee jerk resentment within the Met every time they came under investigation by outsiders, was par for the programme.

'Your brief,' Blaize remarked, tapping a slim folder labelled SOX, 'relates to the investigation of serving Met officers. Do you have evidence to link this savage assault in some way to the Force?'

Taff was about to launch in about Isabel Hartington's fears of a prejudicial Met investigation, but fortunately old Briggs got in first. 'Sufficient for me to notify my Chief Constable of the matter, yes, sir.' He cleared his throat, then added: 'As to any complaint from the Chairman of Balham United, I can say no more at this stage than that I'll deal with the matter as and when it reaches my desk.'

'It happens to have reached *this* desk, Chief Superintendent,' Blaize murmured acidly.

'Then, sir, I imagine you'll observe established procedure regarding special operations such as ours.' He stepped forward, hand extended. 'You have a statement from the plaintiff?'

'As yet, not in my possession.' Blaize's plump cheeks glowed. 'I've merely had the gist of it phoned though to me from the division.'

'Excuse me, sir,' Taff cut in, 'would that have been from the divisional commander?'

'I'll thank you not to interrupt, Roberts.'

'If I could rephrase it,' Taff ploughed on regardless. 'During the course of the interview, Mr Oxted admitted to having a close liaison with senior divisional personnel.'

'Hardly surprising, given the policing levels necessary at that particular football ground.'

'None the less, sir, since Oxted is criminally implicated . . .'

'Really? With what offence, hm?'

'Conspiracy to the assault.' Taff paused, turning to his chief as Briggs tried to intervene: 'Hang it, Guv'nor, Oxted tries to go over our heads, tries to pull rank and hamstring me with a trumped-up complaint. OK, at the very least we've a right to the names of the officers he's got dancing to his tune.'

'Now then, Roberts . . .'

'If they want to start a witch-hunt, let them face the consequences!'

'Thanks, Guv'nor,' Taff remarked as the two men took a much-needed leak in the VIP loo along the corridor from Blaize's office. 'I appreciate the support.'

'Don't take it as a mandate, Roberts,' the Chief growled curtly. 'You're walking a bloody thin line.'

'Don't I know it!'

'Obviously, if I do get a formal statement from Oxted on my desk, I'll have to observe the complaints procedure.' He zipped up and crossed to the washbasin, adding: 'Albeit as slowly as possible.'

The DCI nodded acceptance, reasonably confident that nothing further would come of it. Operators like Oxted far preferred to do things through the old-boy network: a phone call to his chum the divisional commander, who in turn bells Blaize to turn on the heat and scare off this cocky Thames Valley hick. And thank God Briggs hadn't played the hick but had instead called their bluff, duly obliging Blaize to back off.

Yet they both knew it wouldn't happen that way a second time. For instance, it only needed Blaize to learn of Taff's secret trade-off with DC Stan Smith and he'd have everyone's guts for garters.

As they stepped into the lift, Taff further abused his chief's peace of mind by pressing the third-floor button and explaining he had to go to see the spooks.

'What the hell for?'

'Deep Throat told the judge he had pictures linking Bull supporter crews with the National Front. If such links exist, it's possible Special Branch might be able to give me some names.'

'Be warned, lad, being able to and actually doing so seldom go together in their world.'

That fly old chiefie knows it all, Taff reflected ruefully when, over an hour later, a patronizing sergeant with a computer terminal finally condescended to tap in the particulars but then refused to let him see the screen or to give him a print-out.

'Very sorry, Mr Roberts sir, but it's the security rating on here. Provide us with the requisite authority from your guv'nor, counter-signed by the Thames Valley Chief Constable, and you're in business. Otherwise, no can do.'

At least, Taff thought as he headed back to Caxton Street, they seem to have information worth classifying—which could mean the Deep Throat offer of photographic evidence was authentic and not just a sly ploy to lure poor old Vincent into a trap. Supposing, for instance, the Doc Marten mob were the actual crew pictured in Deep Throat's photographs and that they'd somehow found out he was about to betray their links with the NF. They put the clampers on Deep Throat, force him to reveal the rendezvous point, then wait in hiding until the Judge arrives. Boom-boom. Well, at least it was a workable theory . . . except that most tough hooligan crews are only too proud of their NF links and would prefer to parade rather than suppress them!

However, although it prompted a few scornful grunts, the theory proved just persuasive enough for Chiefie Briggs to sign the Special Branch authority and then dispatch it to Kidlington for the deity's counter-signature. Just.

'Got to hand it to you, Roberts, you're an obstinate bastard.'

'Damn it, Guv'nor, the old bloke could *die*.'

66

'If he does, lad, the case'll die on you and all. Blaize'll put a full murder squad on to it. Of course they *might* allow you on to the team. But no bookie'd lay odds on it.'

He found Kate double-parked at the top end of Caxton Street, her face almost the colour of her Polo.

'Bloody traffic wardens!'

'Sorry, sweetheart.' He kissed her, loving the touch of her, suddenly longing to hold her as though all the years and pain had never intervened. 'I hit a slight red-tape problem.'

'That'll cost you another kiss, then.' He went to oblige but she shook her head, pushing him back. 'I'll decide the time and place.'

'So long as you make it soon.' He pulled out the word-processor disk he'd copied of the Judge's report and popped it into her glove compartment. 'The trouble with floppy-disks is they're so easily edited.'

He turned at a sharp knock from outside, then rolled down the window to offer the meter-maid his mangled grin. 'Sorry, mam, but we have to meet here because of her husband. Look what he did to my face last time.' Then, when the warden threateningly pulled out her book, he climbed out, leaning briefly back in for a last word. 'I'll collect you from ITN about five-thirty, yes?'

'Mystery tour?'

'Chiefie Walsh got us tickets to see Balham mauled by Fulham at the Bullring this evening, OK?'

'About that kiss,' she called as she gunned the engine. 'Tonight after the match.'

Which was a prospect which warmed both his heart and his loins all the way to the Temple and Judge Hartington's chambers. It even seemed to make the austere Virginia Cohen seem a shade more fanciable—a view helped by the fact that today's blouse, unlike her previous choker, was revealingly open-necked.

'You had Chief Inspector Lawley to see you?' he asked.

Surprisingly, her cheeks coloured up in embarrassment as she nodded. 'You see, he seemed to know all about you.

At least, he asked when you'd been here and what I'd given you.' Then, with an anxious shake of her head, she added: 'Also he already had a copy of the inquiry report.'

'Forwarded from my office, yes. My chief deemed it relevant as material evidence.'

'I see.'

'Don't worry, Miss Cohen, there'll be no risk of his breaching the confidentiality.'

'You're sure?' She was clearly fussed about it. 'You see, when I heard the radio reports—that they'd got a preview of His Honour's recommendations—I thought perhaps . . .' She paused, frowning in concern, then added: 'Security's so essential with judicial reports like this one. The press get up to all manner of tricks to try for a leak.'

'Right.' Taff nodded. 'Something the politicians deeply dislike, because an advance leak cramps their chances of, shall we say, adjusting it prior to publication.'

'Adjusting?'

'For instance, the Cabinet must hate the Judge's call for local authority involvement in the running of League clubs. Chances are, they'd have come back to him for a rethink on all that.'

'No.' She shook her head emphatically. 'No, he sees the socialization of the game as central to its survival. He'd never budge on that. Never.'

'But then, of course, you already knew that,' he remarked pointedly. 'Because they'd already tried.'

'Who? Tried what?' She stared fixedly at him, her cheeks flushing now with guilt. 'Who?'

'The politicians,' he snapped, 'after they'd had it all leaked to them last month.'

The effect was as if he'd leaned across to rip her blouse wide open, her hands clasping tight across her front as she recoiled in her chair. 'Leaked? What do you mean?'

'Come on, Miss Mole, enough of the playacting. The Judge knew what you were up to. He even understood it— appreciated the expediency, if not your disloyalty.'

'I—I don't . . .'

'He'd suspected you for some while,' Taff cut in to save

68

her the humiliation of lying, 'so he set a small trap just to confirm his suspicions.' Then, more gently as she crumpled her face into her hands: 'He realized it was all set up by those who put you in here to assist him. He didn't take it too personally.'

Yet Virginia Cohen did right then, the cumulative guilt and anxiety spilling from her in anguished sobs.

'It—it's haunted me ever since,' she gasped in catharsis. 'The awful thought that—God forbid!—that maybe, if they hadn't known—that if I hadn't told them—maybe he—I mean, maybe . . .'

'Maybe he wouldn't have ended up fighting for his life in that damned hospital,' Taff concluded it for her.

She groaned in remorse, face buried in her hands as the sobs shook her. The detective watched her for a while, then crossed to the door to ask a junior clerk for a glass of water. He waited for it in the doorway, shielding her from view as the clerk returned.

Virginia had quietened a bit by the time Taff crossed to her. She took the drink from him, gulping some and then rummaging for a tissue. Damn sure, the detective thought, she wasn't the one who leaked it to the Beeb—not with all that guilt and anxiety churning her up.

He waited till she'd stopped sobbing and had blown noisily into the tissue, then he asked who she'd been reporting to. She shook her head, eyes averted, until he snapped: 'It's down to you whether or not we keep this between us, Miss Cohen. But unless I have a name . . .'

'Timpson,' she blurted. 'Alex Timpson.'

It fitted. Influential Tory backbencher, link-man for almost as many lobby groups as he was on parliamentary select and sub-committees; one of Westminster's Mr Fixits. And just the sort, Taff reflected as he left the tearful Virginia and made his way down the stone stairway from chambers, exactly the sort whom Ted Oxted was in the habit of inviting to watch top matches from the directors' box.

CHAPTER 6

From their seats in the south stand, they had a clear view of the glass-fronted directors' box in the huge north stand. Using fieldglasses, they could make out Chairman Oxted hosting it up with his guests—champagne and goodies all round—the occasion more for business deals and PR than appreciation of the Littlewoods Cup match. Whereas several of the faces seemed familiar, Taff could place only the blonde he'd glimpsed at Oxted's mansion. Although he had earlier checked out the particulars and a picture of O Division's Commander, James Blake, also his sports liaison officer, Chiefie Tom Ingram, neither was visible as a guest in the box.

The game, although scrappy and so far without score, was bitterly fought. The Bulls, typical of their aggressive style, had kept the play largely in the Fulham end; but so far rigorous marking of their star striker, Kennie Kent, had paid off. Watching them—the egotistic but daring exploits of the Bulls' frontline, the excitement and pace, the noisy attack and flamboyant histrionics—Taff saw how emphatically they were Oxted men rather than Boss Bryan's tactical robots.

The behaviour of the Bulls' supporters, although fewer in number for the weekday match, closely resembled the provocative and fiercely partisan style of the previous match he and Walsh had watched together. In spite of—or perhaps because of—the recently heightened barrier fences, their abuse was directed more consistently at the visiting Fulham fans than at the ebb and flow of events on the field.

'You see that bearded hombre in the wheelchair,' Walsh muttered to Kate, pointing to the end of the lowest tier of seats. 'That's General Patton and that ain't no telephone he's talking into. It's a walkie-talkie.' He turned to Taff. 'Lend us those glasses and I'll see if I can pick out some of his lieutenants down on the kop end. In years gone by, you'd have seen him down there himself. There were occasions they used tick-tack men to pass on orders in those days. Now, of course, they're all hi-tech.'

'There'll be one of his staff not far off tuned into the police wave-length,' Taff added. 'And you can reckon they'll have at least one tame officer among the coppers on crowd control who'll tip off the General on any shifts of police tactics.'

'Alternatively, Taff, they might have a link with management who's tipping them off in advance.'

'But surely,' Kate protested, 'the last thing the management want is to *foster* spectator hooliganism.'

'That depends,' the retired chiefie grunted dourly. 'It's all part of the spectacle, after all. And this club's got a reputation for loadsa violence and rah-rah carry-on.' He pointed to the television cameras. 'What are your people doing at a Second Division weekday game if not for that, eh?'

Kate pulled a face, but nodded in ironic acknowledgement as Walsh added sardonically: 'We can be sure General Patton's on somebody's payroll. Like the song says, there's no business like show business. It's getting so that you could forget it's supposed to be a *game* hidden away there behind all the big-money entertainment.'

Taff grinned, eyeing his erstwhile guv'nor with wry amusement. Although usually wary and taciturn with the opposite sex, this evening he was all chatty: but was it prompted by Foxy's lifelong passion for the game or by his self-appointed role as matchmaker? Or perhaps by a bit of each, the two having been nicely brought together here in the Bullring's south stand.

As for Kate, she seemed closer in mood to Kathy, relaxed and enjoying herself, excited by the game, her reporter's hat seemingly set aside. Only once did she obliquely refer to the covert interest she and Taff had in the club—in fact after telling Walsh the news, phoned to ITN's sports desk earlier in the day, that Striker Kennie Kent had been selected for the England team in the pre-European Championship friendly try-out the next week in Munich.

'Martin Ford will have a camera team along, Taff, probably tomorrow. It might be of interest, if you want to tag along.'

'Great—provided you're there to hold my hand.'

It was curious to reflect on the contrast between Papa Walsh and the Honourable Vincent. Each in his individual way represented an alter ego for Taff, yet from different corners of the Justice model. Foxy Walsh, the old-style survivor detective who'd slogged his way up through the ranks by playing the system and working the tricks necessary to notch up a glittering conviction rate while staying always just ahead of C-10 and the Police Authority. Yet, for all his cunning and cynicism, old Walshy was every bit as dedicated to the service of justice as the Queen's Bench judge with his fastidious integrity to all that was proper and visibly correct. Yet *was* he? For, if so, what the hell was the Judge up to selecting Stitcher Roberts for the Sox Operation? A paradox there, for sure—albeit one that, come the crunch, the chosen protégé had failed to live up to.

True, whatever qualities Hartington had valued in him, they could hardly be those of a pugilistic bodyguard. Yet, ironically, it was for that role he had summoned Taff here to the Bullring forty-eight hours ago.

He was jolted back to the game by the sudden roar as Kent at last banged one home—in fact between his marker's legs—before as usual disappearing beneath his euphoric team-mates. The chanting of Bully-Bully-BULL! resounded from every Balham throat. But it was to the directors' box that Walsh directed Kate's attention, handing her the field-glasses for a closer look. Sure enough, after a moment, the roars of adulation increased as Chairman Ted came strutting out forward on to an extended section of the balcony. There, his hands clenched above his head, he cavorted and postured in triumph, a grotesque, cheer-leading Mussolini, to the frenzied delight of his screaming fans.

'You'd think *he'd* scored the blinking goal!'

'What I think, Kate, is that, as well as being a multi-millionaire business tycoon, he's also a natural ring-master.'

Crowd tension soared during the remaining minutes of the game, the visiting Fulham supporters irked by wild taunts and abuse from the Bulls. But, surprisingly, General Patton held his lieutenants back from putting the newly-raised segregation barriers to the test. And, in the event, it was not until after the game as they were leaving the ground that his plan emerged.

The police strategy was to marshal the Fulham fans along to the tube station in manageable groups of a hundred or so at a time. Patton's strategy was to assign several of his larger but less militant hooligan crews to harass and taunt each group to the point where, nearing the Underground, their militants broke ranks to give chase down the side-streets—where of course the Bulls' nutter crews were lurking in merciless ambush.

'Patton won't win any Brownie points for this,' Kate gasped as Walsh and Taff hurried her along behind one of the police hoolivans towards a particularly noisy skirmish. 'It's all happening off-camera.'

'The thing is,' Walsh explained, 'his lads like a bit of both. The camera show is all very well for the flashers, but some of these nutters only get their real turn-on by this sort of savagery.' He pointed across to where several Fulham supporters were staggering back, blood-drenched and mauled.

Taff had a protective arm around Kate, watchful for any direct threat to them. Yet, more so, his eyes were sharp for anything remotely recognizable in shape, physique or attire among the few Balham United fans the constables were starting to heave into the hoolivan. Whereas most seemed to conform to the general pattern, however, none clicked in his mind from the assault.

One Bulls' supporter, however, did spark a shock of recognition. It would have been hard to miss the lad, given the abuse and spirit with which he fought the three constables who were trying to wrestle him into the van. And just how, Taff wondered as the fan's heavy boot thumped a PC in the privates, how in God's name do I justify injuries like that caused to police personnel during the course of DC Stanley Smith's illicit undercover op!

*

73

'The politicians are boiling over about my piece on the Hartington report,' Kate chuckled later as they parked outside Taff's box. 'The Minister for Sport demanded an instant retraction *and* threatened to refer us to the IBA for transmitting contentious and irresponsible fiction.'

'The IBA already?' Taff snorted, shaking his head. 'Boomerang time.'

'For me or the Minister?' Kate yelped. 'It was safe, wasn't it? Damn it, I assured ITN's lawyer it was authentic!'

Taff grinned, leading the way into the apartment building. But for Kate's extreme vulnerability over it, he'd have been tempted to tease her. Instead he let her off the hook, promising that as long as she'd stuck to the text on that disk she was fireproof. 'Just call the Minister's bluff. If he does lodge a formal complaint, just refer the IBA to Virginia Cohen. She won't dare give them anything but the original version.'

Kate breathed out in relief, chuckling again as she added, 'Whatever the Beeb got hold of yesterday, it wasn't the full report. In fact, thanks to you, ITN quite upstaged them.'

'Ah. So you're back in favour with your editor.'

'Never! Lawrence is far too much the male chauvinist for that. At best, he and I coexist in a state of armed neutrality.' She gave a shrill laugh, then added: 'He's deeply suspicious of my connivings with the sports desk over Balham. Threatened to put me on the transfer list.'

'Don't let him,' Taff chuckled, unlocking the door of his flat. 'If they take you off crime, I won't be of any use to you.'

'That's a bloody awful thing to say!' she sang out, following him into the flat. 'Anyway, you do have *other* uses.'

With which, as if fully aware of the neutering effect that three years on Indecency had wrought on his sex-life, she kissed him with most unEnglish abandon, leaving her Welsh boyo this time no chance whatsoever to plead injury or headache or any other form of non-arousal.

In the event, having now had several months on Sox and having been lovers before, Taff found he was able gradually to relax and banish the gross mutilations and perverse

74

horrors to which he had so often been privy during those three years.

'Why come here, for God's sake?' she muttered as they broke for air. 'At least there's a real bed at my place.'

'Sorry, Kath, but from something I saw after the match, I could be in for yet another early call tomorrow.'

In the event, they dragged his narrow mattress on to the floor and augmented it with chair cushions. Then there was the business of his injuries—the specifying of no-hold areas, the positions to be avoided and so on—which, as time passed and passions quickened, became no more painful or relevant than the horrors which had haunted him from the indecency unit . . .

There was a moment—that extended, timeless moment— when the feline's claws struck with such force on his dressings that he sensed his ribs had cracked afresh. Yet so what? It was all an exquisite multiple ecstasy—a wondrous physical affinity bridging time and the years and closing those other wounds which had for so long gaped bare.

And yet, and yet . . . in the event, the high joy of it was short-lived. All too soon the aftermath of wellbeing was flooded with the backwash of solitude. Thanks perhaps to the high of their physical reunion, Taff experienced a keen, post-coital clarity of vision, seeing in it the starkness and aridity of his daily life. The vision, in contradiction of his busy, often frenzied life within the Force, was one of solitude and loneliness . . . part of a vast family within which, for all his loyalty to it, he felt increasingly isolated.

Suffering what was known as the Countryman Syndrome, perhaps? That crisis of commitment common to officers assigned to probe the diseased integrity of the Met? That crisis induced by a conflict of loyalty—the result of finding that one's brother officers, supposed to be dedicated to the unswerving service of justice for the people, were in fact flawed and fallible and prey to self-interest? *Quis custodes ipsos custodiat?* Who is to police the policemen? It was a syndrome guaranteed to provoke introspection in a bloke like Taff, reluctant to accept the exalted, holier-than-thou role of judging his colleagues. The more so, indeed, since his last major case at Marlbury had qualified him for the arcane title of Stitcher Roberts. No matter that his botched stitching attempt had been motivated not out of self-interest but solely to counter dire loopholes in the law which amounted to a sex-abusers' charter. The fact remained that he, too, was flawed—was capable of abusing the powers vested in him by the Force.

And now here he was, doing it all over again! Way out of order, bending all the bloody rules, abusing his rank and position to suborn DC Smith, drawing excessively on his governor's sense of loyalty while himself charging around like a one-man band. Oh dear . . .

Yet just how much was all that an over-simplification? Lying there on the floor, staring up at the play of light on the ceiling, listening to the steady breathing of his lover beside him, feeling her nakedness against his limbs—how honest was he really being? It was so easy to blame guilt or an abstract syndrome when in relaity it all went far deeper— like, to the very roots of his past, his childhood and his personality—to all the complex dimensions which had led him to become a copper, which kept him single, which made him by nature a loner, yet which fuelled the gnawing sense of isolation, even of chronic unhappiness, which lurked at bay ready to haunt him in these rare moments of truth.

In the event, the next morning brought no repeat of the panic call. Instead, the two of them shared more pleasure, then arose at their leisure and ate breakfast together. Taff checked his urine and his sputum and, finding both clear of blood, reckoned he could give the quacks another miss. They were relaxed with each other, met each other's eyes without awkwardness and their lips without artifice. Like any other live-in couple, he thought ruefully, purged now of the bitter reproaches which had split them apart and driven him into exile in Marlbury.

'Move into my place if you like,' she suggested as casually as if she was offering to lend him a book as he dropped her off at ITN. 'A different set of neighbours, but otherwise the same old pad as before.'

Sure, just step back through the years as if the fœtus had never quickened! 'Thanks, girl. I'll think on't. Meanwhile, bell me when they schedule the Kennie Kent interview. Oh, and later on I'll brief you with a bit of background scandal.'

'Sounds intriguing.'

'It could make for some fireworks. Ciao for now.'

Her kiss, like so much about the blessed woman, left him unsure of her as he drove off. But which was worse, he wondered: to be in competition with another man or with a jealous flaming career? Not that Kate Lewis loved her career; on the contrary, the combination of camera fright, anxiety and workaholism drove her almost frenzied. The problem was, she *had* to succeed; she *had* to prove not just herself as a person but that she could do the job despite being a woman in a man's world. All rather tiresome and sad, he decided, but no more than he himself would have been obliged to do in her shoes. Perhaps it was in that very similarity between them that their fated attraction lay.

The cryptic signal he got from the Sox secretary warned him that maybe all was not after all as well as he had hoped on the DC Smith front. After murmuring into her desk intercom, she waved him hurriedly on through to the Briggs inner sanctum.

'The ACC sent for *me* this time!' the Chief rasped, letting Taff stand there on the carpet. 'And why the bloody hell couldn't you have told me about your dickhead scheme with that Smith maniac? Well, of course we both know why you couldn't: because you knew I'd have bloody vetoed it! So instead you went and set it up behind my back—hoping they wouldn't find out, hoping if they did, old thickie Briggs'd close ranks and play it loyal again like yesterday. Right?'

Pause. 'Something like, Guv'nor, yes.'

'Prat! Everything—that was our understanding—every-thing out in the open between us. And there I was, stood there like a one-legged man at an arse-kicking competition, mouthing about discretion and privilege and—and meanwhile trying to conceal the fact that you'd blackmailed the muscle-bound oaf into working for us at all!'

He paused, glaring across for an answer, only to cut off Taff's reply. 'Don't give me that crap about a *quid pro quo*! In my book, it's blackmail. Coercion. Precisely the sort of Met malpractice we're here to root out. Dear God, you and your famous Chiefie Walsh!'

'Listen, Guv'nor—'

'Don't interrupt, Roberts. You realize you could well have shot this whole Sox operation in the foot! They don't want us here, as you well know. Blaize and his mob have had the boot ready for us all along. This could prove precisely the weapon they need to see us off the field once and for all!'

Taff nodded glumly, ahead of him on that one, damn it. The only question was whether he had now stretched his chief's tolerance beyond breaking-point.

'Now here's what you do, Roberts: you write me a full report on the incident, specifying your precise instructions to DC Smith and why you saw fit to conceal it from me. I'll submit that, along with my own comments, to CCTVP. After that, it's down to him.'

'Sir.' Taff cleared his throat. 'Might I ask the situation regarding Smith?'

'That's under review.'

'Of course. But what about his cover?'

'You really are obsessed with this case, aren't you. Obsessed. No holds barred.' At least the man's tone of reproach was giving way now to one of personal concern. 'That's always dicey. Be impersonal and detached, Roberts, that's the way to get results.'

'Agreed, sir. However, what with Mrs Hartington's plea and also my own respect and affection for the Judge . . .'

'Tell me one thing,' Briggs interrupted. 'Do you genuinely think the Met are involved behind it or are you just using that to stay on the case?'

'Frankly, Guv'nor, I doubt they were involved *before* the incident.' There was no mileage in trying to flannel old Briggs. Not now. 'However, I can't disagree with Mrs

Hartington about the threat of a prejudiced Met investigation—likely procedural irregularities and even suppression of evidence. In view of that, I feel my pursuing the case falls well within the spirit of Sox if not within its precise brief.'

'Bloody Welsh verbalizer, that's you,' Briggs snorted, holding out an official envelope. 'Here's your Special Branch authority. Now piss off and write me that report.'

Alex Timpson was round and portly, with plump cheeks and an engagingly affable smile. It was only his eyes that belied this geniality, their sharp shrewdness amplified by bifocals, their mobility lending a hint of shiftiness. Or maybe, Taff reflected as he settled himself among bundles of files in the MP's busy House of Commons office, maybe he's got something to feel guilty about.

'Good of you to see me, sir.'

'Cooperation with the police deserves priority.'

In point of fact, the Hon. Member for Carton East had been distinctly uncooperative, dodging Taff's attempts to see him the previous afternoon and presumably giving in now solely because Taff had whistled up the high-powered influence of Isabel Hartington.

Although the detective had ordered Virginia Cohen *not* to forewarn the MP, he was uncertain about whether or not she'd have kept faith with that. Distraught and contrite she may have been; yet, for all the guilt and remorse, she was unlikely to forget who were her masters.

'So what's your line of inquiry, Chief Inspector?' He eyed Taff's warrant card then slid it back across the desk. 'The Thames Valley's a long way from my constituency.'

'I'm attached to the Yard, sir, special inquiries.'

'To do with?'

'Football-related offences.'

'I might have guessed,' Timpson quipped, indicating the detective's bruised face. 'Decorated in the line of duty, presumably.' Then, still grinning, he added: 'Of course, football's hardly my field—no pun intended.'

It was said of Timpson that, despite his benign image

and air of avuncular sincerity, he had failed to earn a place in the Cabinet because he was too sharp. Sharp-witted or sharp practice, Taff wondered. Undoubtedly, he was one of the most influential backbenchers.

'You did sit on the sub-committee reviewing the proposed identity-card legislation.'

Timpson shrugged in dismissal. 'Only as a layman. We got our expertise from the likes of David Evans.'

'Did you happen to give evidence to Judge Hartington?'

It startled him, his eyes hunting involuntarily away to gaze through the mullioned windows towards the grey, rainswept river outside. Evidently Virginia had after all kept faith. 'Well, no, not personally. Again, David Evans was the obvious spokesman, what with his being chairman of the Luton club as well as an MP.' He looked back, cocking his head. 'Why, Chief Inspector? Where's all this leading?'

'I think you know that very well, sir.' There was a pause, the MP easing his buttocks from side to side yet somehow keeping his face impassive. 'Suppose we say it's leading to the name Virginia Cohen.'

Given less personal urgency and a bit more of old Briggs's detachment, Taff might well have enjoyed the politician's mental contortions, his impulse to duck and prevaricate tempered now by the blatant futility of doing so. In the event, he still couldn't resist the knee-jerk evasion.

'You're dead right, of course, Chief Inspector. I might have known that from the start.' Anything to play for time and avoid giving a direct answer.

'Known what, sir?'

'What? Well, why you're here.'

'I presume you mean you'd been expecting inquiries.'

'What? How should I?'

'You'd obviously heard about the attack on the Judge. You must have foreseen it wouldn't be long before the trail led to you.'

'Led to . . .' He uttered a yelp-like laugh. 'What are you . . . I—I mean, surely you can't imagine I'm in some way implicated.'

'It's not my place to imagine things, sir, simply to sort out the facts.'

'Can't you give a direct answer, yes or no?'

That from a politician! 'I think you're ahead on the evasion points so far, sir. However, one fact I have established is that you've been in secret liaison with Miss Cohen.'

'Secret?'

'That's right.'

'Discreet, naturally, but . . .' More buttock-shifting. Come on now, Mr MP, you're up against a moment of truth here; no more wriggling now. 'The fact is, the Prime Minister has high expectations of the Judge's report. That being so, there's a natural reluctance to, well, leave things to chance.'

'The PM wants it ensured that His Honour's findings turn out to be politically palatable?'

'Not the Prime Minister specifically. But in view of her direct interest in the issue, naturally the Minister responsible—well, Under-Minister to be exact—was anxious to, let's say, monitor Hartington's progress.'

'Monitor.' Taff nodded. 'Right, so Ginny Cohen passed it to you and you passed it to the Under-Minister. But then it all went sour, didn't it?'

'What?' Timpson glanced at his watch, doubtless seeking an out. 'Sour?'

'This monitoring revealed a ghastly miscalculation— namely, what the Judge calls socialization of the clubs. Help! Time to press the panic button.'

'What?' No trace now of affability, the face flushed with outrage. 'Just what the hell are you implying!'

Got you, Mr Smug Fat Cat, Taff thought, got you on the run. Now let's get somewhere at last. 'Facts, Mr Timpson. The findings were leaked; they were politically unacceptable; His Honour was lured to a secret rendezvous; an act of violence was committed.'

'And—and, god damn it, you're saying they're linked?' If he was indeed genuinely rattled, the politician contrived to mask it with furious indignation. 'Well?'

'You tell me, sir.'

'I'll tell you this much, Roberts, if it turns out you're

behind all these press leaks and the question tabled this morning by the Labour sports shadow, you'd better look to your pension rights!'

'What question, sir?'

'Demanding a statement on the press leaks and also progress on the assault investigation.'

'Are you acquainted with Mr Edward Oxted?' Taff asked, countering the man's counter-attack.

'What if I am?' he retorted evenly. 'Oxted's a keen Party supporter, high on the social list. Can't be many of us haven't met him at some time or another. Why?'

'You're aware of the report's appendix citing Oxted's mismanagement of Balham United. I have reason to believe he was tipped off about that appendix.'

'Have you, by God, have you.' The MP stood up. 'Then I'll thank you to leave now. I'll say nothing more without a solicitor present.'

'I told you this was strictly informal, sir. You're not under caution.'

Timpson hesitated, then shook his head. 'The answer's no, it wasn't leaked by me.'

'But perhaps by someone to whom you passed the material? Some civil servant or—'

'No, Mr Clever.' He moved to open the door, visibly more confident. 'You want proof? Go back and check with your Miss Cohen. Whether or not she had this appendix on Oxted, it was *not* among the stuff she passed to me nor did she make any mention of its existence. Good day to you.'

Oh dear. Lucky in love, unlucky in war—or, on this occasion, in detection. However, as Chiefie Walsh liked to say, the best cases seldom solve easy. Whether or not there was a link between the Balham chairman and the Honourable Member, it wasn't going to tie Oxted to complicity in the assault. None of which did anything to help ease the detective's problems. Whereas it was not yet proving terminal, this latest aggro over DC Smith had undoubtedly sharpened Blaize's axe. It would be honed sharper still if Timpson now added to the clamour for Taff's head.

He crossed Parliament Square and hurried up Victoria Street heading for the Yard. On the third floor, he asked for the Special Branch sergeant, then handed him the authorization. The result, although he was promptly ushered into a senior spook's office, duly emphasized that Taff had even fewer friends around the Yard than he'd thought.

'Before we talk, Roberts, you can just listen to this.'

The man, whose rank was as unstated as his name, switched on a tape-recording of a BBC news report detailing the latest effects of the teachers' strike. He immediately switched briefly to fast-forward then came back to normal speed on the tail end of a report on a NATO meeting. Finally he nodded in satisfaction, turning up the volume and then switching on an adjacent tape-recorder with twin tapes as:

The mysterious circumstance surrounding last Monday's assault on Judge Hartington took a sinister turn today when it was learned he had gone to Balham United's stadium to rendezvous with an informant. The BBC is reliably informed he had been offered photographic evidence of links between hardcore groups of Balham United supporters and the National Front. Additionally, it is understood he was expecting information on links with right-wing activists both in Germany and in Spain of a type frequently associated with massed demonstrations on the terraces. It is understood that similar links have been under investigation by officers of Scotland Yard's Special Branch who had reputedly given evidence in camera to the Hartington inquiry. Meanwhile, in a bulletin issued this morning by the hospital medical authorities, the Judge's condition was described as stable but with as yet no sign of his recovering consciousness.'

CHAPTER 7

The Special Branch man clicked the bulletin to silence but left the twin tapes turning so as to record the ensuing interrogation. Tall, moustached and military-straight, the man had the air of an ex-SAS officer. Due perhaps to his air of confident superiority, Taff found his manner even more disconcerting than the taped news-report.

'You are Chief Inspector David Roberts on Yard attachment from the Thames Valley Police and you have just heard this BBC news recording. What observation do you have to make?'

'I'm surprised by it.'

'Why?'

'Because, apart from myself, the Judge's wife and the man who telephoned the Judge offering information, no one else knew about the National Front aspect.'

'You are sure of that?'

'Other than my superior, DGS Briggs, no one.'

'You withheld those details from DCI Lawley of O Division despite his being in charge of the assault investigation?'

'I did, yes.' Then, to try and get off this line, he added: 'The BBC report is inaccurate in respect of the German and Spanish connections. According to what the Judge told me just before the assault, he'd been offered only the photographic evidence on the NF link.' Taff cleared his throat, irritated to find he was sweating. 'Incidentally, his wife later confirmed to me that that was all he was offered.'

'Did Hartington say if he was acquainted with whoever phoned him to fix the rendezvous?'

'He knew him only as an anonymous voice on the telephone. He'd nicknamed the caller Deep Throat.'

'Deep Throat. Well, well. Then had he received information before?'

'Yes.'

'Concerning?'

'Irregularities by Mr Edward Oxted relating to the future of Balham United Football Club of which he is chairman.'

'To what end?'

'The club's financial ruination with a view to amalgamation with Chelsea so as to liberate the Balham ground for commercial redevelopment.'

'Mr Roberts, did you pass this information to the BBC or any other branch of the information media?'

'I did not. Nor, sir, in view of the extra material about foreign right-wing links and also Special Branch activities, do I believe it to have been leaked by Mrs Hartington.' Again Taff cleared his throat, longing for a drink, longing to sit, longing to get the hell out. 'That would appear to leave only this Deep Throat character or those associated with him in one way or another.'

'One way or another? Explain that, please.'

'The Judge said the man's voice sounded strange—muffled, distant and scared. That suggests either that it was an impersonation or that the man was under duress—perhaps being forced deliberately to lure the Judge into the trap.'

At last there was a pause. The interrogator reached for and glanced at some notes but remained otherwise formal and remote.

'Incidentally,' Taff added, 'the Judge contacted me to accompany him to the rendezvous as a precaution. He'd never actually arranged to meet Deep Throat before. You'll doubtless be aware that I'd been liaising with His Honour with relation to Operation Sox.'

Another pause, longer this time, before the man's hand at last snaked out to switch off the recorder. He removed one of the duplicate tapes, signed and dated it then slid it across the desk towards Taff.

'You may go.'

'Unofficially then, sir, had your people been investigating NF links with Balham United supporters?'

Pause, the atmosphere glacial. 'They said you had a damned cheek.'

'I also have a signed authority, sir.'

85

Pause. In the event, the spook's reply was no more direct than the politician's. 'It's possible. If you think about it, it's almost inevitable. But, of course, what you're really asking me is whether this Deep Throat's offer could have been authentic.' Pause. 'But that presupposes you'll be continuing your investigation.'

'It does, yes. Which happens to be a decision for my guv'nor and the TVP Chief Constable. The same two who signed this authority.' Pause. 'Do I get an answer?'

Whether through lack of progress or else his own compulsion for secrecy, finding an answer genuinely seemed to pain the spook. In the event, to Taff's frustration, he gave an equivocal headshake. 'The NF have contacts with most militant-supporter clubs like the Bulls. Naturally, this department takes an interest in all such links. So, you see, the answer's wide open. But, on the balance of probabilities, I'd say no.'

'No, the offer wasn't authentic?'

'Unlikely.' Abruptly, as if having broken faith, he stood up. 'Why not do yourself a favour, Roberts? Stop trying to play the super sleuth. Stop withholding evidence. Just hand it all over to DCI Lawley and let him get on with the job.'

'That's down to my superiors, sir. Thank you for your co-operation.' Taff pocketed his copy of the tape and moved to leave, wryly reflecting that he really must have been a lot luckier in love than he'd realized.

At Kate's request, Boss Bryan had agreed to set up Kennie Kent's ITN interview at the Bulls' supporters club. The venue suited Kennie just fine, the lad being every bit as much a showman as a sportsman and hence glad to be surrounded with those guaranteed to laud his talents and boost his personal following.

A good-looking and articulate Cockney, Kennie had been groomed by his agent to cultivate the standard Frank Bruno repartee along with the good-family-boy image. To this end, his fur-clad mum, stepbrother Mervyn George and girlfriend Sharon were all prominent in the impromptu club celebration framed as backing to the interview.

Given the number of fans, PR people and club staff crowded into the club bar, it was easy for Kate to ease Taff into the place as an ITN researcher—although, with his smashed-up face, he could well have passed for an ageing supporter.

Martin Ford, primed in advance by Kate, planned to widen the scope of the interview. So, after letting Kennie crack on about his training regime and new game tactics, his diet and his love-life, the sports interviewer steered across to aspects of the club—the team's prospects and general morale, gate revenues and, inevitably, the reputation of its supporters.

'Greatest bunch of lads a team could ask for, Martin. I mean, like, you've got to know they're red-blooded and virile; likewise, they enjoy a good knees-up. But, all said and done, it's the pride they take in us, innit. I mean, OK, so once in a while they may go a touch over the top with the old patriotism, like. But that's the price you got to pay, know what I mean?'

'The price, Kennie?'

'Price of loyalty. Price of their pride in their team.'

'Some might argue it's a heavy price to pay.'

'Don't see why.'

'It's costing the game its status as a sport. It's costing the club a lot of goodwill alongside most other League clubs, especially when you get reports flying around like the one this morning about links with the National Front.'

'Well, I mean, Martin—' the superstar managed a wry snort of derision—'anyone who believes stuff like that, they've got to be bonkers.'

'True or false, you can't deny the Bulls have a very bad name.'

'They're my mates, Martin, so what can I tell you? Not the nutters, of course, but—well, here they all are, God bless 'em.'

He broke off to the familiar chant of Bully-Bully-BULL! Nodding, the interviewer turned to the stepbrother, as squat and powerful as Maradona, yet wild-eyed and tense—and visibly unnerved to see the camera swing towards him.

'How about it, Mervyn? Care to speak up for the club's supporters?'

Pause, the man turning in desperation to Kennie who moved to hug an arm around the broad shoulders. 'No sweat, Merv, tell it to 'em.'

'Like you said, Kennie—the club—it's our life. S'what we live for. Ain't nothing else. Put up wiv a crummy job, see your neighbourhood going yuppy, get slagged off all round.' He shrugged, shaking his head in dismissal. 'None of that matters, like, 'cos this is where it's at. Pride, like you said, Kennie.'

'OK,' the interviewer nodded, 'but, apart from this latest National Front report, what about the club's future? The reports of insolvency? The rumoured merger with Chelsea? The virtual death of your beloved club?'

The supporter winced, stepping back as though from a knee in the crutch—hardly surprising since Kate Lewis had planted the bombshell with her fellow reporter only an hour or so before the interview.

'Dunno what you're on about, mister.'

Neither did the rest of the lads. To the consternation of the sound engineer, a surge of resentment mounted throughout the room.

'What rumours?'

'Who says we're bust?'

'Yeah! Freaking lies!'

'*Sub*merge Chelsea, you mean!'

'Sounds like Ponse Perry talk.'

'Right, Ponse! That freaky fanzine of yours!'

Attention shifted to a lanky young man seated near the entrance who promptly grimaced, shaking his head in denial. 'Rumours? Rumours ain't my style.'

'What about it, Boss?' Kennie called across to where Bryan Walton was leaning against the bar. 'Us and bloody Chelsea?'

The manager spread his hands, shaking his head. 'Go and ask in the boardroom, Kennie, not me. Mr Oxted's the big financier.'

It wasn't the flat denial they'd have liked, the hubbub of

resentment intensifying. And most vocal of all, indifferent now to the camera, was Mervyn George, the fan thrusting angrily forward at the interviewer.

'Where'd you get all this crap, then? Come pushing in with a swinger like that. Who put you up to it?'

'A reporter never reveals his source, Mervyn, you know that—'

He broke off as the youngster grabbed his lapels, heaving him close. 'I asked you a question! Now you bloody answer!'

The moment of threat was instantly defused, Kennie stepping in to intervene, laughing as he eased his stepbrother back. 'You prat, can't you see he's just winding you up?' He turned to the startled interviewer. 'Right, innit, Martin? Just stirring up some on-camera aggro.' He moved to place his hand over the camera lens. 'OK, so we fell for it. You got what you came for. That's your lot now.'

'You run the Bulls' fan magazine?' Taff asked, sitting down with the beanstalk they called Ponse. 'That must keep you busy.'

'Busy today,' he nodded, looking up from his notepad. 'Where'd you lot get all that about insolvency and mergers?'

'Like Martin Ford said, our source is our secret.'

'That how you got the face job?' the youngster asked, nodding at Taff's bruises. 'Working a wind-up trick like this one, was you?'

'Today's was no wind-up,' Taff exclaimed in mock indignation. 'Come on, running a fanzine, you must be the first to hear the rumours. You originate half of them, I'll bet.'

Ponse Perry smirked, flattered for all his ingrained cynicism. 'No comment, guv.' He indicated his notepad. 'Not till our next issue.'

'Come on, surely you'd an inkling about the club's finances if not the Chelsea prospect.'

Ponse examined his fingernails. In contrast to his ear-ring and wavy hair, his arms were heavily tattooed. Finally he nodded, glancing briefly at Taff. 'Yes, I'd heard. Snag is, Obersturmführer Oxted has big boots. It's more than our fanzine's worth to take him on.'

'But if he's killing off the club . . .?'

'Thanks to your lot bringing it into the open, guv, I can now splash it big. Maybe it's anyway time to declare open war. Maybe we run the next issue, then go underground. Snag is, most of these apes in here are either so brainwashed or brainless they can't see Oxted as anything but the club's big white saviour. They swallow all this mouthwash he gives 'em about being a super-fan. They think 'cos he's always upfront and yacking about being Mr Balham United—they believe he'll fork out the bread to bail us out, buy in more talent and that. The apes think with their feet, right.'

'But you know better.'

The editor nodded in conspiracy, lowering his voice. 'Like, there's talk of a big sponsorship deal with Associated Distillers. Big money. But ten per cent'll go straight into Oxted's pocket in commission and most of the rest'll go into paying off *his* loans to the club rather than into transfer fees. Naturally the geezer's a super-fan. Anyone would be if they'd milked the club for a fortune.'

'What about when they finally realize he's betraying them?'

'You heard the buzz earlier. That'll be more like Hiroshima, come the big bang. Much good it'll do. Get 'em all mobbing his mansion up there by the Heath and so what? They'll be dog's meat.' He leered, apparently finding the prospect quite attractive.

'Do you reckon it's already too late?'

'Dunno.' He shrugged his thin shoulders. 'What the board *should* do is vote the Führer off and then get Council money in to bail out the club.'

'But what chance if he's got all the board members in his pocket?'

'OK then—' his sly eyes narrowed—'maybe there's another way.'

'Like what?'

Ponse opened his mouth to answer, only to check at a cough from Boss Bryan, the manager moving to join them. 'You do realize, lad, you're speaking to the fuzz?'

*

Lucky-lover Taff Roberts felt like creeping back into the Sox office on his knees; but in the event, Chiefie Briggs did no worse than call out for a progress update. Presumably the MP had decided on discretion and the spook had decided to reserve his trump.

Taff was about to breathe in relief when the secretary handed him a phone number with a cryptic message to call NATS. National Association of Technical Staff? Northern Athletic Training Service? In the event, it turned out to be Stan in reverse.

'What-ho, Guv. I got you the goods.'

'I should bloody hope so, Smith, the trouble you dropped me in.'

'Oh, yeah, well, sorry about that, Guv.' The Detective-Constable paused to stifle a giggle. 'Thing is, getting in wiv their toughest crew, I had to make it real, know what I mean?'

'I know what I told you about using Sox only as a last resort!'

'Thing is, Guv, I was just putting on this big Tarzan act when some burke of a PC cops on to the end of me toecap. Wasn't intentional, honest.'

'I was there, Smith! I saw it happen! You didn't give a monkey's who got hurt! Just a crazy nutter having it off!'

There was a disconcerted pause before: 'Had to look natural, what with half the crew nabbed along wiv me.' Pause. 'Sorry about that, Guv—about dropping you in it. Anyhow, the good news is, it's got me in wiv 'em. And listen, it's better'n we thought. The word is, they're really tooled up!'

'Arms? Weapons?'

'S'what one of 'em told me, yeah. Dead scared he is and all. He wants out but he don't know how. So I told him I knew this copper. Married to me auntie, I said.' He snorted. 'Sorry about that but how else could I know the Filth? Anyhow, he's all jacked up for a meet, OK?'

'How soon? This evening?'

'Ah, well, Guv, he's *very* nervous. The meet's got to be on his terms or not at all. He'll name the place and the time.'

And just how far, Taff wondered, could he trust DC Stan Smith, let alone this reputedly nervous Bull supporter.

'You've got to be kidding.'

'Take it or leave it. Frankly, mate, since I'm up there in the firing line wiv yer, I'd as soon you left it.'

Another pause, longer this time, Taff perspiring for the second time that day. The pain of those boots smashing into him was still too bloody recent, the ache of his cracked ribs still too sharp a reminder. But against that, the sting of failure and betrayal. Ribs would heal and memory fade, but not the sense of guilt if he now bottled out.

'One thing this kid said,' the DC added after a moment, 'he reckoned this whole frigging arsenal they've got hid away—it all come via some Paddy they met through the National Front.'

'You crime wallahs,' Martin Ford grumbled as he and Kate returned to the news-room, 'you're all as bent as the criminals.' Then, as Kate exclaimed in indignation, he added: 'I'll be lucky to use more than a smidge of that Balham stuff.'

'But it was magic—real-life drama—ITN's stalwart sports reporter grabbed by yobbo fan, then saved by super-star Kennie Kent . . .'

'A cheap media wind-up,' Ford retorted, shaking his head. 'Calculated provocation.'

Kate gestured in wry self-defence, knowing he was largely correct. 'Except, Martin love, it's all true about the insolvency *and* the merger plan.'

'Except, Katie love, since you can't substantiate it, the lawyers won't allow us to air it. End of real-life drama. Spiked.'

'Just hang on to it. Its time will come.'

'Oh, sure,' the sports editor groaned. 'A gem for *It'll be All Right on the Night*.' He laughed, none the less, tickled by the whole bizarre episode. If nothing else, he was determined to keep a copy for his private collection.

He headed for the sports desk, only to be confronted by

a rather flustered researcher, a hand pressed tight over the mouthpiece of her phone. 'I've got a woman here asking for either you or Kate Lewis. Says she's got information about the assault on Judge Hartington.'

Kate was quick to take command, contacting the switchboard to transfer the caller to the crime desk, then hurrying to switch on the tape-recorder before picking up her receiver.

'Saw you there at the club, Miss Lewis.' The woman spoke rapidly, rattling out the words in short, nervous bursts. 'You've got to understand, you do this our way or not at all—right?'

'Do what, caller? All I know is it's something to do with the assault on the Judge.'

'A witness who wants a meet, OK? Now do you do it our way or not?'

'Depends . . .'

'Yes or no, Miss Lewis?'

'All right, then.'

'See, it's my boyfriend what was there.'

'One of the muggers, you mean?'

'No questions. Just listen, OK? Thing is, they went too far. He didn't want no part of it—not that sort of aggravation—no way.'

'You mean, he's scared the Judge might die?'

There was a sharp exclamation and then the line went dead. Kate swore. She switched off the tape and hung up but continued to sit beside the telephone.

'You blew it,' the sports reporter groaned. 'You frightened her off.'

'Want a bet? With informants like this, it's best not to let them have it all their own way. If you make it clear from the start that it's a two-way trade, they're far less likely to get camera shy later on. Also—' She broke off in relief, switching on the tape and lifting the phone as it rang again. 'Kate Lewis speaking.'

'I told you no questions. It's hard enough this end without you getting smart. Understood?'

'Yes.'

'He's scared. He wants to make a statement, but he don't trust the Old Bill. Savvy?'

'Yes.'

'He's agreed to meet you. On your own. Get that? Alone. Understood?'

The sports reporter was shaking his head in open disagreement but Kate gestured in dismissal.

'Whereabouts, caller?'

'Go to the Vauxhall tube and walk along Nine Elms Lane. Stay on the bit beside the river.'

'When?'

'Soon as ever.'

The line went dead. Kate switched off the recorder, removed the cassette and then headed for the news desk with the sports reporter in tow bleating about risk factors.

'No risk, Martin,' she winked, tapping the side of her nose. 'You can come along and watch the action from the camera car if you like.'

In the event, however, Kate ended up as the one with egg on her face. They reached the rendezvous without traffic hold-ups. Kate walked up and down beside the river like an early tom. She even had one hopeful punter slow his car to ask her price—only to recognize her face and speed away. But there was no sign either of the nervous woman caller or of her remorseful Bully boyfriend.

CHAPTER 8

'Come in and sit down, Bryan. Drink?' It was the invariable opening to all their sessions, no matter how negative the Chairman's reasons for summoning his team manager. The order to sit was so that little Oxted would then be higher; the offer of a drink was merely an excuse to pour one for himself. 'I heard you landed Kennie a television interview.'

Pause, Bryan Walton bracing himself for the Gamelord's inevitable rebuke.

'Selected for an England friendly after all.' He accepted the half glass of champagne and as usual set it on one side to leave untouched. 'I think it went reasonably well, all in all.'

'Do you, by God, do you?' The Chairman took a pull from his own glass, then stared in thought before moving to gaze out of the big vista window with its panoramic view over the London suburbs. In contrast to Walton's office, the Chairman's suite was sumptuous: calf-leather upholstery, Swedish design furniture and fittings, space for a full board meeting, kitchenette, cocktail-bar, wall-to-wall extravagance. 'Would have gone one hell of a lot better if you'd followed our normal interview procedure.'

'They asked specifically to record at the supporters' club.'

'Not surprising in view of what they'd got planned!'

'It was Kent they wanted to interview, not you, Mr Oxted.' The manager's response was unusually sharp and defiant, stopping the tycoon in mid-stride around his desk. He took another drink, staring keenly at Walton, then shook his head.

'And just who do you suppose got him that selection, eh, Walton? I swung a thumping lot of influence to get him this chance.' He grimaced, drinking again. 'All right, so that's not something to brag about to the press. None the less, with hindsight, you can see why you screwed up, eh? Why you should have cleared it with me first.'

'A trivial issue like that?'

'Trivial, was it? Trivial?' Then, overriding the manager's reply: 'You blew it! As usual. By all accounts, they took us to the cleaners.'

'Since you weren't even there—'

'No, I wasn't there, damn it! If I had been, they'd not have got away with it!'

'Away with what, Mr Oxted? Whatever account of it you heard, it sounds wildly inaccurate.' He reached none the less for the wine, lifted the glass, then quickly replaced it.

'Oh, no doubt you've got your "trivial" version all prepared, Walton. But what I heard—in fact from that git editor of the fanzine, and subsequently checked with two others who were present—was that the TV people concocted a load of rumours about insolvency and a proposed merger with bloody Chelsea. More, instead of denying these rumours, you simply referred them to *me!*'

'Ah.' This time he did take a drink, slurping some in the process.

'Ah, what? Ah, you'd set it all up with ITN? Planted these bloody rumours? Planned some sort of lunatic sabotage! The same way you've been leaking all these lies to the BBC!'

'What lies?' Walton jumped up. 'What in the hell are you on about?'

'Scurrilous crap about links with the National bloody Front, that's what! Don't pretend you hadn't heard!'

'Sure, I heard. Martin Ford referred to that as well. Doesn't mean it originated from me!'

'*No?*' Oxted was crouched forward now like a boxer on the attack. 'So where else do you expect me to look, eh? For years you've had the knife out for me! Ever since I stepped in to try and save the club, in fact. Right from the very first. And it ain't hard to guess why! You want the Bulls to go to the knackers like Millwall, don't you? Fancy your chances in a Council tie-up, right? See your way to getting a seat on the board that way, don't you?'

Curiously, Walton had stopped trying to deny it, was merely standing there, arms crossed and shaking his head, as though to counter the rantings of a child.

'Well, tough!' Oxted rapped, jabbing a finger at him. 'Ted Oxted's here to stay. Take more than a sly little worm like you to see me off!'

Oddly enough, for all his ranting and apparent venom, the Chairman said nothing about dismissal or handing in notice. For his part, the abused manager said nothing of resignation, simply swearing in muted denial before swinging round to walk out.

The City pub was crowded with hyped-up youngsters trying to unwind from the stock listings and currency shifts on their terminal screens. Cocky, ostentatious fat-kits, Taff decided as he eased among them looking for Papa Walsh.

'Pint of Guinness here, son.' The man and the pint were both awaiting him in one of the chintzy booths. The familiar leathery grin greeted him like a warm hug. 'Welcome to yuppy land.'

'This your local, Guv'nor?'

'They're all as bad round here,' Walsh apologized. 'This one just happens to be the nearest to my office.'

In the three years since retirement from the Met, Chiefie Walsh had built himself a handy little empire managing security for one of the City's middle-range merchant banks, Klein Holdings. Through a blend of contacts, bluff and cunning, he had accessed his way into a wide range of information networks, including an illicit link with Criminal Records. It was, as he'd explained to Taff, his main source of job satisfaction, a modest compensation for the loss of active field work. He also had a substantial slush-fund allowance for 'entertaining' snouts and also his Yard contacts, principally personnel from the Serious Fraud office. As ever in his life, the *quid* trade-off was a feature of his success, several insider-dealers and one corporate raider having already gone down as a result of tips passed on by Foxy. Fortunately, his employers had the good sense not to inquire either into his methods or his expenses.

'How did you make out after the match last night then, boyo?'

'You getting porno-minded in your dotage?' Taff grinned, shaking his head. 'Cracked ribs, all bashed up, and I'm fit for fun and games?'

'It never stopped you before, you Welsh ram!'

'Honest, Guv'nor, I don't know where you get this image of me.'

Papa Walsh chuckled, raising his pint in a wry toast before pointing to the seat. 'The envelope folded into that newspaper confirms most of the share dealings you wanted checked, including one unexpected little gem I chanced on.' The lean face creased in satisfaction over it. 'The nominee owner of several very large Chelsea FC holdings turned out to be a *femme fatale* by the name of Mrs Patricia Johns, using her parents' address in Islington. Turns out she is now

97

divorced and using her maiden name of Patricia Craine to live in sin with Teddy Oxted. Whatever his plans for the lady now she's divorced, he's invested a *lot* of trust in her. All right, so he'll have the usual co-ownership safeguards on the share titles; but it's a fact she could hold him to ransom if she chose, both over sale *and* over voting rights.'

'A tenner says she's blonde and leggy and one hell of an eyeful.'

'You mean the bird he had with him yesterday in the directors' box?'

'Observant as ever, eh?' Taff grinned and took a grateful pull of Guinness. 'Anything else?'

'Apparently there's been quite a lot of smart money deserting Oxted's ship in the last couple of days. Wherever the rumours are coming from, the City suddenly got shy of Oxted Securities.'

He paused to check his Filofax, then nodded. 'You asked about Associated Distillers. An intriguing one, that. They were gobbled up by that American liquor giant a couple of years back, remember? Well, it's known that the Yankee end, in a tradition dating back to Prohibition days, has a lot of Mafia involvement. Presumably as a result, Associated has been getting increasingly lavish of late. This sponsorship deal with Oxted is typical. Their expenditure's said to be way out of line with profit ratios. Splashing cash around like there's no tomorrow.'

'You think they're laundering?'

Foxy nodded. 'That's what the Fraud Squad lads reckon. Brimming slush funds, sponsorships all round, limitless perks and entertainment budgets. It's got to be coming from somewhere.'

'Bastards!'

'Now then, Taff lad, now then, remember the basics: distance, dispassion, objectivity.'

'Listen, Guv'nor, you try a holiday in Gambia. See the sharks sunning themselves beside the pool, then drive out into the bush and get mobbed by skinny black kiddies without even the price of a bloody pen.'

'You know your trouble, my son: you've seen too much

villainy and corruption.' Walsh sighed, genuinely worried. But for his anxieties for the future of the Force, he might have urged the DCI to pack it in, read Law and become a fat cat himself. Conscience was all very well but not when it tilted investigation into crusade.

'I'll survive, Jack, don't you worry.'

'But will you? Look at the bind you got into over that pervert Snow. Rotten little wanker wasn't worth the time of day, yet you risked your all to put him away.' He shook his head. 'That sort of Robin Hood lark's way out of line.'

'Whatever risk I took was for the kids,' Taff retorted. 'Couple of dozen little girls he'd savaged over the years. All admitted in TICs. Left to it, Snow would have done a Colin Evans, gone over the top and killed some poor little Marie Paine. Call it a crusade if you like, but someone had to stop the animal!'

He managed to pull himself up at last, embarrassed by his emotion and aware of the validity of old Foxy's concern. Distance, dispassion, objectivity. Yet, damn it, what was there left if you didn't care? If you cauterized emotion? If you let yourself become a Kate rather than a Kathy?

'So you stopped Snow; and now you're going to stop Oxted. That how it is, lad?'

'*Oxted?*' It checked Taff in mid-drink. 'You kidding?'

'The fat cat tycoons were never favourite with you, as I recall. You could generally boil up a fair head of steam over the City's venal hypocrisy.' Foxy was getting pretty passionate himself now. 'For God's sake, the Indecency Squad should have cured you of all that—got your priorities sorted. But the way you're going at this one, all it did was start you down the Stitcher slope!'

'I'm obliged to you for seeing me so promptly, Mr Venables.'

Taff had got the man's name from the Judge's Deep Throat file, Foxy duly establishing that, although not a full director of Associated Distillers, Venables was an executive accountant of sufficient seniority to be in the know. He turned out to be engaging and jokey with a big horsey grin and a six-handicap stoop.

'An urgent inquiry to do with our sports-sponsorship programme? Not by any chance Inland Revenue or VAT, I trust.'

'Not tax, sir, no. I'm here because of your company's dealings with Balham United.'

'Ah.' Just a touch less grin at that, perhaps. 'Mr Oxted referred you to me, did he?'

'As it happens, no, sir.' He needed to shock the guy; there wasn't the time for tiptoeing around. 'In point of fact, because of His Honour Judge Hartington.'

'Ah.' No visible sign of shock, unfortunately. 'Does that make you a lawyer or what?'

'Detective Chief Inspector, special duties attachment to the Yard.'

The toothy grin just about stayed fixed but the bland composure was in disarray, strongly suggesting to Taff that the executive had indeed been corrupted and drawn into the laundering caper.

It could, after all, be excessively tough for middle-class Brit suburbanites like Venables when, in the wake of all the takeover anxiety, they were confronted with the trauma of illicit practices. OK, buddy, we're happy for you to stay on board so long as you understand how we do things Stateside . . . a fat salary hike in return for three-monkeys loyalty to the company . . .

'As I told the Judge last week, Chief Inspector, United's sponsorship is yet to be finalized.' He cleared his throat, turning to tap away at his console until he produced the draft contract document on his screen. 'We're looking for exclusive drinks cover, which means Mr Oxted has to terminate several related publicity agreements. But the main sticking point is on transfer fees: he's pushing us for a no-strings percentage involvement in all player transfers, but our people feel that at the least that merits a seat on the club board.'

He glanced up from the screen. 'I have to tell you, Mr Roberts, what with that gruesome attack on the Judge in the Bullring car park—frankly, we've been having second thoughts. In the liquor industry we get a bad enough press

100

without risking being tarred with any sort of, well, hooligan scandal.'

'I'm sorry, sir, I don't follow you.'

'The whisper in the City is that Judge Hartington had unearthed something a touch murky to do with Balham United. Nothing specific, but what with the precedent else-where—property speculations and so forth—it's enough to make us nervous.'

'You and the stock market both.'

'Money talks, as they say,' Venables affirmed, the grin on the executive face of Capitalism now back up to full strength. He wiped the contract from the screen with a gesture of dismissal. 'So, in summary, the answer is: not yet and quite possibly not at all.' He stood up. 'I can't imgine that advances your inquiry very far. I need hardly say, Associated Distillers's fiscal record and integrity remain as ever our paramount concern.'

'They've got to substitute Community for Commerce,' the Judge's voice told Taff from the cassette-player on the way back to the Sox office. 'Community sponsorship via local authority ties is the only long-term way of keeping the game as a sport. Unfortunately, it will have to be imposed by legislation because the money's too big for the top League clubs ever to accept it voluntarily.

'Yes, of course there'll always be a commercial element. Local councils owe a duty of thrift to their tax-payers, after all. Revenues from gate-money and occasional television may still need to be augmented by such as product sponsor-ship, especially when the all-seat regulations finally kill off the terraces. But it will be commerce with propriety rather than the blatant profit-grubbing of the enterprise culture. The professional foul, the rake-off percentage, the covert fostering of hooliganism—these are the ugly face of modern League football. They're all symptomatic of the fatal cancer which will have to be cut out, and very soon, if the patient is to survive, ha.' Hartington's abrupt guffaw punctuated his iration. 'Forgive me, Roberts. Time was, as a young barrister, I used to wax lyrical at the sight of a fee. But

101

whenever you hear a judge resorting to metaphor, it's a dangerous indication of passion.'

And why shouldn't the old gent get passionate, Taff thought, switching off the tape. He's a sportsman himself, a rugger Blue, no less! Whatever other reasons they had for appointing him to this judicial inquiry, his lifelong sporting ties surely figured. Dame Elizabeth for Cleveland, Taylor for Hillsborough, Hartington for football's future. They might have misjudged his individuality and his politics; but they'd got the right man for the game. Or was that in itself a mistake? Given less commitment to sport, maybe he'd have given them more politically palatable conclusions. Hence Miss Watchdog Cohen perhaps.

Once again, returning to the Sox offices, Taff got the warning signal as their secretary pointed him through to the chief's room. Oddly enough, however, although Briggs had received yet another complaint about his maverick Welsh sidekick, he dealt with this one more in a spirit of resignation than rebuke. The old bloke being worn smooth, Taff decided, by the persistent drip of water on stone.

'Serious Fraud office this time, Roberts. That doesn't leave many feathers on the Met fowl you haven't ruffled. How about Traffic next?'

'What's their complaint?' Taff asked, for once more worried than his chief. 'To do with my visit to Associated Distillers already?'

'It is indeed,' Briggs confirmed, 'and registering about point six on the protest scale because, wouldn't you know it, they've had the company under covert investigation for months. The last bloody thing they wanted was a pushy DCI waltzing in there ringing alarm bells, alerting the Distillers' accountants and, worse, their American masters.'

Taff grunted, still frowning and anxious. 'OK, Guv'nor, I apologize for that and I'll keep totally clear of them from now on. What I don't understand is how the Fraud lads knew. I walk into AD House and within half an hour they're belling you about it.'

'Maybe they've got a mole in there.'

'Come on, Guv'nor, even Serious Fraud don't have those

sort of resources. Anyway, I went straight to Venables, and damn sure he's no mole. Nor would they bother bugging his office. So how did they know? Even in the improbable event that they had the building under surveillance, they'd hardly have identified me going in there.'

'Someone watching who knew you from your Met days?'

'Thousand-to-one shot, Guv'nor.' He shook his head and swore. 'I just don't get it.'

'And I don't get why you're suddenly so twitchy, lad. Usually so unflappable.' He grunted, baring his tobacco-stained teeth in unaccustomed humour. 'Getting to you, is it? Don't like them all breathing down your neck?'

'Me, Guv'nor?' Taff gave a tense, high-pitched giggle. 'That's the big turn-on.'

It was a bit of wry banter he was to recall soon after. Just then, however, they were interrupted by the Sox secretary, buzzing through to relay Taff two urgent messages—the first to make personal contact at Klein Holdings, the second from Isabel Hartington to say that her husband's condition was deteriorating.

'Where are you calling from, Taff?'

'Car phone. I'm on my way to the hospital.'

'Ok then, I suppose this is no more of a risk than our meeting up somewhere.' Walsh paused, and for a moment Taff thought they'd been cut off.

'Guv'nor?'

'They're gunning for you, son. I got back from the pub to find a plummy-voiced chiefie from C-10 playing with my computer. Worse, he'd got himself into my CRO link. Naturally, he used that to put some very heavy elbow on me. And it won't surprise you to hear what he's after in return for not pulling the plug.'

'Ohhhh shit.'

'In a word, yes. On you. He insisted on digging right back to that prison-riot case we cracked together. Everything. Illicit expenses, your liaison with madam, the lot.'

'With Kate? For God's sake, what did you tell him?'

'Don't panic, son. You know me: I'd as soon get publican's elbow running a pub than split on you. Mind you, they seem to know an uncanny lot already. Like the fact that we all three went to the match last night. In fact, I have to tell you, the amount of mouth he gave me, I reckon they want you spoon-fed.'

'Come again?'

'They knew I'd bell you like this. They *want* you to know you're on the spot.'

'To scare me off? That what you mean?'

'It's a well-worn trick, son.' He guffawed. 'I used it meself once or twice.'

'The bastards!' Already Taff was looking in his rear-view mirror, scanning the vehicles behind him to see which they might be in.

'They'll try to jerk your strings, boyo. But don't let them con you. I told it to them straight how you're the Kleenex Kid and there's absolutely nothing they can find on you. Nothing. So just hang in there.'

This time the line did go dead, Taff's nerve along with it. They would find out. If Vincent Hartington could find out, one judge to another, so could they, one copper to another. Stitcher Roberts would come unstitched. End of Sox and, worse still, end of the Hartington case—sod it—which was, after all, their objective. If you can't deflect it, shoot it down; the Met's knee-jerk response to having its closet searched. After all, no one knew better than they did how everyone above the rank of woodentop has something hidden away somewhere.

Meanwhile, his alter ego the Judge was in crisis, possibly already dead; which, ironically, would jolt the investigation from assault to murder, leaving him anyway outranked to continue it on his own. The best he could then hope for would be to have Chiefie Briggs at the helm. And the chance of the Met brass accepting that was an implacable nil.

'I blew it, Lawrence,' Kate groaned in a rare moment of confession. 'I misread the signals. I should have registered how jittery this mystery woman really is and gone in there solo without the team.'

104

'Nonsense, woman.'

Yet for all the editor's denial, the use of her gender said it all. Had it been a male reporter, he'd have been expected to go in solo and then negotiate camera coverage as part of the deal. Instead, as a woman, she was barred from any such initiative. True, Kate had once set an unfortunate precedent by getting herself taken hostage by a crazed prison officer wanted for the murder of an IRA bomber. The incident had ended with her being all but blown up and subsequently forbidden by Lawrence Cawley ever to go in solo again.

'They're probably contacting the Beeb right now! Kate Adie will go in solo. You wait and see!'

'Cool it, darling, this isn't like you.'

'It is! What do you mean, damn it?' Then, abruptly laughing at her own outburst: 'All right then, all right. But I've got to have something to give my fella in return. He's out on a limb. He's got to make this case or they'll screw him. The brass at the Yard can get *very* vindictive. OK, Lawrence? So next time . . .'

'We'll see.'

'Next time, I go in solo.' She pulled a face, moving away. 'The same way I'm going to interview Oxted this evening: wired but otherwise naked.'

CHAPTER 9

Isabel Hartington sat beside the bed, clasping her husband's hand, her eyes on his ashen face. The scene could almost have been posed: a classic Pre-Raphaelite entitled *Vigil*. Yet, glancing at the monitor screens and dials, Taff saw they all seemed much as they had on his previous visit. Also, when the wife registered his arrival and moved to welcome him, she showed few symptoms of distress. Tired-eyed, indeed bordering exhaustion; but not tearful or distraught. Whatever the crisis, it had apparently receded.

'The old dog's got bottle,' she confirmed, smiling. 'I'm so sorry to have cried wolf.'

'No problem.' Taff grinned, relief surging through him at this reprieve from the ultimate guilt.

'Your secretary was all for interrupting your meeting if I'd let her.'

'Ah well, she knew I was back in the doghouse, that's why. She wanted to get me off the hook.' He gestured in dismissal at the woman's frown of concern. 'It was no great hassle, just my boss relaying the latest complaint against me.'

'Complaint?'

'First it was Ted Oxted, via O Division; DACC Blaize, both yesterday and again this morning; this afternoon's was Serious Fraud, and next in line could well be Special Branch. It really only needs Alex Timpson for the full house.'

'Oh dear.'

'So far, he's exercised his politician's discretion—presumably thanks to the influence you brought to bear on him.'

'Ah.' That at least seemed to amuse her. 'Well, if so, I'm delighted. I suppose it's a help knowing how to play the Establishment game, however much one may disapprove of it as a system.'

But does she really disapprove? Taff wondered. It's always so fashionable to knock the system despite being a child of it. Moreover, would she have done so before her husband's defiance of the Establishment and his conceivably falling victim to it?

'So they're all gunning for you,' she remarked, serious again as she eyed him in the subdued light of the ward. 'I'm sorry, David, my fault, I'm afraid.'

'Like hell it is.'

She smiled, shaking her head in denial, holding him with that direct gaze of hers. 'So, aside from fighting off the long knives, how goes the investigation?'

Taff grunted, rubbing his chin in evasion and wondering if her husband had really taken a turn for the worse or whether she had merely invented that to get him along for a progress report. Well, tough, Madam Justice, the only

106

person privy to that progress, what little there was of it, happened to be Chiefie Briggs. 'To use police spokesman's jargon, ma'm, no arrests are as yet envisaged. And you? Did you pick up anything of interest?'

'It's hard to say. Yesterday, for the second time, a young woman rang the hospital masquerading as my daughter. I tried to draw her out, but of course the moment I asked why she was so interested in Vincent's condition, she rang off.'

'Unlikely to be a reporter then or she'd probably have tried to brazen it out.'

'I agree. In fact, she sounded scared and also genuinely upset.' Isabel Hartington paused, glancing at the detective before nodding in decision. 'Also I've had another visit from the Met, but not that pushy lad Lawley. More senior and, now that I think about it, I suppose he must have been fishing around for information about you.'

'Wonderful!' It was like standing in a forest watching the trees close in. But was it anything more than routine Met paranoia? The irony was that, if only they could stop wasting manhours watching their backs and instead get on with the job of protecting the public, they'd have a lot less to be paranoid about in the first place.

Paranoia breeds paranoia, Taff concluded, watching his rear-view mirror rather more than the road ahead during the drive back from the hospital. He failed to establish if anyone was tailing him, but he succeeded in giving a van in front of him a modest bumper-shunt.

However, it was easy enough to pinpoint the man watching from a car parked opposite the Sox office. Suspiciously easy, Taff thought, recalling Papa Walsh's spoon-feeding theory. Face averted, Taff stepped inside a nearby shop for a few moments, then returned the way he'd just come before crossing the road and edging closer so as to suss out the car and its occupant. In point of fact, being a new model Jag, the car definitely didn't fit—other than perhaps for Special Branch surveillance! Nor, when Taff eased closer, did the watcher fit either. On the contrary, he was middle-aged, smartly turned out and alarmingly familiar . . . a man Taff had indeed visited in his office week by week over the preceding three years to discuss indecency prosecutions.

'Far too much of a coincidence to find you here, Mr Harris,' he remarked, easing into the Jag beside the flustered branch Crown Prosecutor. 'Whatever could have brought you to my doorstep?'

Taff of course knew the answer all too well; yet he had little sympathy for the lawyer and the reasons which had panicked him up to Caxton Street.

Harris's professional caution and his ambitions within the Crown Prosecution Service had come dangerously close to undermining their combined conviction of the child-molester Leonard Snow. In the event, the lawyer's involvement in the conspiracy had been largely by default; yet already he had benefited from the Snow case by promotion from Berkshire to one of the prestigious outer-London branches.

'I've been waiting outside here for nearly an hour,' Jeremy Harris complained irrelevantly.

'I was at the hospital to see His Honour Judge Hartington,' Taff replied with equal irrelevance.

'Heavens, why?'

Taff indicated his battered face. 'I happened to share some of his punishment.'

'Good God. But I understood you were investigating corruption within the Met.'

'As a side issue to His Honour's judicial inquiry, yes.'

'I had no idea.'

'Very few people have, sir. So what is it brings you to wait for an hour in the hope of catching me?'

The lawyer fidgeted, unwrapping a toffee before also offering one to the detective. 'I've had some inquiries regarding a case we were involved in together. Initially a request, by way of the Chief Crown Prosecutor's office, asking for the case file. Then today an officer—I presume he was from C-10—putting some very probing questions to me about the strength of the police evidence.'

'Which case would this have been, sir?'

'Damn it, man, don't pussyfoot around,' the lawyer snapped, his anxieties surfacing in anger. 'You know very well it's the Snow case. Specifically, the officer wanted to know about our evidence from the forensic people, from a witness called Darroch and also from yourself.'

An inspired bit of targeting, Taff thought. Yet only he and Harris had known for sure. So long as Harris hadn't bottled out, no one could actually *prove* anything.

'So what?' Then, when the prosecutor blinked in surprise, Taff added: 'There's been no appeal by Snow; there's no question of anyone reopening the case. Provided you gave them the same answers we gave when briefing counsel before the trial, no one can possibly dig up any mud.'

'You—you're a cool fish, aren't you, Roberts.'

'I've no trouble with my conscience, sir, if that's what you mean.' Then, as Harris again shook his head, he added: 'Damned sure, you'll not do either of us any good panicking up here to lurk outside my office like this.'

'What do you mean?'

Taff nodded towards the line of parked cars opposite. 'Likely as not, someone's snapping pics of us right now. Possibly this C-10 bloke of yours. See him anywhere around, can you?'

The effect on Harris was convulsive, the lawyer shrinking down in his seat while tensely scanning the cars. 'Blast you, Roberts!'

'I really can't see why you're being so hostile, sir.' Despite the threat to his own position, Taff was having a job keeping a straight face. 'It's standard Met procedure whenever threatened to dig around in search of a *quid pro quo*. Pragmatic policing, that's the euphemism: blame it on manning-levels, market forces, declining public morals, Thatcher's enterprise culture—the whole bagful of excuses.' He nodded, repeating it. 'Pragmatic policing à la Met, right?'

'You should know, Roberts, since the Met was where you first cut your teeth.'

'All I know,' Taff retorted, shaking his head, 'is that I'm damned lucky they aren't doing a John Stalker on me. At least, with me, they're trying to dig up some dirt first instead of suspending me and *then* trying to find a reason for doing it.'

'I remember—' the prosecutor's head was still wagging—'I remember warning you that it's a slippery slope.'

'The fudge game? Yes, I recall that, too. A warning I took very much to heart, both then and ever since, rest assured.' He opened the car door to leave. 'By the way, sir, congratulations on your promotion. One step closer to the DPP's job, eh?'

Harris's face as he closed the car door was flushed with anxiety. And rightly, Taff thought: lose his cool and blab about Snow, and they'd both go down together. There'd be nothing public or out in the open; it would all be dealt with discreetly, behind closed doors; but they'd both lose their entire stock of Brownie points.

The atmosphere in Oxted's sitting-room was about as hostile as any Kate Lewis could recall since leaving the *Manchester Evening News* for television journalism. Oxted's surliness apart, the silent presence of his lawyer, notepad in hand, was distinctly disconcerting. After all, had Oxted allowed a camera team along, he might have had grounds for nervousness. But since this visit was really no more than exploratory, why the legal eagle? Not that she objected in the least to the presence of a third party; on the contrary, given the tycoon's reputation with women, it was a big relief.

'So that we don't waste any time, Miss Lewis, suppose you state your areas of interest.'

Kate nodded, determined to yield nothing. 'General and wide-ranging, OK? To begin with—'

'Hey.' Oxted was equally determined not to grant her the initiative. 'That's no answer.'

Kate stared at him in feigned surprise. 'In the absence of an ITN camera, I'd say it was ample answer. However, if you plan to start spelling out no-go areas—' she stood up to leave—'I agree, don't let's waste each other's time.'

'You'll allow me some precautions, Miss Lewis.' He had

shifted position so as to obstruct her departure. 'I'm not accustomed to having crime reporters interview me.'

'I'm not accustomed to having lawyers present, least of all at preliminary interviews such as this.' She forced a half-smile, moving back to the chair. 'Suppose we call it quits, OK? Now, for a start, what comment do you have to make about the recent sharp fall in the value of Oxted Securities on the stock market?'

Briefly, the little man's face flushed with anger as he stepped across to point down at her. 'Don't think you can come pushing in here and get smart with me, missie. You're not dealing with one of your cheapo villains now, you know!'

The rapid-fire of his words checked in response to a warning murmur from the lawyer, reinforcing Kate's relief at the man's presence. It was not so much the substance of Oxted's words as the latent aggression in his manner. And just what was his relationship with his mother, Kate found herself wondering; just which female was it in those formative early years that he has to keep putting down?

'Right, then,' the man resumed more quietly, 'you want my comment, I'll give it you. Share investors are sensitive, and rightly so given that they've a lot of money at stake. When they hear wild rumours floated by irresponsible media people trying to hype up a story, do you wonder they start to sell?'

'You're referring to the rumours about the solvency of Balham United, sir, and its possible merger with Chelsea?'

'Scurrilous bloody lies! And worse, cooked up by you people so as to provoke an on-camera incident at the supporters' club!'

'Excuse me, but that part of the Kennie Kent interview has *not* been transmitted, nor is it likely to be.' Kate paused long enough to add a wry shrug. 'Not, that is, unless these so-called rumours are later confirmed.'

'You what?' Oxted glared across from pouring himself a brandy. 'Is that meant to be some sort of a threat?'

'Simply a matter of fact, Mr Oxted. Dramatic moments such as a physical assault on ITN's sports correspondent

111

are naturally handy for possible future use.' She cocked her head in query. 'Why? Am I to take it the rumours *are* true?'

But for the presence of the lawyer, Kate reflected, she'd never have risked being half as audacious. Indeed, for the second time, Oxted came visibly close to losing control as he strode across to stand over her.

'Really fancy your chances as a clever bitch, don't you, missie!'

'When I call you a bastard, Mr Oxted, you can call me a bitch. Until then, kindly try to be more civil.' The two glared it out in mutual antagonism before Kate renewed the attack. 'I repeat, are the rumours about the club's bankruptcy and a proposed merger true?'

This time the tycoon managed to bite back his response, instead turning to the lawyer. 'Morris, remind me never to let ITN interview me on camera again.' Then, resuming to her, he replied evenly: 'The club's finances are always open to scrutiny. As for a merger, since Chelsea are the senior club in terms of League placing, I suggest you ask their chairman. OK, Miss Steel Trap?'

'So you're not denying either possibility?' Kate retorted. determined to sustain the pace of aggression. Then, when Oxted merely waved two fingers in reply, she added: 'What about His Honour Judge Hartington? Do you admit or deny that you had a rendezvous to meet him at the Balham United ground the night he was assaulted there?'

'Surely to God, Morris, that has to be actionable provocation!'

'A simple yes or no would help,' Kate persisted as the lawyer shrugged in equivocation.

'No, damn you!' Oxted yelled at her. 'The man's a personal friend!'

'Really, sir? I find that surprising in view of his recently reported recommendations for the future of football in this country, not least the running of clubs such as Balham United.'

'Just what the hell are you trying to imply by that?'
'By what?'

'Clubs such as Balham United, that's what!'

'Clubs, for instance, with a reputation for rampant hooliganism among their supporters.'

'Ah, so I'm to be held responsible for the behaviour of the Bulls' supporters?'

'It appears that your friend Judge Hartington intends to suggest something to that effect in his impending report, yes.'

'God help me, woman!'

He got no further. This time, however, it wasn't the lawyer who stopped him but the arrival of a tall blonde woman—Patsy Crane, his female companion of three years. She came in quickly, crossing without hesitation to greet Kate, making no bones about the fact that she'd been listening outside.

'Perhaps I should shout Cut, Miss Lewis. Isn't that the word you film people use to interrupt the action?' She shook hands, her grip firm and determined, ignoring Oxted as he tried to gesture her aside. 'Always a treat to meet a TV celebrity.'

'You're Patricia Crane, yes?' Then, at the woman's look of surprise: 'Our library doesn't usually get these things wrong.'

'Terrific,' the woman responded flatly. 'And just how does your library classify my relationship with Mr Edward Oxted? Live-in floozie? Plaything?'

'That'll do, Patsy, that'll do.' He moved firmly between the two women, a hand propelling Kate towards the door. 'Our celebrity, so-called, is already overdue leaving.'

Kate only just managed to drive clear of the Hampstead mansion before braking to a stop and slumping over the steering-wheel with an anguished cry. It was all very well to play the tough cookie upfront like that. But there had to come a break point—a moment to unwind after all that adrenalin and dread. Taff boyo, she vowed, if you and I are half worth our jobs, we have to nail that bullying little monster!

*

As experiences go, Taff reflected, this present one would be a lot better without the residual aches of all those bruises and cracked ribs.

He had been on the kop before only as a uniformed constable on crowd control, certainly never as a spectator packed shoulder to shoulder with hundreds of other spectators. His nearest to this had been the stands at Cardiff Arms Park chorusing Welsh patriotism alongside fellow rugger fiends. Now, standing incognito among the kop-end rabble at the Den, submerged in their midst, swaying whichever way they swayed, chanting their chants, supporting Millwall because he happened to be in among the home fans—now he began to experience the real meaning of the spirit of the terraces.

It had less to do with the skills of the players or the tactics of play as with the mood of those pressing tightly around him. It was theatre in the raw and in the round, and far more a participation experience than when he'd sat with Kate and Foxy Walsh in the stands. In fact, vulnerable though he felt, Taff was glad not to have the fearless old Arsenal supporter with him now. For all the massed submergence of individuality, his awareness of those crushed against him was acute. The voice pitch and passions, oaths and abuse of those in his close proximity were by now intimately familiar to him. Not their appearance, his vision being held by the force of the action on the field, but their shared emotional kinship had hold of him, the stronger with each pulse of cheering.

Thus, Taff reflected as the sensation dominated his senses, thus was Hitler sustained in howling adulation, not through force of intellect but by the brutish manipulation of massed emotion.

The policeman was not in fact as totally alone as he felt within the womb of this intense and heaving Den. DC Smith's cropped head was down there among the blue-and-yellow gear and the other cropped heads in front of him. None the less, Taff was sharply conscious of what a suicidal rendezvous he had agreed to—and what a pig's ear it would be to try and justify at any subsequent disciplinary inquiry: It was agreed for reasons of security, sir, to make contact with the informant outside the stand's south-east gate in the aftermath of the Millwall-Arsenal match—It didn't occur to you the detective-constable might be, as the phrase goes, fitting you up?—Damn bloody right it did, sir, YES!

For the moment, however, thoughts of trickery or betrayal were held largely at bay by this mesmeric piece of raw theatre which was exclusively the Terraces Experience. In the event, the two First Division teams held each other to a hard-fought and unusually clean three-all draw, allowing both sets of supporters equal measures of pride and chagrin as they jostled and heaved their way from the ground.

Throughout the match, the Lions' self-stewarding efforts had enabled the police to remain largely out of sight and had limited abuse largely to verbal outbursts. However, as with the match to which he had taken Kate, it was open season once out in the streets surrounding the ground. Whereas there was a highly visible police presence near the exits, they were making no attempts as yet to marshal the provocative Arsenal fans into convoys.

Taff's arrangement with Smith had been that, although keeping a mutual eye on each other, they would remain apart during the match. Should they lose touch when leaving the ground, they would liaise at the corner of Hunsdon Road and Cold Blow Lane. Foolproof enough, or so it seemed until the youngster whom Taff followed out of the ground and well past the corner turned out to be a clone of Smith. Inevitably, returning against the flow of the crowd, he drew the sort of attention he'd wanted to avoid and was twice challenged by militant groups, twice having to swear allegiance to Arsenal.

It was during the jeers and shoving of the second of these that Smith at last made contact—painfully so, a knee jabbed into his rump along with the curt message to follow him back up the lane. This, so it soon emerged, led to the chosen jousting ground for the militants of both sides to square up to each other—certainly no place for the faint-hearted to stray into.

'Here, lad, hang about,' he called from behind the swaggering DC.

'Losing your bottle, dad?'

'In preference to broken limbs, yes.'

'Listen, you,' Smith snapped, swinging round to grab his coat and jerk him close with an extremely convincing show of aggression, 'our skylark's just ahead. If you want to hear him sing, suppose you stop whingeing, OK?'

It was while the two were still up close like frozen lovers that Taff glimpsed the figures racing towards them. No time to voice a warning or do more than swing Smith heavily back against them before launching into furious retaliation.

They were not the same crew who'd done for the Judge. Their fighting skills were nowhere near as slick. However, they had the advantage of numbers, enabling them to overwhelm the two detectives just as the transit van reversed fast from nearby, its rear doors gaping open in readiness to engulf them.

Kate Lewis checked the street plan at the entrance to the tube station then set off for the nearby square. She was aware that of course they were watching her—again—the knowledge churning inside her like a gut full of worms.

And just where are you, Taff lover, now that I need you? However, since their agreement was that Taff would make contact as and when, he could hardly be blamed for failing to ring before the mystery woman had once again belled her at ITN with a rendezvous and an angry earful about this time not trying to play clever with hidden camera cars!

Not that Kate was under any sort of obligation to Taff, damn it. It was simply that the last time—the bomb time which could so easily have proved fatal—he had been furiously upset, making her promise never to take such a crass risk again.

Also, of course, Lawrence Cawley would have less grounds to get all twitched up if she'd had her copper along as back-up. Hey-ho. But there it was: she had not got him, Taff was not shadowing along behind her; and as a result, although the square was brightly lit and there was a reassuring number of people about, she was still tensed like a bow-string as she walked across to sit on a bench under the plane trees.

She was still deeply ambivalent about her Taffie. While he'd been away in Marlbury things had seemed just fine; indeed, the traumatic process of the abortion had seemed to purge the man as much as his child from her system. Now that fate had drawn the two of them back together, however, Kate was in a renewed turmoil, torn between her extreme emotional and physical attraction towards the man, in conflict with the moral strictures and rectitude of the policeman. She wanted to mother the child she saw in him, she wanted him as a lover the way a desert thirsts for water, she wanted his company and his approval and his sense of fun. What she couldn't take was his criticism—any more than she'd been able to cope with the expectations he had set on her as prospective mother to their child. Essentially, it was the same old conflict, were she to acknowledge it, which he defined as Kate versus Kath.

But how to resolve it? How to reconcile these two distinct and irreconcilable faces? How to foresee any lasting solution to the tussle within her which, in truth, had commenced that night almost four years earlier when she had first let herself fall in love with the then DI David Roberts? What possible future was there if she could neither get rid of him nor accept him other than on *his* terms?

Abruptly she found herself recalling a joke-riddle Taff had told her, perhaps of more significance than she'd realized at the time, about just how to make God laugh. Answer: tell Him you're reviewing your future plans.

CHAPTER 10

'Check them out.'

Taff's first impulse when Stan Smith had urged him earlier for Christ's sake not to carry his warrant card had been to point out that the contact would expect proof he was meeting a genuine copper. Well, tough, Guv, Smith had replied, you come naked, with no card and no wire, or we scrap it. And just as well, too, Taff reflected as the pugs frisked him. It might not save him from surgery or even burial, but at least there wouldn't be an inquest into the fate of his precious bloody card!

Further retaliation was out now that they were secured in the rear of the transit van. The knives were out in menace, after all, so what else but damage-control measures? Besides, it was as yet unclear to what extent their cover was blown. After all, if the crew were merely suspicious over Stan's asking so many questions, they might yet bluff their way out of it. On the other hand, if the contact had been luring Smith into a trap with a lot of bullshit about firearms and CS gas, that could put them both heavily into injury time.

'Right then, dad,' the leader snapped once the body search had failed to produce any identification, 'what's your game?'

'Just trying to mind me own . . .' He gasped as they hit him, bracing himself in case the next blow caught his injured ribs. 'What's up with you bastards? I thought you was coming to help me out with this puffball and then . . .' This time it was a karate chop across the upper arm which, for an excruciating moment, he thought must have broken the bone.

'No more shit now, OK? Herbert says you're family—an in-law of some kind, he says.' He turned, lunging a mean boot at the DC's crutch. 'Right, Herbert?' Then, resuming to Taff: 'But that ain't how we figured it, see. All these questions about the Front—that's got to make you and him something else, savvy?' So the whole set-up was exactly what it had looked from the outset: a crudely set trap, baited with info on lethal weapons, into which Taff had let himself be led like a sacrificial goat to the altar of over-commitment, diawl! 'Come on, dad, do we have to knee-cap you or what?'

This time Taff anticipated the blow, minimizing its force by riding it sideways. The move lurched him hard up against one of the van's rear doors, doing so at the precise moment that something whacked heavily against it from outside. Birefly, the impact left him all but stunned. Then, as his head cleared, he registered sounds of violence outside—and at the same instant saw Stan Smith try to dodge clear of the knife at his throat while kicking out in frenzied retaliation.

Instantly, Taff corkscrewed backwards against his own knife ape. In the event, the timing worked well for him, coinciding with the van doors being wrenched violently open. Next second he and the pug were rolling out to crash down and struggle on the ground. Somehow Taff managed to keep his hands locked on to the knife wrist, his knees, elbows and forehead all flailing for a target despite the shards of pain stabbing his side where his ribs had rebroken with the fall. Real pain would doubtless come later with the ebbing of adrenalin; right now the priority was survival.

His adversary evidently felt the same for, abruptly releasing the knife, he wrenched free, rolled clear then leapt up to sprint away into the night.

Taff heaved to his knees only to sway as pain and shock threatened to overwhelm him. Despite his confusion, he made out several figures groaning nearby on the ground. He also realized the van doors had been wrenched open not by a whole rival crew but just two blokes . . . moreover, the skill with which these two were now tackling the bruisers from the van was familiar to Taff from his level-one Support Unit training. Certainly they lost no time subduing the others, heaving a couple into the back of the van as the driver hurriedly gunned the engine and careered off, hooting his way wildly through the crowd. They chased the remainder off up Cold Blow Lane, then came back to drag Taff to his feet, checking him over before doing the same for the dazed and blood-soaked Smith.

'Walk, can you? Hospital's just along Hunsdon Road. You'd best get this woodentop along to Outpatients sharpish.'

Taff started to ask them which outfit they were with but was instead pushed firmly across to support Smith.

'Just do us all a favour, guv. Just take your tame monkey and fuck off out of here?'

*

119

Kate had sat in the square for twenty despondent minutes before she heard the telephone start ringing in the nearby callbox.

'Go to the pub across the street,' the woman's voice told her when she answered it, 'through the main bar and along to the toilet.'

Luring me out from the bright lights and away from the people, Kate thought as she crossed the road. Although the bar was moderately bright and busy, the doorway labelled toilets led into a gloomy passage, the Ladies equally dour. Kate waited a minute or so in there, leaning for support against the washbasin until she at last heard an outside door open at the further end of the passage and footsteps approaching.

'Out the back,' the young woman ordered, beckoning to her from the doorway. She was a platinum blonde of thickset build, her small, anxious eyes all but concealed with heavy make-up. 'Quick!'

Quickly into the trap, Kate reflected, following her along the passage and out through the rear door. There was an unlit yard behind the pub with a couple of cars parked in it. The rear door of the nearest one swung open and the woman waved her towards it.

'This here's Ronny,' she said, indicating a dark figure in the back. 'I'm Sharon. Want to get in?'

Kate hesitated. The last thing she wanted was to be confined in there, at risk of being driven off somewhere. Wasn't last time enough for you, girl? When will you ever learn? About the only reassuring thing about it all was that Sharon and the blokie peering out at her were both young and, for all their precautions, clearly felt scared and out of their depth.

'Come on,' Sharon snapped. 'We ain't going nowhere.'

'Aren't you going to search me for hidden video cameras?' Kate quipped, hoping to ease the tension. It didn't.

'Don't get clever, OK?' Sharon waited as Kate at last climbed in, then closed the door behind her before getting into the driver's seat. 'You've had two second chances already, so don't push your luck.

'The one thing I have brought,' Kate said, eyeing the

youth beside her on the back seat, 'is a disclaimer form, guaranteeing your anonymity. No names or identification unless you end up giving evidence in court.' Normally, she'd have held the form back as a bargaining ploy for later, but for once her priorities had shifted. This time, it wasn't the story which mattered so much as getting the guy singing to her Welsh copper.

She took it out and offered it to him; not surprisingly, it was Sharon who switched on the light and took it from her. Looking at Ronnie, tall and droopy, with languid eyes and a crop of well-attended spots on his face, Kate reckoned it was Sharon who made the decisions. Hardly into pumping iron, she thought; indeed, it was surprising he had enough umph to get in with what Taff reckoned must be one of the Bulls' toughest crews. Maybe he made up in brutality what he lacked in wits and physique.

'So you were in on the mugging at the stadium cark park, but it went further than you'd expected, yes?'

'I didn't do nothing meself.' Ronnie swallowed, rubbing at the ripest of his spots. 'Just on watch, like.'

'So you want it on record that you're clean, is that it?'

'S'right, yeah.' He nodded, glancing at Sharon as she handed back the contract.

'You realize you'll have to name them—identify those who did commit the violence.'

'Grass on 'em?' It seemed a totally new and appalling thought to him. 'You kidding?'

''Course you will, meat-head,' Sharon snapped before turning to Kate. 'I keep telling him, if that old geezer croaks it, he's in complicity to murder, which is a life stretch just for being there. That's right, miss, innit? You tell him.'

'Absolutely right. And don't imagine you can get off the hook simply by grassing on them, Ronnie. If any of them are arrested and name you, your only hope is to turn Queen's evidence and testify for the prosecution.'

Seeing the sweat glistening now on his face, Kate hoped she hadn't scared him off to the extent of defying Sharon, the young woman clearly being the only element of good sense and moral force in his life.

121

'What I can do,' she added hurriedly, 'is get you together
with a totally reliable police officer—one you can trust to
protect you. If you cooperate fully with him, I guarantee he
won't let you down.'

'How?' Sharon demanded sharply. 'How you so sure
about him?'

'Because, ducky, he happens to be my boyfriend, OK?
He does what I say or he gets the boot.' Kate found she was
even adding a Cockney accent to reinforce the persuasion.
'Better still, he's on attachment from the Thames Valley
Police, so there's no chance of anyone pressuring him.'
Unlike me with my damned editor, she thought; so what
does that make me? A whore or just another bloody journal-
ist? Assuming there's any difference?

'So what's he called,' Sharon asked, 'this Mr Wonderful
of yours?'

'No names, ducky, not yet. And I'll tell you this, the meet
will have to be on *his* terms, not yours. I may be the sort of
idiotic git who'll risk toddling into a corner like this, but
he's got more sense.'

'Anyone with even half a brain would have given football a
miss for a while, mate. Specially Millwall at home to
Arsenal. Always let the one lot mend before wading in for
another bashing.' The casualty sister, as formidable as any
of the hooligans they'd just encountered, waved him off the
inspection trolley, peeled the hospital gown to his waist and
started to restrap his ribs with all the delicacy of a Sumo
wrestler. 'Some sort of kink, are you? Enjoy having the boot
go in?'

'I—*ah*!—you see, I'm doing this thesis on violent subcul-
tures. In fact—*AH*!!—I could add a section on Casualty
Staff.'

'Hurting you, was I? You should have said. See, dealing
with all these drunks in here, you can get a bit casual.' She
guffawed. 'Casual for Casualty, get it?'

'You should be in the theatre.'

'I tried but it wasn't me. Nowhere near butch enough.
All those camp anæsthetists.'

122

'I meant on the stage.'

'Oh! Here, fancy coming to our panto?'

'I'd rather go and see that young bloke I brought in.'

'Herbert? Why not? He's all stitched and had his transfusion. Just needs doctor to check his X-rays. Third cubicle along.'

Clad in hospital gown and with a pressure bandage around his cropped head, DC Smith looked almost saintly, stretched flat on his trolley as if lost in pious contemplation. He gave a dour grunt as Taff pulled a chair close but otherwise held his peace.

'By rights, Smith, that knife should have sliced your carotid. You should be laid out in the morgue downstairs.'

'You alongside me, Guv'nor,' he quipped mordantly. 'Good job someone had them two minders watching out for us.'

'Sure.' Taff nodded. 'Any ideas who that someone might have been?'

'S'obvious, innit?' Smith gave him an old-fashioned look. 'You said it was a suicidal place to meet.'

'You think *I'd* got them lined up?' Taff pulled a face and shook his head. 'Granted, it's what I should have done. Would have, perhaps, if I'd been working with the Met instead of investigating them.'

'Oh yes.' The DC didn't look particularly convinced. 'So just who do you reckon it was betrayed us?'

'What?'

'Someone blew the whistle—did a Judas on us and tipped off them Bulls with the transit. Okay, Guv'nor, you know who your enemies are. You work out who.'

Taff could, of course, think of several—O Division and the Special Branch to name but two—just as he could speculate on who might have put the two minders, so-called, on to tailing him. However, there was another potential enemy far closer to hand who seemed the more probable Judas. An enemy Taff had brought on himself, yes, but no less bitter and reckless for that.

'You want to know how it looks to me, Constable Smith, I'll tell you. I think you knew full well what we'd be walking into at that rendezvous and you didn't give a monkey's! You went into this cover job like a madman, taking care along the way to drop me in it with my superiors; next you ploughed around the Bulls with all the subtlety of a Sherman tank and then you set up this suicidal bloody rendezvous. Deliberately drag me into the Lions' Den, *right*?'

Taff had to pause for a sudden agonizing bout of coughing which left him doubled forward and gasping for air. The only consolation was that he didn't seem to be coughing up blood. He'd had to tell several lies to the casualty officer in order to get his damaged ribs restrapped and avoid being kept in for observation. The danger now, apparently, was less from a lung puncture so much as a chest infection due to the strapping preventing him from breathing properly. As for the pain-killer jab he'd wangled out of Sister Sumo, either it was slow-acting or not potent enough to ease the agony of coughing.

'For the risk to yourself,' he continued as the spasm finally passed, 'you didn't care. Get yourself into a red-hot scrap, why not? Loads of agg and knuckle, great! Prove your bottle, yet again. The vital thing was that you'd be getting your own back on that blackmailing sod DCI Roberts!'

The constable had received all this impassively, lying back on the trolley, eyes closed and motionless. Finally he opened one eye and mimed the pointing of an imaginary pistol at the senior detective. 'I suppose this is how it gets you, eh, Guv'nor—working on an operation like Sox, sifting for shit on your fellow officers. Gets you so screwed up you can't trust no one, suspect your own father if you knew who he was.' He grinned in irony, pulling the trigger of his imaginary gun. 'Don't forget, I could have bled to death on this caper of yours. Call it quits, shall we?'

Kate Lewis leaned back in her car and tried to relax, her eyes fixed on the dark windows of Taff's flat. Ironically, for all her fears of a trap and also Lawrence Cawley's rebuke over the risk she'd taken—for all that, she felt far less stressed right now than she had after confronting animal Oxted. The cut and thrust of a hostile interview like that was, after all, far tougher and more demanding than walking into Sharon's rendezvous, no matter how vulnerable she'd felt.

All she needed now was a kiss and cuddle with her man of the valleys and she'd be back up to full strength. She was not, she believed, stroppy by nature, only by profession. Successful reporting, particularly of crime, required a robust and at times aggressive approach. How else to deal with devious toads like Oxted, it being the only style of approach they respected?

The aggression, such as it was, lay solely in the Kate side of her personality—in that determined obstinacy which drove her to insist on scoring tops against all the odds in a man's world. Damn it, she'd forfeited her first marriage for it, and she'd insisted on the abortion because of it. Nor was it because she needed the fame or the ego trip or even because she liked the work, but essentially because of the challenge to succeed . . . not the most healthy of compulsions, perhaps, but no less compelling for that. The high price of ambition. Yet, disconcertingly enough, the longer she sat here thinking of her Welsh boyo, anticipating his return, wondering where the hell he could be and whether he was safe, the more excessive that price began to seem.

At last she saw him drive up and park, waved and sang out as she went to join him in the entrance to the apartment block. His kiss seemed somewhat restrained.

'What happened to you, Taff? I've waited hours.'

'I'll find you a spare key. Sorry.'

'But where were you?'

'Later, OK? Right now all I can see is a pot of strong tea substituting for a Scotch bottle.'

In the event, Kate couldn't even wait for the kettle to boil before launching into the account of her own evening; and in no time, although she'd tried to play down the element of risk, Taff was raging at her.

'Bloody idiotic woman! Indulging in crass heroics like that for—for nothing!

'Nothing hell! I got you your witness!'

125

'Along with another scoop, of course! Don't let's forget the glory! ITN's intrepid crime correspondent—'

'No!' She was shouting now to top his anger. 'No scoop— no story! I did it for you, damn it, *you!*'

It stopped him at last. Instead, he swung away to churn hot water around the teapot before setting it to brew. 'You should have waited till you could contact me—'

'There wasn't time! They were jumpy as hell. If I'd tried to stall them, they were going to cry off. I honestly had no choice. And anyway, who the hell are you to tell me what risks I can and can't take?'

'Who? I'll tell you who! I'm—' He checked, swinging away as a renewed bout of coughing tore at his chest, doubling him back on to a stool, unable to conceal the agony of it.

'What the—?' At last, with a surge of guilt, she registered the fresh damage to his face. 'Taff, what the hell happened? For God's sake!'

'I—' He gasped to stifle more coughing, continuing in a hoarse whisper. 'I went prancing into a meet about a hundred times more risky and stupid than yours, that's what.'

'Oh . . .'

'Ended up in Casualty, more X-rays, more pills, stay off the booze, watch your urine.' He paused to swallow back another spasm. 'I know! I know what you're thinking: He can do it willy-nilly, but when I do it, boom-boom! Well, sorry, Kate, but that's the way it is. Call me a chauvinist pig by all means. But that's how it's got to be because— well, because that's how I feel about you, that's why! I'm telling you not to take risks because, damn it, I'm the dumbo who happens to love you. So fair enough, that doesn't give me privileges or rights, but it most certainly gives me feelings! And, diawl, Katie, it makes me see bloody red when you take risks like that—whether it's for me or my lousy job or yours or whatever!'

At last he shut up, puffed and still in pain, and cursing when his hand shook all over as he tried to pour the tea. To his enormous relief, she didn't retaliate. Instead, after a moment's silence, she leaned close to kiss him, cradling his face in her hands.

'You bastard, you could at least say thank you.'

'Will this grass of yours tell us the lot? All their names and a full statement?'

'If his girlfriend tells him to, yes. And she will if I tell her.'

'Well then, love—' he creased his swollen face to a grin— 'thanks a bundle. Sounds like the first real break in the case.'

Yin and yan: for every plus a minus, every brightness a darker side. The two lovers were just attempting very gently to consummate their shared euphoria when the doorbell rang.

'Ignore it.'

'Sweetheart, apart from Foxy Walsh, no one but my office knows where to find me.'

'Oh.' Pause. 'What about the mattress?'

'Let's just hope it's Foxy,' Taff said, groaning as he pulled on his towel robe, then nodded her into the bathroom before heading for the door.

It wasn't Foxy. Worse, in his urgency to communicate, Chiefie Briggs came bustling in and all but fell over the mattress and cushions.

'What's all this, Roberts? What the devil are you up to?'

'Er—oversprung bed, sir—only way I can get comfortable . . .'

'Don't bullshit me. You've got somebody here.' He pointed at Kate's clothes on the chair. 'Where is she?'

'Hardly your business, sir . . .'

'Maybe not,' the Chief snapped, swinging round on his junior, 'except what I have to tell you is too urgent and too sensitive to be overheard.'

'Too urgent to use the phone?' Taff asked, lifting Kate's skirt from the back of a chair.

'Too confidential,' Briggs retorted pointedly. Then, in concession, his eyes on the bathroom door, he added: 'I suppose we can go and talk outside.'

127

'There's a development you ought to hear about first, sir.' Taff moved to tap on the bathroom door, then handed Kate's clothes through when she opened up. 'Someone here you have to meet, love, sorry.'

'Before you do,' the Chief murmured, turning away, 'the fact of it is, ACC Blaize pulled rank to get you off the case.'

'Ah.' Although it was no more than Taff had expected, the impact was still devastating. 'Ironic, Guv'nor. Sacked at the very moment I've got hold of a witness.'

'Really? How strong?'

'My lady-friend's been acting as go-between. She reckons he'll go the distance—name the assailants, if not those behind them.' He turned as she emerged from the bathroom. 'Right, Kate?'

'Provided you keep to your side of it, yes.' She shot Briggs a big smile and held out her hand. 'Sir, how do you do?'

The Chief ignored her hand, instead groaning as he swung to confront his Sox junior. 'Still pulling your damned Met tricks, eh, Roberts? Reckoning to buy some sort of insurance through the bloody media, are you? God preserve us . . .'

'Miss Kate Lewis, DCS Don Briggs,' Taff interrupted formally. 'Kate and I have a longstanding friendship, sir— dating back well over three years, in fact. As you'll have gathered from the, er, bed, it's a very close relationship.' Then, hurrying on before Briggs could add anything more offensive: 'As I was saying, Kate found me the witness, in fact via her job. However, I'm under no sort of obligation to ITN. That's never been the way we work. Well, naturally not, given the Yard's Press Office guidelines.' He cleared his throat, conscious of his chief's persisting scowl. 'Look, Guv'nor, for heaven's sake have a drink and let's talk this through, OK? Scotch in the sideboard, Katie.'

To his relief, Briggs accepted a glass, taking a hefty gulp as he adjusted to this fresh dimension of the Roberts nightmare. Definitely a meaty one for his memoirs, Taff reflected, assuming the poor old sod could stave off a coronary long enough to retire.

'You say Blaize pulled rank?'

Briggs shrugged. 'I imagine so. I simply had a memo,

special delivery from the TVP Chief Constable, saying you're to hand the case over to the O Division team.'

Taff grunted and pulled a face. Over to bloody Lawley after all. But at least they hadn't resorted to the full John Stalker treatment of suspending him—not yet! But, hell, if they did then the implications were appalling: not just his own career under threat but the heat going on to Foxy Walsh and even Kate as well, both dragged into playing Kevin Taylor to his Stalker!

Kate was shaking her head, close to melt-down, but he gestured for her to stay quiet as he resumed to the DCS. 'So, er, you're not officially here, is that it, Chief?'

Briggs groaned yet again, eyeing Kate. 'Your boyfriend is *not* an easy person to work with, Miss Lewis. Thirty years I've served in the Force and never . . .' He shook his head, leaving it unsaid.

Kate nodded. 'Too much Welsh initiative, Mr Briggs. He's either ahead of his time or too late.'

'Let's hope it's the former.' He turned curtly to Taff. 'Should you fail to call in tomorrow morning because you're chasing this witness, there's not a lot I can do other than carpet you later for breach of reporting procedure.' He drained his Scotch and stood up to leave. 'I was never here this evening, Miss Lewis. I look forward to the time we can meet for real.'

CHAPTER 11

'It has to be this way, Taff. Unless I'm there, nothing happens.'

Taff grunted in irritation, hunching back in the passenger seat to stare at the rush-hour traffic ahead. Aside from the fact that he had a headache, he disliked having to accept terms and conditions, especially when they meant endangering his girl.

The previous evening, because he found Kate so hugely sexy, they had managed to make love despite all the medicines and new bruises and chest pains. And just as well, since it had allowed him that most powerful and restorative of sleeps that only love-making can engender. None the less, he had woken heavy-headed and with the pain intermittently aggravated by bouts of coughing. But for the force of his obligation to Judge Hartington and now the Briggs deadline, he would have liked nothing better than to collapse for a totally lost weekend.

'That's the pub,' Kate said at last, driving past in search of a way round to the yard at the back. She found an alley but then had to reverse awkwardly back out again to give way to a departing brewery truck. Then, when she finally got them round the rear, the yard gates were shut.

'Terrific.'

'Turn the car round and we'll wait,' Taff told her. 'Chances are, they'll be watching from somewhere nearby. What are we looking for?'

'An old red Cortina. Blonde girl and spotty hooligan.'

'He can have spots, squares, circles and webbed feet so long as he delivers.' He coughed again, groaning and sweating, and then morbidly examining the sputum on his tissue—spots of greeny phlegm, but at least it was still clear of blood.

In the event they were faced the wrong way to see the yard gate swing open, both starting at the short hoot from behind them. Sharon was there in the gateway, beckoning them across to the red Cortina.

'There's someone else in the back,' Taff warned, his hand out to restrain Kate. 'Bald bloke.'

'Probably the lawyer I told them to contact,' she answered, climbing out to confirm it with Sharon before waving Taff across.

'Recognize me, do you, Ronnie?' Taff rapped as soon as they were all five inside the car.

The youth blinked in alarm. 'Here, you're the geezer what was with the old Judge.' He swung to face Kate. 'What's goin' on?'

'You're about to make a full witness statement, that's what,' the copper told him firmly. Then, to head off any

130

objections, he added: 'The damage your mates dished out to the old Judge left him dead. Heart still beating but otherwise dead. Brain-damaged, comatose and paralysed, his internal organs ruptured and useless. Technical murder and likely to become actual murder at any time.'

He paused, holding out his warrant card for the lawyer to check. 'Right then, let's get on with it, shall we?'

In the event, the lawyer amply earned the fee ITN would be paying him, confirming to Ronnie that a full statement was in his own best interests before then spelling out certain client safeguards to Taff, then in due course writing out the agreed wording of the witness statement—its detailed description of the assault and names of all those involved—writing it out, moreover, on a pad with several carbons to provide extra copies.

'Let's just recap from the time they phoned you,' Taff said after they'd covered most of it. 'This bloke Wilson—Spud Wilson—rang you to get tooled up and then down to the club. By the time you arrived, all the others were there and you headed off together to the stadium.'

'Right.'

'What did you expect to happen? What was said to you at that stage?'

'Just told us there was this geezer visiting the club what had to be sorted out.'

'Did they say who or why?'

'Said the scab was goin' to do for the club. Said it was that Judge what was makin' the report. Said he'd got it in for the Bulls on account of us bein' in with the Front and them.'

Taff got him to repeat all this so the lawyer could get it down in full, then asked the key question. 'Who was it, Ronnie? Who told you all this?'

The youth grinned, rubbing at a spot, only to jerk as Sharon nudged him into answering. 'Like, it was mostly Spud, but he was only sayin' what Mervyn had told him already 'cos a lot of the time Merv was addin' bits.'

'Mervyn's the one you described earlier as the ringleader,

131

the boss of the crew.' Then, when the lad nodded: 'And he's the stepbrother of Kennie Kent, the team's striker.'

Ronnie nodded again, smirking to Kate. 'The same as shook up that sports-reporter git of yours down the club.'

'And the addresses of these eight crew mates you've named,' Taff resumed, 'presumably we'll be able to get them from the supporters' club register.'

'Sure. Ain't no rush, though.'

'What do you mean?'

'None of 'em won't be home till Sunday night.' Then, gawping at their frowns of confusion, he added: 'Munich. The friendly warm-up for the championship, OK?' He gestured, turning in desperation to Sharon. 'And if I don't get my arse over there with 'em fast, Merv'l put two and two together and clock me as Sonny Supergrass.'

'Very much obliged to you for seeing me so quickly, sir.' Taff braced up as smartly as his injuries would allow. 'Be sure, it is extremely urgent.'

Commander Blake shot him a rueful glance. James Blake was a proud man—proud of his rank and prestige, his physique and health, his family and children. He had risen through the ranks by hard work, by a flair for exams and by managing to keep his nose cleaner than those around him. His deepest fear was of scandal surfacing in O Division during his period of command. This was the extent of the background Foxy Walsh had been able to unearth on the commander. Although not much, it was enough for Taff to take a gamble on him.

'Spoken to your guv'nor this morning, have you, Roberts?'

'No, sir. I should explain, I'm here about fresh infor-mation on the assault on Judge Hartington and myself at the Balham United stadium.'

'DCI Lawley's case.'

'Sir, I have communicated substantial evidence already to Ian Lawley. However, due to the sensitivity of this latest information, I need assurances at a higher level.' Then, inclining his head: 'The highest level.'

'Not content with going over Lawley's head, you're top-

132

ping his chief as well.' Then, when Taff bridled at putting it so baldly, he snapped: 'Chief Inspector, I'm aware of the maniac way you've been behaving over this case.' He snorted. 'Earned yourself quite a reputation.'

'With respect, sir,' Taff answered, wondering if he'd got it wrong from Walsh and was trying to beard the wrong lion, 'what those Bull hooligans did to the Judge has caused me a great deal of grief. If I appear over-zealous, it's because this case simply has to be cracked.'

'Not supposed to be your case at all!' The retort cracked across like a bullet. 'Moreover, had you spoken to DCS Briggs this morning, you'd have heard it no longer *is* your case.'

'Really, sir?' Taff attempted a show of surprise. 'Well, as it happens, this morning I took a statement from a crucial witness.' He pulled out a photostat of it. 'From one of the actual assailants.'

'That so?' Blake eyed but didn't reach for the document. 'Then give it to DCS Lawley, not me.'

'Certainly, sir, subject to certain conditions.' Then, hurriedly heading off the Commander's angry rebuke: 'Whereas it's not actually a murder case—not yet—the implications from much of the evidence suggest it should be taken over by a more senior officer. Preferably, Ian Lawley's guv'nor, Chief Superintendent Ingram.'

It surprised the Commander even more than Taff had expected it would. 'Listen, son, don't you try to get clever with me!'

'Sir?'

'Pretending you didn't know about Tom Ingram's prior contacts with Mr Edward Oxted.'

'In that he was the officer who processed Mr Oxted's complaint about my conduct, you mean?'

'In that he oversaw Lawley's investigation of Balham United several years ago and has been their liaison officer on crowd control and security more or less ever since.'

'All the more appropriate to involve him at this stage, sir.'

'I said don't get clever! ACC Blaize told me about your

suspicion that the club chairman was somehow behind the assault. Whether or not you have valid evidence against Oxted, that's bound to make you, let's say, uneasy about Tom Ingram.'

'One question before I reply to that, if I may, sir. Presumably it was also Chiefie Ingram who allocated Ian Lawley to the assault investigation?'

The Commander cleared his throat, evidently in considerable conflict. 'I'd have to confirm it from the duty rotas,' he muttered, 'but, yes, it's probable.' He shrugged, his chin out. 'So what?'

'So Chiefie Ingram is the right man for the case,' Taff replied blandly. It had all fitted together, piece by piece. That he was now having to compromise by coming to Ingram's commander was only mildly frustrating—providing, of course, the Commander didn't risk anything stupid to try and shield his subordinates. 'Set a sprat to catch a mackerel, sir.'

Blake's scowl was knee-deep, his patience long spent and only his natural caution holding him in check. His desk intercom buzzed, but he ignored it, instead glaring dourly at Taff. 'The sprat in this instance being?'

'Commander, I'm not suggesting Chief Superintendent Ingram is guilty of anything worse than, say, an indiscretion. Allowing himself to be compromised by his contacts with the club chairman—'

'And Lawley tarred with the same brush,' Blake cut in. 'Come on, stop beating about the bush. What do you want?'

'Simply, as I said, sir, assign the case to Tom Ingram.'

'And?'

'Tell him that, because this key witness refuses to trust anyone but me, he's to take me on board in place of Lawley.'

'Ha! Quite the wheeler-dealer, eh. You should be in the bloody City, Roberts, not the Force.' He pointed in anger. 'Entrapment, that's what it amounts to. Pushing old Tom Ingram into a compromising situation and with you behind him as his bloody watchdog!'

Taff paused over his reply since it had to be the clincher, make or break. 'A lot tidier like this, sir. Keep it within your

134

division. A lot easier to handle as an internal matter.' He paused, attempting to soften the implied threat with a smile before adding: 'This way, you can remind Ingram of the need for discretion regarding Balham United's chairman.'

'Oberkomissar Günter Braun,' Ingram exclaimed, 'with the Bundes-Kriminalamt in Karlsrühe. Ideal for this job. I met him at that conference on hooliganism in Italy last year. A real stormtrooper.'

Taff sat back in surprise. Whatever cautionary briefing Ingram had just received from his commander, he showed little sign of diminished enthusiasm. On the contrary, he seemed delighted with the case as a chance to win glory and promotion points: gung-ho over to Munich for the massed, upfront arrest of Mervyn George and his crew by the German police . . . a highly visible gesture to the spirit of 1992, a PR coup for the Euro-Cops lobby, didah-didah-didah . . .

'Technically, sir, it's going to be far simpler to arrest them once they're back here, so why not simply wait and nab them at their port of re-entry?'

'Listen, lad, if you'd had as many years' experience as I have dealing with these football louts, you'd know *never* to wait. They have very good information channels. A lot of contacts inside the Force—fellow supporters, moles—a lot. Set up an operation at the ports, and the chances are they'd hear about it. No, no, we go after them—fast—you and me in co with the well-armed resources of Oberkomissar Braun.'

As well as enthusiastic, Taff decided, Tom Ingram was far more of an opportunist than his commander. He was also more jokey and relaxed, which, although of no relevance to his integrity, made him more pleasant to work with.

'I don't like that cough of yours, David, not at all. At the very least, you should get yourself on to antibiotics.'

'I am already, thanks. The doc put me on them when I insisted on having all this rib strapping.'

'Of course. I forgot you'd been Jackbooted.'

'You what?'

'Mervyn George's crew—surely young Ronnie told you?—they're called the Jacks.'

135

Taff was tempted to thank the old rogue for the timely rescue which his two gorillas had staged outside the Millwall ground the previous evening. Whereas the two *might* have been from the Yard, he was prepared to bet after his session with the Commander that they were in fact from O Division. However, since Ingram had chosen to give him such a warm welcome on to the case, for all the world as if he'd actually requested the Welshman's assistance rather than attempted to block and subvert him at every turn over the last few days, Taff decided he'd as well continue in the role of provincial hick.

The Chief Super dialled through to clerical requesting priority contact with Günter Braun in Karlsrühe, also three reservations on the next available flight to Munich.

'Who's the third seat for, Chief?'

'Kate Lewis, of course. I presume you'll want her along.' There was no hint of irony in his tone; he might as easily have been referring to a PA or even a fiancée. However, seeing Taff's blink of surprise, he added: 'Your reputation precedes you, boyo. Famed for the notorious company you keep.' Then, still routinely casual, he added: 'Obviously, with the big match tomorrow, there'll be a camera team already available over there for her to call on.'

'Either he's red-hot on PR and reckons to show British viewers how the Force are cracking down on soccer hooligans . . .' Taff paused to hold his cup across to the Lufthansa air hostess for a refill. 'Bitte.'

'Or?'

'Or he wants you along as a form of insurance.' He gave Kate a lopsided grin. 'Reckoning to compromise me.'

'He seems too nice for that.'

'That from a seasoned old journalist?' He dodged her retaliatory lunge, the move triggering yet another bout of coughing. 'Which,' he wheezed as he finally got it under control, 'is why *I* wanted you along: as nurse and protector.'

'Great.' She gestured towards lthe throng of enthusiastic football fans rehearsing patriotic chants at the rear of the plane. 'Heading for one of the biggest British invasions since

136

1945 and lumbered with a case of first-degree pneumonia!'

'This lot aren't all bad,' Taff told her, pointing towards the rear. 'In fact, many of them maintain they're ambassadors, here to restore Britain's flabby image. Show the world the Brits are first and fearless! Show them who's top of the Bottle League.'

Kate nodded in mock relief. 'I knew it couldn't just be mindless hooliganism.'

'I'll play you a tape of a couple earnestly explaining how, although she had to *pretend* disapproval, Maggie Thatcher's actually very proud of the performance put up by British fans abroad. They genuinely associate with the Thatcherite principles—her win-win materialism, her pride in Britain's potential, the Falklands victory, the whole enterprise culture. They're not wearing those Union Jack T-shirts and hats as part of the NF uniform so much as national flag-carriers issuing an open challenge. Showboating, it's called.'

'Terrific,' Kate sighed. 'Really makes one proud of one's origins.'

The landing was every bit as smooth as the cabin staff had been in dealing with all the provocative 'ambassadors'. Let *Die Tommies* jeer and posture and display; after all, there remained no doubt as to the ultimate victors.

They filed across the tarmac to the transit buses, enjoying the fine clear day and the view across to the snowy Austrian alps little more than an hour's autobahn drive away. There was a high police presence in and around the terminal building, alert for drunks, druggies and vagrant backpackers, the techniques of the cops markedly less tolerant than those of the Lufthansa staff.

There was an ITN contact man waiting to meet Kate and her cameraman and whisk them off to their hotel. There was also a huge, bearded Rhinelander waiting to greet Tommy Ingram with a hug and a ringing laugh before turning to crush Taff's hand in welcome. The Oberkomissar managed to give the impression he had been poised for years, ready for Tommy's call and the chance of collaboration.

137

'How strong,' he wanted to know on the ride into town, 'are their links with the Fascist organizations?'

'As yet unconfirmed, but probably very strong,' Ingram assured him promptly. 'His Honour the Judge and Herr Roberts were expecting to receive evidence of those links when they were attacked in the stadium car park.'

'So?' Günter Braun turned in wry curiosity to Taff. 'Your injuries—these are the maulings of *Die Tommies*, ja-ja?'

'They like to leave their mark,' Taff confirmed, looking in vain for signs of duelling scars behind the German's beard.

'And this evidence?'

'The Judge was promised photographs of meetings with National Front people. Of course they may just have been a pretence to lure the Judge into the trap.'

'You also, Herr Oberinspektor.'

'They were only expecting the Judge. I'm afraid I was called in for his protection.'

'As bodyguard, ja?' He shook his head in sympathy, indicating the leather holster of his gun. 'Carry these and you would stop them.'

'Unlikely, sir. They had the element of surprise.' Taff shook his head in denial. 'More likely I'd have had it stolen.'

'You should carry them,' Braun insisted, patting the holster. 'For authority, ja.'

Taff shrugged, reluctant to be drawn into the debate. What with policing the miners' strike and Wapping, and doubling up as ambulancemen; with the scandals of Kent and Greater Manchester and the Guildford Four; with barely a week passing without an officer convicted of fraud or negligence or drunken driving, of extortion or rape or blackmail; with morale at rock bottom and pay the sole motive for many—what with all that, why add side-arms to the controversy? At least at present the thin blue line still had a reputation for personal courage, if not courtesy.

'So now,' their host announced as they arrived at central police headquarters, 'I will take you to top-floor accommodation. With this big match, there is no more any hotel rooms. But German police enjoy also comfort, as you will see. You will take refreshment and a shower. Then this evening we will visit the bierkellers around the old part of town to seek out these neo-Nazi Jacks, ja.'

It was Kate who found them first—or rather, she found Mervyn George surrounded by a bevy of rowdies including Ronnie. She also found herself in the tricky situation of being recognized at the same moment by another member of the crew who pointed her out to Mervyn, then waved her a big two-up in welcome.

'Come on over, Miss Lewis! Want a drink?'

She shook her head, cursing her carelessness and forcing a smile as she crossed to their table in the corner of the big crowded bierkeller. Briefly she glanced back to see if the cameraman was on to the situation. She needn't have bothered: the lads had already seen him, waving their tankards at the camera and aping around. Apart from Ronnie who appeared frozen with shock, only Mervyn remained quiet, his broad Maradona frame hunched low in his chair.

'Here for a follow-up on that ruck you pulled down the club?' he asked her. 'Show the animals up to their tricks in Fritzland?'

'If you want to wreck the place, Mervyn, that's fine by me. Go ahead and win the Jacks a piece on *News at Ten*.'

The direction of the camera along with the antics of the fans had caught the attention of the local toughs, who promptly started to call out in mock challenge, '*Achtung! Koming Die Skins! Run Tommies!*'

Meanwhile, almost without seeming to move, Mervyn's hand shot out to snatch Kate's wrist, pulling her close. 'Know a lot about us, don't yer. What's your game? Got the knife out for us? Part of the big conspiracy?'

'Let go or I yell the place down!'

'You do and you'll get this glass in your face!'

For a second his eyes held hers; and instantly she was

139

back years to the eyes of the killer who had held her hostage—held her not by force or locked doors but solely by an inner paralysis, freezing her with the instant hypnosis of terror.

Then everything became a blurred jumble of shouts and movement—whirling and crashing, pushing and shoving, sirens and bullhorns—the harsh, chaotic eruptions of riotous affray.

Mervyn didn't stay to fight. Instead, he used her as a ram to force his way through the mob; then, veering towards a side entrance, he tried to drag her outside before finally releasing his hold so that she was able to plunge blindly away, buffeted by the heaving throng all round her, punched and elbowed and kicked ... until, with an abrupt resurgence of terror, she felt herself hoisted clear off her feet in an embrace from which, struggle as she might, there was no release.

'Kate love! KATE! It's me!'

Taff was gasping for air even as she registered it was him, stumbling and falling back with her into a mass of ornamental shrubs on the edge of the crowd. Then the coughing took charge, convulsing his body as she clung tight in shock and relief.

'You OK?' he gasped at last.

'No!'

'What?!'

'Taff, I—I'm *sorry*!'

'What? Why?'

'I lost you the bastard!'

He shook his head, once again unable to speak, but less now through coughing than laughter.

'So long as you're OK,' he gasped, shaking his head. 'Mind, I can't answer for the Kraut cops. They hate to be shown up as inefficient. You won't be popular with Herr Oberkomissar Braun.'

CHAPTER 12

'We should have waited for you to arrive,' Kate repeated, her body close against his in the hotel bed. 'Typical of me: Pushy-Pants, wanting to jump the gun . . . find the gang of them first so we could scoop the action when Braun and his boys came storming in.'

Taff gave her earlobe a teasing tug. 'Well, at least you got your piece on to *News at Ten*: Intrepid ITN sleuth Kate Lewis roughed up by Brit football louts in bierkeller riot.'

In fact, he had been deeply impressed by Kate's determined professionalism. For all the shock and trauma, within minutes she had recovered enough to write and then tape a piece for the *News* on how gangs of British hooligans were rampaging in the Gartenstrasse in anticipation of a sweeping English victory the next day . . . and how, when trying to interview a bunch of Balham United fans, she herself had become embroiled in the violence, as seen in this sequence filmed by cameraman Jason Moyle, himself jostled and slightly injured during the ensuing mêlée . . . 'And this is a somewhat battered Kate Lewis in Munich returning you to the ITN studio.'

'One thing, Kate, how did you know where to look for them?'

'Tom Ingram, of course.' Then, seeing Taff's sharp reaction: 'Oh dear. When he phoned, I thought it was odd he'd called us instead of you.'

Taff grunted sourly. So much for his trying to play the role of sly manipulater and out-score O Division at their own game. 'Nothing odd, really. It all worked out exactly as Ingram anticipated: unleash the media hounds to frighten off the quarry.'

'Oh God! And Pushy performed exactly as programmed. Damn!'

The detective shrugged, shaking his head in dismissal. 'Listen, love, I've seen plenty of blundering incompetents in the police force, but it's a unique experience to work with a senior officer who actually *wants* to screw up a case.'

'But why should he, Taff? You think he's in Oxted's pocket?'

'That's certainly the way it looks,' he admitted, hoping to God he hadn't scored an own goal by getting the man on to the case.

'That devil Mervyn,' Kate recalled, 'seemed to think I was part of what he called a big conspiracy.'

'Interesting.'

'But conspiring with whom?'

Taff shrugged. 'Maybe he was talking about Judge Hartington. Remember what Ronnie said about the old bloke having it in for the club. That could well have originated from Chairman Oxted when he unleashed his dogs on the Judge.' He shrugged, frowning over it. 'It's certainly one question I'll put to Mervyn.'

'But *when*?' Intolerant of failure, Kate hated it most of all in herself. 'Between us, Ingram and I managed to scare him and his Jacks right off.'

'Merely delayed things a bit,' Taff corrected, reaching gingerly out to switch off the light. 'After all, we know exactly where Mervyn and his crew are going to be tomorrow afternoon. Packed in with a mere 75,000 other fans.'

'Excuse me, Oberkomissar, but it can only be this way.' Taff had gone to elaborate lengths to intercept the man before Ingram could get to him, waiting down in the vestibule of police HQ until he arrived. 'All right, so we'll give your men photographs of the Jacks. But I can personally identify at least two of them. I have to be there to direct your squad.'

'The gates—'

'Watch them, of course. But access to that north end stand involves monitoring an awful lot of turnstiles.'

'Oberinspektor Roberts, your health—you are unwell.'

'I'll manage, don't you worry.' He gestured in apology. 'Of course, if you're saying it'll be too wild for your squad to risk going in there . . .'

142

'Fer satan!' Braun checked, conscious of the heads turning in curiosity at his indignant denial. 'This is Munich, not Manchester or south London. There is still here respect of police.'

'Except, sir, that north stand will be a highly patriotic corner of England.'

'They are wanted on disorder charges from last night's riot on Gartenstrasse,' Braun retorted stiffly. 'You identify them, we will arrest.'

'One final favour, Obersport,' Taff grinned, thumping the big Rhinelander on the shoulder. 'Tommy Ingram's ordered me off sick, so just keep our arrangement a secret between us, jawohl?'

The great Munich stadium was built for the 1972 Olympics to a daringly futuristic design. Set in an 800-acre lakeland park, the pitch sits down the bottom of a massive bowl and looks like a twenty-first century bedouin tent draped across a fertile oasis. There are spacious seating areas on the bowl's east and west sides plus more traditional open terrace areas north and south. Kate had managed to wangle herself and Jason Moyle a last-minute place in the subsidiary press and television box at the back of the south terrace. It suited them well enough, in fact, giving a direct view of the north end terrace assigned to the British fans.

Kate managed to bully Jason up into the box a good hour before kick-off; but already most of the British fans had arrived, their flags, club ensigns and symbols filling the choicer positions, their chants already beginning to find voice.

Moyle hooked up to playback so they could review a copy of the tape he'd shot in the bierkeller, then froze the picture on the posturing Jacks moments before the fighting broke out.

'About the only one whose face you can't see in there,' Kate remarked, 'is the ringleader, sly wee Merv.'

'The one you're masking.'

'Yes, Jason dear, because the bastard had grabbed hold of me, that's why!' She shivered, recalling the paralysis of terror, then she nodded across to the fans already crowding the north end stand. 'So long as we can pick out one or two of his villainous crew, we should find Merv along with them.'

She sat back to watch the monitor screen while Moyle focused down to a tight shot on the individual faces in the crowd. Then, panning very slowly, he commenced the methodic scanning of each level—left to right then up, right to left, then up again, and so on, pausing occasionally to check a particular face or else a group wearing the Bulls' distinctive colours, until he had reached the topmost rear level and then swivelled the camera down to start once again at the lower left corner.

'If you ask me,' Moyle remarked, taking a break after half a dozen fruitless scans, 'since they know we recorded their little rumpus last night and could have supplied the local police with a copy of the tape, they'll likely have decided to lie low.'

'They may keep a low profile and come muffled up or whatever,' Kate replied, passing him a Wurstburger and pickle, 'but there's no way Merv will miss the spectacle of stepbrother Kennie striking for the English team.'

Taff consoled himself with much the same thought as, with less than a quarter-hour to go before the whistle, he decided to leave the turnstile area and try and spot them in the crowd.

The vast tentlike structure of the roof over the west seating area extended round in the shape of a crescent to shield the top ends of the north and south terraces. It was made of hundreds of clear acrylic plastic panels, seeming to Taff to magnify the crowd noise. As he pushed his way into the the crowd packed inside one of the entrances up on the rim of the north terrace it was like a mega-raucous Last Night at the Proms, fans from numerous different clubs vying with each other for the loudest rendering of their particular chant. From the huge numbers already massed around him, it was clear the tout ticket-forgers must have made a killing. Taff grunted, his confidence of an easy collar taking a dive.

There was a sudden surge of noise as the two teams came jogging out to line up on the pitch for the national anthems. Taff managed to force his way a few rows down an aisle, then across to just below the centre before speaking into his radio for news from Kate.

'No joy, sorry. We're both square-eyed up here.' She sounded tense and low-spirited. 'Whereabouts are you?'

'Top centre about three rows below this side's TV position.'

There was a pause as she relayed his position to Moyle. Then he heard her giggle as she remarked: 'Despite the woolly hat, you still stand out like a eunuch at an orgy.'

'Thanks!'

'Listen, all we can tell you is the position of the main group of Balham supporters—roughly twelve rows down and to your right. But if the Jacks are anywhere near them, they must be in disguise.'

It seemed unlikely, given the tradition of showboating. On the other hand, it was possible Mervyn had been alerted, if not by the previous night's ruck, then even by a tip-off from one of the German supporter groups. Despite the animosity with which the groups from rival countries abused and fought each other, their leaders had established an intricate network of links, particularly for use on occasions such as the World Cup.

'OK.' Taff knew that, besides the camera's powerful zoom lens, Kate had some fieldglasses. 'Keep looking.'

'Be careful, Taff.'

'Eunuchs usually are.'

The patriotic yelling of *The Queen* was dying away as he zipped the walkie-talkie inside his ski-jacket and turned to start thrusting a way down the aisle steps. Given the density and liveliness of the crowd, also the state of his ribs, it was no easy process. Moreover, the analogy of an orgy seemed even more apt when, as he was midway down, England kicked off to an intricate manœuvre which surged their forward line through to the German defence and a clever lob from Kennie Kent which all but slipped home. It was during the ensuing eruption of enthusiasm that Taff was suddenly tugged to one side by a leering fan.

'Watcher, copper, slumming it again?'

For a moment he mistook the lad for one of the two minders from outside the Millwall ground. Then he recognized the gaunt face and earring.

'I thought you'd be up in the press box, Ponse.'

'The day they give accreditation to fanzines, Guv, I'll eat my word-processor.' He paused, glancing at the pitch as the crowd roared again, this time in encouragement of a run by Steve Bull. 'Besides,' he resumed as Steve ran into a blitzkrieg of German defence, 'here's where it's at.'

'The sharp end, huh.'

Ponse nodded. 'Doubtless why you're here and all, eh, Guv? Also, I dare say, why you was storming the Gartenstrasse last night.' He fixed Taff with a keen stare, eyes sharp and unblinking, beaky nose thrust forward with the intensity of a heron. 'Something me and my editorial team can help with?'

Taff hesitated, surprised by the offer. But then, he reflected ruefully, since he was supping with one jurnalist already, why not feast with them all? From their prior meeting he recalled the bitter contempt in which Ponse Perry held the club chairman, so maybe he'd feel the same about Oxted's wilder supporters.

This time there was a roar from the German fans, their team at last hitting form with a determined surge from their mid-field. It was stopped at last but at cost of a lot of ground.

'That rather depends, Ponse, on how you align with the Jacks.'

The fanzine editor nodded, his lip curling in satisfaction. 'I guessed they might be the mob you was after, what with your, er, friend Miss Lewis mixing it with their Merv last night.' Then, seeing Taff's surprise and unease: 'Supporters clubs are awful tight-knit and incestuous. Nests of gossip. Anything happens, everyone knows.'

'Does that mean you know where the Jacks are right now?'

146

There was another roar from around them, but this time the editor's eyes remained fixed on the policeman. 'You're asking one hell of a lot.'

'Agreed.' Taff nodded. 'But I'll tell you this much: the survival of your precious club could very well depend on it.'

Ponse gave a grim nod, his fears confirmed. 'You'll find Mervyn George and Spud Wilson staying with the leader of Die Skins. Ceremonial, OK, like visiting heads of state. But right now they're somewhere up at that top north-west corner.'

Watching this exchange from the press box, Kate recognized Ponse Perry from the ITN interview session at the supporters' club. It was torment to watch the two men but without being privy to what was being said. Restlessly, she swung the heavy fieldglasses back along the rows of excited spectators, their attention fixed as one on the match.

Ironic, she thought, to be watching the crowd when, by simply turning her head, she could witness a spectacle being avidly followed by tens of millions of German and British viewers. She was dimly aware that, as a contest, it must be of a high standard; so much was apparent merely from the tension in the television box, let alone the voluble excitement from the stands.

The prospect of a possible English victory, however, was a matter largely of indifference to her. Kate Lewis, like most women who have toiled their way up to celebrity status, was too pressured to have much room left either for spectator sports or patriotism. It was less a case of her being selfish or egocentric, however, so much as driven. It had long been so. Even during her childhood, her lazy and demanding father would often complain that young Katherine would be busy even at her funeral; and in the event, to her abiding guilt, she'd been too busy to go to his.

Focusing back on to Ponse Perry, she saw he and Taff were both peering across towards the top left-hand corner of the terrace. Hurriedly, seeing Taff unzip his coat to pull out his walkie-talkie, Kate reached for her own in anticipation.

147

'You there, Kate? Take a close look at the upper west corner.'

'Will do.'

She raised the fieldglasses, fine-tuning the focus on the area, and promptly realized there was something different from when she'd scanned it a few minutes earlier: the spectators were now bunched much more densely together in the space near the top corner entrance. Scanning these newcomers, she was disappointed to see from their red-and-white colours that they were Liverpool fans. She concentrated on the area immediately around them, densely packed with the pressure from the entrance. Still no luck. She was just reaching for her radio when Barnes brought on a sudden roar as he at last broke through and, dancing round his mark, crossed for Kennie Kent to crack it into the net. In the event, the ensuing burst of euphoria was the Jacks' undoing, the crew forgetting to maintain their disguise as Liverpool fans in the frenzy of celebration. And there in their midst, most prominent of all, Kate saw Mervyn George, his clenched fists flailing in triumph . . . only to convulse in a paroxysm of rage when the ref ruled out the goal as off-side.

Given the deafening howls of protest and abuse, it was some while before Kate was able to convey the vital information to Taff. She confirmed the identification as positive, then watched her fella turn to force a way across to the nearest aisle and through the fans thronging the steps. Then, tense with excitement, she turned to point out the Jacks' position to Jason Moyle, alerting the cameraman to be ready to tape their arrest. As she turned to retrieve the powerful fieldglasses, someone called to her from the rear of the press box and, turning, she was startled to recognize Chief Superintendent Ingram.

'Just what's going on?' he asked, moving to sit beside her. Then, when she gestured with forced innocence towards the game, he took hold of her arm, leaning close. 'Don't flannel me, please. Roberts was supposed to be up here out of harm's way with you. Now tell me what the hell he's playing at!'

She was just launching into a fiction about his having a

relapse and going for medical attention when the invalid himself barked into life on the walkie-talkie beside her.

'I can't seem to contact Braun on the radio.'

'Taff, your chief's just arrived. Here he is now.'

'Roberts, where are you? What's this about Günter Braun?'

There was a pause during which Kate thought Taff had decided to break contact. But then this voice came on again, punctuated with coughing. 'Yes, sir, good. Radio the Oberkomissar to assemble his squad at the top of the north terrace on the west side. Repeat, west side. Full strength.'

Taff, although alarmed, could really foresee no way the Chief might now jeopardize the operation. Whatever message Ingram radioed to Braun, Taff could still if necessary make contact with the Oberkomissar by way of the local officers situated in groups around the terrace—assuming, of course, they were prepared to accept the authority of his warrant card.

He pushed his way through the final mass of spectators and at last moved out through one of the central entrances on to the concourse beyond the terrace. It was a relief to move without the near-constant buffeting on his cracked ribs—and a relief, too, to distance himself from the constant roar of the crowd.

Not surprisingly, the area beyond the bowl of the stadium was deserted as he hurried across past other entrances towards the one at the extreme west corner. However, as he neared it, he noticed a kid peering intently at him over the rim of the perimeter wall. Just then he heard a shout from behind him and, turning, saw Günter Braun now in leather police coat accompanied by several of his men as they hurried across to join him.

'You have tracked them, ja?'

'Just inside the entrance there. The whole crew, but disguised in red and white as Liverpool fans.'

'Ver goot.'

'Where's the rest of your squad?'

'Coming, coming.'

149

Taff turned back and noticed that the youngster had gone.

'Best move in right now, OK?' Then, at the Chief's frown: 'There was a kid on the wall—looking this way instead of at the game.'

Günter nodded in concern. 'I saw him go.' The Oberkomissar caught sight of a couple more of his men across by the further entrance and, yelling for them to hurry, turned to head for the entrance.

'They'll be armed,' Taff warned as he followed. He was well aware that, even if the crew were tooled up, it wouldn't be with firearms; but he reckoned there'd be a whole lot less aggro if the police had their guns out for the collar.

In the event, there was no collar. Evidently the kid must have been keeping watch-out because, by the time Taff and the squad reached the thunderous crowd inside the west-corner entrance, Mervyn and the rest of the Jacks had flown.

'They suddenly all scattered,' Kate confirmed over the radio. 'I *think* Mervyn may be heading for the central entrance.'

Taff had already turned and was racing back out to the concourse area, Günter Braun and one of his sergeants following. No luck. They reached the next entrance along and forced their way inside but could see no sign of Mervyn.

'Hello, Kate? See anything of him?'

'He was at the very back—pushing his way along towards the centre and then—'

'Kate? Lost you.' The crowd were going wild over yet another English attack. 'Kate?'

'Sorry . . . Yes, yes—that's him!'

'Shout, love! I can't hear you!'

'I said I can see him!'

'Where?'

'The roof! He's up on the roof! Going like a cat—heading for the motorway side. Heading east!'

The roof? It seemed impossible. Staring up at the huge tentpole-like supports with their steel guys, there seemed no possible way . . . But then, looking out to where the edges

150

of the vast tentlike crescent dipped down along the rear rim of the terrace, Taff realized it would indeed be possible to leap up and catch the rim.

'The concourse!' he yelled to Günter, hurrying back out of the entrance and pointing east to the furthest tip of the crescent. 'Quickly!'

They weren't at their fastest, thanks to Taff's chest infection and the heavy leather coats and gear of the police. Even before they reached the next entrance along, Taff saw the dark figure drop down from the lip of the crescent and race off across the concourse towards the distant autobahn bridge. Günter Braun bellowed out *Polizei*, warning him to stop, but it was a lost cause.

'Where's your car?' Taff gasped, his chest a furnace of pain. Then, when the Oberkomissar indicated a special police park way across the huge concourse, he added: 'He's staying as a guest of Die Skins. If you can find the address of their leader, it's worth us checking there.'

Braun ran off ahead to get busy on his car radio while Taff responded to the insistent bleeping on his walkie-talkie.

'I'm sorry, Guv'nor, but Mervyn George slipped the net.'

'We've got a couple of them pinpointed across on the terrace. Leastways, your lass reckons she has.'

'A word with her, please.' She came on immediately, and he told her to brief Braun's sergeants re the whereabouts of her two Jacks. Then, watching Braun way across the concourse, he added for her ears only that they were still after sly wee Mervyn. He passed his radio to the sergeant with a hurried explanation, then started to wheeze painfully after the Oberkomissar.

'You should not be chasing around like this,' he was told as they took off up the slip road from the ground. 'You are being foolish. You should look on it just as a job. Why must this operation have such importance to you, huh?'

'Their victim is effectively dead. He's an Oberjudicator and, as it happens, a friend of mine. More like—well, almost like a father to me.'

Braun gave a curt nod and, switching on his flashers,

rocketed the Mercedes down the autobahn into town. 'Then we must both be foolish, ja.'

The address was in a well-to-do district of tree-lined streets and modern houses built to traditional styling, the whole area tasteful and prosperous . . . and no great surprise for Taff over that. Even in England, the conventional cloth-cap image of the football supporter was on the wane; all too often, the maniac war-game organizers, the generals and their staff, emanated from Yuppy Land. They were compensating, according to the sociologists, for the absence of physical contest in their desk-bound lives.

'What about some back-up?' Taff asked, calculating from the map that they were only a few minutes away from their target.

Braun shrugged, then reached for the radio, duly barking out the request for a support vehicle before turning to explain. 'We have here the latest in command control. Computer monitoring of all car positions. Instant support units, ja.'

'Right.' Taff nodded, pulling a wry face. 'And by next year, come the completion of mega-stream cabling, Britain's Bobbies just may catch up with you.'

As they approached the street, they saw a taxi turn out of it. Instantly the police chief braked, signalling for the driver to stop, then crossing to question him.

'A good hunch, David,' he confirmed, hopping back behind the wheel. 'He just delivered "ein frightened Engländer" to number four.' He radioed in for news on their back-up, then grunted in irritation as the control operator apologized for the delay. 'So much for the hi-tech latest!'

'In England, all car crews would have unplugged and be watching the match on TV in the nearest bar.' Then, when the Oberkomissar snorted, reluctant to concede to an equivalent lack of discipline among German police, he added: 'They're only human. Besides, those Münchners who aren't actually at the match will be watching it at home.'

'Ja, ja, ja, Oberinspektor, while the professional criminals take the opportunity to get busy.' He tried the radio again, this time delivering a blast when the operator repeated the apology. 'We shall miss him again!'

Taff nodded, reaching to open the door. 'You go to the front door, I'll cover the back, OK?'

Braun's hesitation was only brief. He was a big man who kept himself in good trim. Moreover, like senior officers the world over, he welcomed the occasional chance of once more making a collar on his own.

'Give me exactly three minutes,' Taff said, checking his watch. 'Oh, and, Ober, if it comes down to shooting, *please* don't kill him. It's what he's going to tell me that's important.'

'You are so sure he will talk?' the German called as Taff got out of the Mercedes.

'That may depend on you, sir, and how slow we can be over taking him into formal custody.'

There was an unmade access track along the rear of the back gardens, much of it masked from the houses by garden trees and bushes. Taff worked his way along to the rear of No. 4, then chose a spot behind thick shrubs beside the swimming-pool's changing hut—a vantage-point where he could watch for the Mercedes to arrive as well as covering the rear of the house.

He was barely in position before Braun drove up and hurried to the front of the house. After a moment, Taff heard heavy knocking and Braun shouting that it was Police and to open up. More heavy knocking. Then at last he saw the crew leader's squat figure run from the rear of the house and, after a hurried glance around, dart down the garden towards the pool.

For a split second the fugitive hesitated over which side to come round. Then, hearing the Oberkomissar shout from beside the house, he darted towards the changing-hut corner.

Briefly, unsure which side of the hut to expect him, Taff braced in readiness against the centre of the rear wall. Then, hearing the crunch of foliage, he spun round to find the two of them face to face. For a shocked second, Mervyn froze.

153

Then, unexpectedly, he flung himself low at Taff, his bullet head smashing the wind from the policeman. Somehow, as he plunged backwards under the impact, Taff's rugger-playing instincts prompted him to lock on to one of the man's legs, clinging on to the ankle while Mervyn smashed his other foot frantically back at his head and face.

The desperate assault, although seemingly endless, in fact lasted only seconds before Günter Braun crashed round behind the changing hut. He yelled for Mervyn to stop, then promptly emphasized the order by firing his pistol inches from Mervyn's ear.

Abruptly, Mervyn obeyed, petrified by the shot. And with the sudden cessation of violence, Taff was once again engulfed with pain, groaning out what felt like quite definitely his last ever breath.

CHAPTER 13

'Right, boy, this is off the record. You've not been cautioned yet nor properly arrested. Nothing you say here in the car is official. However, the fact is, we've got you bang to rights on the assault charge. Let's call it murder—at the very least manslaughter—because, if Judge Hartington isn't dead already, the medics say he can't last out the week.'

Taff paused for emphasis, eyeing the sullen prisoner beside him in the back of the Mercedes. 'Murder, manslaughter. For which, as the boss of the Jacks, you'll face a near-certain life-sentence. However, I'll see it goes a *lot* easier for you if you tell me—now, unofficially—who was behind it. Who was it put you up to the assault in the first place?'

'Sod off, copper.' Mervyn worked his dry mouth in vain for phlegm to spit in Taff's face. 'Get stuffed—'

He broke off, shrieking in pain and shock as Günter Braun's gloved hand suddenly thrust in to clamp on his testicles, the big man growling into his ear as he did so. 'This is Germany, not England! No Police and Criminal

154

Evidence Act to protect you here. Less even than that. Until we get you into police headquarters, you risk very much injury, received while so violently resisting arrest.' The warning was punctuated with yet another shriek, the police chief glancing as though in mock surprise to Taff. 'Now sings he, ja.'

Taff nodded, his grin lopsided as he tried to conceal his unease. He was fast coming to understand why it was that Chiefie Ingram had such a high regard for the Oberkomissar: thin on scruples, the pair of them.

Whereas Taff harboured no sympathy whatsoever for the manacled bully between them in the back of the car, his own deeply-ingrained abhorrence of violence ran heavily against such use of physical torture . . . unlike the big Rhinelander who, to judge from his relaxed expression, clearly had few if any qualms. Maybe, Taff reflected as their prisoner gave yet another wild shriek, this time followed by convulsive sobs—maybe Herr Obersport merely has a thing about Engländer football thugs.

He took another sip of schnapps from the flask Braun had handed him as a temporary painkiller once they'd got Mervyn handcuffed and into the car. After that, the chief had radioed in to cancel his fruitless request for back-up before driving them to this quiet, non-residential part of the city near the canal for what he'd described as 'a bit of small-talk'.

The raw schnapps brought on another bout of coughing, harsh and persistent and, Taff felt sure, every bit as painful as having one's pills crushed. When the spasm was finally spent, he returned the flask and, giving Braun a discreet nod, turned to resume his own more British line of persuasion.

'I'm offering you a deal here, boy. You tell me the exact details of why you and the crew were waiting there at the Bullring to sort out the Judge. Who tipped you off? Exactly what did he say? The lot. You come clean with me, right now, and—well, for a start we can do without what's known in the trade as the Hidden Persuader.' He nodded for a reminder from Braun to underline the point, then waited uneasily for Mervyn's agonized sobs to abate. God help

155

them all if the Kraut butcher went so far as to rupture one of them!

'The second point you appear to have overlooked in all the mayhem and excitement is your stepbrother Kennie. Doubtless at this very moment he's scoring his way to international fame and glory, while you, through obstinacy and a misplaced sense of loyalty, smear that glory in shit.'

This got home all right. The sobs stopped, the dark piggy eyes glaring fiercely back at Taff's as the thickset head shook in rejection.

'I agree, it's a big burden to live up to,' the CID man persisted. 'Such a talented young member of the family, everyone so proud of him. Mum and Dad, your stepsister, the neighbours, the whole street, your mates at work— quite some procession. Worth preserving, eh, lad? Worth concealing the fact that another member of this esteemed family is notorious not as a great sportsman but as a second-rate, violent little thug!'

With an animal cry, Mervyn lunged forward in a furious attempt to head-butt his tormentor, only to heave convulsively backwards as Braun shouldered him, harshly renewing the grip between his legs.

'What I'm saying, boy,' Taff resumed evenly once their prisoner's sobs had abated, 'is that the choice is all yours. Refuse to cooperate now and the world's press will have it in full: Kennie Kent's stepbrother arrested on suss of the ultimate crime. But if you cough us the lot now, I guarantee no one will make the connection. There'll be no press release until your first remand back in England sometime next week, and even then you'll just be Mervyn George, n.f.a., member of the Bulls' supporters' club. No link to the Kents, nothing.'

There was a pause, Mervyn biting his lip in uncertainty before grimacing in rejection. 'They'd know. Be bound to come out.'

'No, boy, not until the trial. Which could be as much as a year away. A long time. Time enough for him to become King Kennie, big enough to ride out the scandal relatively unharmed.' He paused, eyeing the bully for a reaction before deciding to play his final card: 'The other reason for urgency is to do with the thing I believe you're even more passionate about than young Kennie.'

'Wha's that, then?'

'The club. The fact that its future is critically in doubt.' Then, persisting over Mervyn's denials, he added: 'Judge Hartington had obtained rock-solid evidence of Mr Oxted's plans to bankrupt the club and force a sell-off along with a planned merger with Chelsea. No, listen to me, hear me out. Oxted must have known the Judge had that evidence. And it's my belief it was Oxted who put you and the Jacks on to sorting us out that evening. Oxted told you the Judge had it in for the club, right? But in fact, nothing could have been further from the truth. Judge Hartington wanted to try and *save* the club—to try and stop Oxted destroying it.'

There was an even longer pause. The German police chief glanced in query to Taff, who hurriedly shook his head. He knew there was a tight limit on the length of time they could stay out here incognito. But a further squeeze now could prove one too many, simply hardening the lad's resolve in inverse proportion to the state of his privates.

'Only one way you can know so much,' Mervyn muttered at last. 'Someone's squealed. One of the crew's grassed us. Right then, you tell me who it is and I'll cough on Oxted.'

'Again you've missed the point, boy. I'm offering you a chance to *save* your precious bloody club. Bring down Oxted—discredit him—and it's likely his plans to dispose of the club will collapse overnight.' Pause. 'It was him who contacted you about the Judge's visit, yes?' Pause. 'That's right, isn't it?'

Taff had expected a straight confirmation. Instead, disconcertingly, Mervyn merely shrugged his thickset shoulders. ''Course it was him. Wasn't no one else could of bunged us all that info and sent us all them freebie tickets and that. No one. It had to be him.' He shook his head. 'Just don't ask me to prove it, that's all.' Then, anticipating Taff's query, he added: 'We never met! 'Course not! Can you imagine Mr Fancy Chairman mixing in with the most notorious crew in the club? Slipping us info on police tactics at matches, giving us a rah-rah when we done a bundle on the opposition, winding us up to have a go at the Nigs or the cop-creepers or whatever? Oxted may be all sorts of things, but he ain't stupid.'

He paused, nodding at the flask. 'Here, give us a snort and get old Fritz to quit the groping.'

Taff glanced at the Oberkomissar, who scowled in reluctance before finally removing his gloved hand from the nether region. It was scant pleasure to Taff that Mervyn's greedy gulp of schnapps promptly set him choking.

'How long had he been feeding you this information?'

'Couple of years. Always by phone. She'd ring about the time I got back from work.'

'*She?*'

'So it was some scrubber of his. Wife, mistress, how should I know? Posh talker, though. Posh and stiff, know what I mean? Like she didn't fancy having to do it for him. Wouldn't answer no questions neither. Right royal cow.'

Taff grunted, realizing there was no prospect even of a voice identification. 'What about these tickets he sent you?'

'She'd tell me where the drop point would be. Always different places. Sometimes there'd be a wad of bread in with 'em—much as a half grand one time. That was after we'd screwed the Fulham lads. Always rewarded a victory, he did. But, like she used to tell us, he always preferred it upfront and splashed on the Box. Wasn't no good 'less Wimbledon and them could *see* who'd got the most bottle. See it on the screen, that's what he wanted. Bully-Bully BULL!' He shook his head, reading the frustration on Taff's face. 'Never no proof, like I said. Maybe the money would have had his dabs on it—if ever we'd kept any.'

'And the evening he sent you to sort out the Judge? What was the message? Something to do with a conspiracy, was it?'

'Right.' Mervyn nodded. 'Come on wiv a lot more mouth than usual, she did—telling how the Judge was going to force all clubs to sell out to the council, have all-seater stadiums, all-weather pitches. Kill off the game's spirit and

158

in partic'lar kill off Balham United. Give us the evil, she did, then promised there'd be a cool grand in it if we toddled down there and give him a little greeting.'

'Did you get paid?'

The crew leader snorted, shaking his head. 'Mind you, to be totally honest wiv yer, that could be 'cos we went a bit over the top wiv the job.'

Taff swallowed down the remnants from the flask, fighting back the urge to choke, then wiping away the tears it brought to his eyes before asking: 'You gave him a warmer greeting than you were meant to, huh?'

'Listen, man, we was just going to duff 'im up,' Mervyn retorted with sudden force. 'On my life, we wasn't reckoning to screw him nowhere near so heavy as it turned out. Just that . . .'

'What? You didn't know your own strength . . .'

'First off, we didn't know *you* was going to be along wiv 'im. And second—' he wagged his head with a show of regret—'I mean, who'd have reckoned an old beak like him was goin' to ruck back like he did? I tell yer straight, beforehand, we wasn't all that bothered—just going to put the frighteners on him and push him around a bit. But, like, half the lads was took up wiv you, and then the stupid old sod freaking well had a go back at us! Clobbered old Spud, didn't he? Floored him wallop. Then freaking near screwed me an' all.'

Taff gave a grim nod, reflecting on the mindless savagery which old Vincent—rugger Blue, Guards, all-round athlete—had so unwittingly unleashed. As he had once joked to Taff: 'An Englishman is never fairly beaten.' But the modern moral? Never take on a brutal animal like Mervyn George unless you know enough tricks and deceits to be sure of winning!

Taff squirmed in vain to try and get comfortable on the overcrowded flight. It didn't help that they were in the very last row of the Tristar and the Force 8 turbulence was heaving the back end around like a roller-coaster. At the time it had seemed a piece of luck to find a couple of vacant seats on the London-bound club charter. Now they were up, however, he was far from sure.

'They shouldn't allow flights to take off in weather like this,' Kate groaned.

'Anything else but a charter full of English football fans, they probably wouldn't. In fact, if England had won, I reckon they might well have reopened the gas-chambers.'

Kate waited for her stomach to catch up with her after a particularly massive lurch, then asked: 'Any chance of hearing how you came to get all smashed up yet again?'

'Sure.' He nodded, sliding her a painful half-grin and gently touching her in a way that was special to them. 'It might even be an idea to get me to a TV studio and ask me on camera.'

'Ha! Bruised your brain as well?'

'Seriously,' Taff remarked, half meaning it, 'we've got to force some action somehow.' He went on to explain how, Oxted had cultivated his own pack of pet jackals, over the years supplying them with endless hand-outs and anonymous phone calls, culminating in the fateful command to greet Judge Hartington in the club car park with their own special brand of hospitality. Great, terrific, his suspicions emphatically confirmed ... except, of course, for the tiresome little matter of proof.

'I told Mervyn to tell Chiefie Ingram nothing—not a single word. Flat denials of everything except that he wants a lawyer. That way, at least we should keep Oxted guessing.'

'Meanwhile hyping up the pressure,' Kate cut in approvingly, 'with a TV report of the arrests.'

Taff heaved aside as an air hostess careered past him down the aisle, all but crashing her runaway server trolley into the rear loos. His evasive action did little to ease the numbing ache in his chest. 'There have been times during this case,' he groaned, 'when I've begun to suspect I'm the target of a violent conspiracy.'

'It's the natural paranoia of working alongside the Met,' Kate remarked. Then, abruptly concerned, she added: 'Listen, they'll never approve it—not for you to go on screen. Not without approval from Ingram. I mean, yes, if we'd thought to stick you in a Munich hospital bed and done the injured-police-hero interview, but it's about 35,000 feet too late for that now.'

'It won't even be hospital if this turbulence gets any worse,' Taff grunted, accepting a low-alcohol lager from the flustered hostess as she struggled back up the aisle. 'Anyway, you're right about the press office not allowing me on screen.'

'So don't do it,' Kate insisted, leaning close to kiss one of the few unkicked parts of his face. 'As soon as we get back I'll work out a piece for tonight's News. Jason Moyle caught some great footage of Braun's SS arresting those two Jacks during half-time. You give me some Police Spokesman stuff to tie them solidly in with the assault on Judge Hartington and, bingo, we'll have the Prince of Darkness sweating blood up there in his Hampstead palace.'

She waited while Taff took a long pull of the no-no lager before nodding agreement, then she asked the question that had been bugging her all along: 'One thing, Supercop, how come you managed to crack a hard nut like Mervyn George?'

She saw the blink of evasion in his eyes—evasion and, with it, guilt—and it shocked her. It was less the principle involved—why not fight fire with fire? violence with violence?—so much as the loss of what she had always believed to be impregnable in him. In contrast to the shabbiness and deceit she so often had to use to crack a story, the rock of Taff's integrity had always stood out as a formidable example. Now, reading his moment of guilt, she was saddened at the loss; like realizing one's beloved daughter is no longer a virgin, she reflected ruefully. And yet, yin and yan, for every bad there's a good: at least she now knew he was human and fallible and real—something she'd never been fully sure of hitherto.

'Actually,' her man replied with false casualness, 'he's not entirely hard. It was just a case of finding the right way to handle him.'

The arrest of three British fans during the friendly in Munich marks a dramatic development in the investigation into the vicious assault on His Honour Judge Vincent Hartington. The three were all Balham United supporters and part of the notorious Jacks crew. Their arrest by officers of the special German anti-hooligan squad based in Karlsrühe was caught on film by ITN cameraman Jason Moyle, seen in this sequence during half-time. It was not by chance that Moyle captured their moment of arrest since he and I had been isntrumental in shadowing the Jacks' movements ever since their arrival in Munich.

Following these arrests, it can now be revealed that ITN's interest in the notorious Balham United crew was first aroused as a result of an incident filmed at the Bullring Supporters' Club during an interview with Kennie Kent soon after his selection as the England striker. Asked by our sports correspondent Martin Ford about the wilder elements among Balham's supporters, Kent called on his stepbrother, Mervyn George, to speak for the fans. Mr George was one of the three men arrested at Munich. As can be seen here at the interview, his rising excitement over the issue led to a partial loss of control during which he grabbed hold of Martin Ford and had to be constrained by Kennie Kent.

ITN's suspicions about the Jacks, of whom Mervyn George is the acknowledged leader, were reinforced shortly after this when ITN was contacted by an informant who claimed to have been present both at the supporters' club interview and, more significantly, during the vicious assault on Judge Hartington. The informant was particularly frightened that the Judge might die and thus render those responsible, himself included, open to charges of murder.

However, the informant was reluctant to approach the police directly for fear of duress, instead seeking ITN's help as mediator. It was in this capacity that I contacted one of the senior officers on the case, Detective Chief Inspector David Roberts. It can now be revealed that this officer in fact accompanied the Judge during the ill-fated visit to the Balham United Football Club and was himself

162

severely injured trying to fight off the assault, suffering multiple bruising and five broken ribs.

Chief Inspector Roberts was also present at Munich during the mini riot in a Gartenstrasse bierkeller. Mr Roberts is briefly visible at the end of this sequence filmed by Jason Moyle when I attempted to interview Mervyn George and the rest of the Jacks crew on the evening before the match.

Mervyn George and the other two Jacks, Patrick Wilson and Harold McQuinty, are currently being held on public-order charges following the Gartenstrasse incident. Whereas their cases are due to be tried before a Munich court on Monday, I understand from a reliable police source that an application can also be expected for their extradition to London to face serious assault charges, including unlawful wounding.

Meanwhile, the senior officer on the Hartington case, Chief Superintendent Tom Ingram, is currently in Munich, where I understand he has been granted access to question the three men in custody.

'The latest medical bulletin on Judge Hartington's condition, issued at the Balham Infirmary earlier this evening, reveals no improvement. The Judge, currently on a life-support unit, has been in a coma ever since the assault last week. This is Kate Lewis for News at Ten.'

'Kate Lewis—she's the one who I met here?'

'Pushy cow,' Oxted confirmed. He switched off the television set, then headed for the drinks cabinet. The ITN report had clearly shaken him, flushing colour to his face, his fists clenched tight. 'The bitch was pushing to tie me in with that Hartington business.' He took a deep gulp of brandy. 'Bitch.'

The woman crossed to pour herself a soda-water, eyeing him coldly. 'Mervyn George, Patrick Wilson, Harold McQuinty. All a bit near to home, eh, Teddy.'

'So what?' He took another gulp. 'There's nothing to tie them in with me.'

The woman remained standing, her eyes fixed on him

163

almost as though mesmerized, the glass held in both hands but as yet untouched. 'That poor old man.'

'Vincent? Yes. And his prospects not improving, apparently.'

'A coma. Imagine.' She was strikingly beautiful, her slim figure, dense ash-blonde hair and delicate features all finely groomed and clad without regard to cost. Although aware that he kept her as a fancy status doll, there was always the secret consolation of knowing that their relationship, so-called, was no more permanent than the tin-pot Napoleon's empire. 'Why'd you do it, eh? How could you have set them on to him like that? Dead vicious—'

He stopped her, his hand gripping her wrist, ignoring the glass as it fell to the floor. 'Do what, Pat? Don't talk shit.'

'The Jacks—they're your little rat pack, right?' She pulled free of him, rubbing her wrist and glaring at him, for once indifferent to his mood. 'All those phone calls I made for you. Tell them this, tell them that. Set them on the blacks, warn them about police infiltrators, order up a new chant.'

'So?' He gestured in dismissal. 'Didn't put them on to poor old Vincent, for Christ's sake!'

'Didn't you? *Didn't you?* Naturally, you didn't tell your little Patsy to phone them like usual. She'd have known too much if you had. But you knew the old Judge was bad news for you and your lousy game plan. You knew . . .' She dodged back from the blow he swung at her, promptly snatching up the brandy bottle and holding it poised to retaliate should he come after her. 'Too near the truth, am I, Ted? Too near the mark?'

'For Christ's sake, what's got into you?' he retorted, hands spread in a show of mystification as he shook his head. 'Do a thing like that to a man who's my friend? What's up with you?'

'Disgust, that's what!' She replaced the bottle but moved towards the door, knowing the danger of his impulsiveness. 'Disgust and shame.'

She would have liked to say more: to tell him of the cumulative loathing and contempt she had generated for him over the years; yet to do so would have been to reveal her own duplicity in the affair. Sufficient now to savour the bitterness of rejection in his face, to force him for once to eat his own arrogant cocky bloody egotism. 'I'm leaving you, Teddy mate. You've made your lousy bed, now you can lie in it!'

Taff swore as the telephone jangled him back from oblivion, fumbling around beside the bed to locate the intrusive thing. 'Roberts speaking.'

'Sorry to disturb you, David, but I just heard the report on the TV.' Regardless of her enduring ordeal since the attack, Isabel Hartington sounded as calm and controlled as ever. He could imagine her sitting back and fondling the ears of the Labrador pups; then he remembered the magazine at the hospital which, although held erect as a shield before her, was upside down. *Appearances, Tibs dear, appearances; matter of duty, what.* 'Arrests, they said.'

'That's right, Mrs Hartington. We've picked up the three principal thugs involved.'

'And?'

He sighed, switching on the light and working his way painfully up in bed to a sitting position. 'Not a lot more to tell you over and above what Kate Lewis just reported.'

'I see.' Pause. 'I must say, David, that did surprise me just a little: hearing such a comprehensive report from ITN.'

'Largely a *quid pro quo*, in fact. The informant made contact with Miss Lewis—for protection, if you follow me. Anyway, as you'll have gathered, things paid off in Munich.'

'And?'

'Sorry?' Yet he knew there was no evading her: senior magistrate, daughter of a judge, wife of a judge. 'And what?'

'What about whoever's behind it? Vincent wasn't the victim of a random mugging.'

'No. Right. Well, give us time, eh.'

'The three thugs you've got—they didn't say anything? Name anyone?'

'You'd expect me to tell you if they had?' His head was aching again. Then he heard the key in the door and Kate called out, surprised that he was still awake. 'I'm sorry if

165

that sounded a bit abrupt, Mrs Harrington. The answer's yes but with no proof or evidence to justify an arrest. Not yet.'

'Political? Was I—David, I have to know, was I right about that?'

'Not directly, no. He may well have been forewarned about the substance of His Honour's report, but . . .'

'Warned by Alex Timpson, you mean, after the leak?'

'But if so,' Taff persisted, waving to Kate as she eyed him from the doorway, 'I doubt there was anything sinister in it. Nothing more than an Old Boy warning on the House grapevine.'

'Ha!'

'Don't forget, Virginia Cohen only leaked Timpson the report, not the appendix about Oxted's plans to destroy the club.'

There was a pause while she considered this. Kate, having slipped out of her coat, came in to snuggle him.

'Last time we met, David, you said they had the knives out for you. Now it seems you're working under some chief superintendent—Ingram, they said on ITN. Who is he?'

Taff told her, explaining merely that the man was DCI Lawley's chief, but concealing the deal he'd made with the O Division commander. She was suspicious, wanting to know the strength of the evidence against the three fans arrested in Munich, wanting to know if Taff had been in some way compromised.

'Mrs Hartington, trust me, OK? I understand how you must feel: unable to do anything but sit around and wait. Please, just trust me. We've identified our main suspect; we've got a strong lead to follow up in the morning. What I need now is some sleep.'

'Of course, yes, I'm sorry. Good night.'

'What about that bulletin on your husband? Anything else you can add?'

'Only that—well, I'm afraid they're talking about further surgery. Good night, David.'

'What was that about a strong lead?' Kate asked as he rang off.

'Nothing,' he groaned, pulling a face. 'About the only prospect for tomorrow is yet another carpeting. Before Madam rang, I had Chiefie Briggs belling me to say he's had the Yard Press Office on to him about your little scoop tonight and what the hell?'

CHAPTER 14

Chief Superintendent Ingram's flight landed at Heathrow shortly before 10.0 the next morning. He seemed surprised to be met by Taff and, behind the cheery smile, uneasy.

'Sick leave, David. That was an order. Gluttons for punishment, you Welsh.'

'Just gluttons for justice, sir,' Taff retorted as he led the way out to the car. In fact he was feeling desperately ill, but there simply wasn't time to lie down. 'We're very close to clear-up on this one.' He paused to show his warrant card to a sullen traffic marshal, then asked the chief what success he'd had with the interrogations.

Ingram shrugged, wagging his head in equivocation. 'McQuinty cracked to some extent—claimed Mervyn George had got them all wound up about the Judge. Needless to say, neither George nor Wilson was saying anything more than lawyer, lawyer, lawyer.'

All of which sounded to Taff as though Günter Braun had also kept mum about their productive bit of 'small-talk' with Mervyn in the car, perhaps not so surprising, given the hidden persuasion the German had applied.

'Kate Lewis,' Ingram announced curtly. 'I gather she got excessively voluble on *News at Ten* last night. I had the Press Office phoning me at God knows what hour to ask how much of it I'd authorized.' He glanced at Taff, waiting while he filtered the car into the tunnel queue. 'Presumably you received much the same query.'

'I was woken up, yes—in fact by my guv'nor. He wasn't best pleased.'

'Your guv'nor? Slight slip of the tongue there, Roberts.

I'm your bloody guv'nor, remember? I'm the one you should have consulted before talking to the media.' He was tense and angry, the jovial front now abandoned. 'I'm fully aware that Miss Lewis brought us the witness, so you owed her for that. But, let's get this fully understood now: so long as I'm running the investigation, you clear anything and everything with me. Not just your contacts with madam, but every move you make. All right?' Then, when Taff remained silent, preoccupied with entering the M-4 access roundabout, he added less sharply: 'Sorry to pull rank, especially with an officer on attachment from another force, but this is how we do things in the Met.'

Taff waited until he was up to speed on the motorway before spelling it out. 'I'm afraid, sir, this is no longer fully under the Met.'

'What isn't? Don't try it on with me now. I've heard a lot about you, Roberts. Cocky sod, that's what I heard. Arrogant bloody Welshman.'

'The fact is,' Taff resumed more forcefully, 'DGS Briggs is still my guv'nor, not you. This investigation is being conducted under the Sox operation—'

'Is it, by Christ, is it! We'll bloody see about that!' He reached for the car radio, then thought better of it and remarked: 'Soon as we get back to Division, we'll clarify this once and for all with *my* guv'nor!'

'If you're still sure that's what you want when you've heard me out.'

'Don't try it on, I said!'

'Suppose you just *listen*!'

Taff's contempt for corruption was dangerously close to the surface, obliging him to pause briefly in order to simmer down. Not that Ingram's was corruption on the grand scale; merely the level of petty graft and compromise, cynically known as perking, all too common among the older officers in many of the Met divisions. Often it had started quite early in their careers as opportunism, such as pocketing one or two nice pieces for the wife when investigating a smash-and-grab raid on a jeweller's: scant risk of a come-back, the whole loss anyway covered by insurance. Perks.

And, from this, only a short step to the hand-outs and freebies which, with time and habit, could grow insidiously to the level of outright bribes.

'His Honour Judge Hartington was leaked inside information on Mr Edward Oxted's conduct as chairman of Balham United—principally, his plans to bankrupt the club with a view to a massive property-development scheme of the ground.'

Ingram gaped at him, shaking his head in shocked denial, genuinely appalled, and more so as Taff continued.

'Also leaked, sir, were details of Mr Oxted's other, more shady practices: such as running a pack of particularly violent fans known as the Jacks; such as compromising the integrity of the divisional football liaison officer by lavishing hand-outs and freebies on him to the point where that officer has become vulnerable and hence open to manipulation.'

'No proof! Nothing!' The curtness of Ingram's response told Taff the man must have been half-anticipating these accusations, perhaps ever since Oxted had first contacted him to get the damned Welsh DCI off his back. 'You and your holier-than-thou attitude! You should try asking your beloved Foxy Walsh about perks and hand-outs! Him and his mates set the bloody style! On the take left, right and bloody centre! Bent as hairpins, the lot of them, sonny, so don't come round me with all this crap about being compromised!'

'I'm not . . .' Taff had to pause once again to recover his cool. 'I'm not pointing the finger or coming on holier-than-thou as you put it, sir. Merely reviewing the situation to see where we go from here.' Then, topping the chief's response: 'I'm not making any judgements re how bent or compromised you may or may not be. Nor is it intended to refer the evidence to C-10 or the Police Authority. All I care about is nailing your friend Oxted. Understood, *sir*?'

His friend, Taff thought, that was the rub. They'd socialized together, met and drunk and joked together; possibly shared family outings or even short holidays together; done each other favours, given presents; been friends. Doubtless, most of the hospitality had come from Oxted, but cheerful

Tommy Ingram had for sure contributed. And now his football chairman chum was suddenly under investigation, and Tommy was being told he must be nailed. Whether or not Tom Ingram yet fully appreciated all this, he gave little sign, merely glaring sidelong at the junior officer who had suddenly taken command. Taff let it sink in for a while, waiting until they were off the Hammersmith flyover and heading up Cromwell Road before he resumed.

'First thing is to get a phone warrant. Since you're the senior investigating officer, we apply for it in your name. Once all the phone taps are operating—his home, his City office and the ground—you bell chummy and you warn him. You tell him Mervyn George has been singing his head off and has also come up with strong corroborative evidence, both cash and an unused match ticket, currently with forensics for checks. You tell him that in addition there's a whole mass of evidence to establish his motive, namely that the Judge was about to blow his development plans for the Balham ground wide open.'

He paused, again waiting for a response, his feeling of contempt giving way now to a measure of pity. It was a bitter shock for the bloke to hear just how dismally he'd misjudged his friend: to learn that, behind his up-market, Establishment image, the Gamelord was in fact both an unscrupulous vandal and every bit as much a cruel bully as the club's worser hooligans.

Yet, hang it, why bleed for Ingram? Provided he now played the hand Taff was dealing him, the senior officer could even end up with a spectacular collar to boost the twilight of his career. Twilight it would be, since Taff would ensure the facts of his misconduct and 'perking' were recorded on his personal file—which, in all probability, would lead to his being advised to take early retirement. But the upfront version for his memoirs and his family and his *other* friends would be esteemed and honourable.

'You warn Oxted, sir, that his arrest is imminent for conspiracy, either to unlawful wounding or, most likely, to murder. And you tell him you're sorry, but there's nothing more you can do to help him other than suggest he does a runner.' Pause. 'You'll have a document, signed by Commander Blake and DCS Briggs, confirming that what you say during the phone call was prearranged and is without prejudice to your integrity.'

Yet another pause. It was Harrods before the chiefie finally spoke, his voice flat and dispirited. 'You're damned bloody sure it's Ted Oxted, aren't you!'

'Yes, sir, having regard to the weight of evidence against him, yes, I am.'

Had Taff been less ill, also less emotionally involved and *also* less the victim of his City fat cat prejudices—had he been able to take Papa Walsh's advice about being detached and clinical in assessing the real weight of that evidence—he might well have acknowledged that he as yet had nothing factual on Oxted. Circumstantial, yes—loads of motive and also the means—but no actual hard evidence. And most certainly a long way short of persuading the DPP into court proceedings.

Ted Oxted was already nervous. That damned TV report of the arrests had been bad enough; but it was far, far worse to have had Patsy Craine walk out on him because of it. Whereas his feelings for Patsy went little further than physical lust, it came as an intolerable rejection to have her leave him. For all his money and power and possessions, the little man had a deep need to feel respected and wanted and admired by those close to him; and, since the death of his old mother, there had really been no one closer than Patsy.

For all that, he knew surprisingly little about her other than that she originated from Huddersfield and had once completed some sort of course in fashion design—something of which she was much more proud than of her subsequent success as a top London model. He had felt no regrets at all over breaking up Pat's marriage, confident that, as a photographer, Andy Johns was bound to be suspect, if not a raving gay. All right, so Patsy wasn't exactly top-drawer, but no more was he. On the contrary, since he was inclined to trade on his tough origins, presenting himself as a slum graduate, it could have exposed him to ridicule were she too upmarket. Moreover, aside from her stunning looks, Patsy had good taste, along with the wit to appreciate his jokes and his acumen; as such, she as all round satisfactory, not only in bed but also as hostess and companion.

So what the bloody hell did she think she was at, walking out on him over this nonsense with the Jacks? How in hell could she imagine he'd be so stupid as to initiate such mindless violence? All right, yes, it was true that just occasionally, when he'd overdone the brandy, he might have manhandled her a bit; also there was a side to his more intimate impulses in which perhaps he really shouldn't have expected her to participate. But even so, to reject him and the lifestyle they had shared for nearly three years just because of an unproven suspicion over the Jacks? Damned faithless cow!

All of which, during the course of a largely sleepless night, had spawned ugly suspicions about Patsy Craine, fears that perhaps she had been planning this departure for some while and had merely seized on the Jacks nonsense as an excuse to quit.

The suspicion was barely formed before he was out of bed and downstairs to check the wall safe. This was the devilish price of cohabitation: the need to yield an unreasonable degree of trust to one's bed partner. With a shudder, he recalled Tommy Ingram's once telling him what a high proportion of young villains from burglars and car thieves right down to dole fiddlers were eventually copped not through police ingenuity but by being shopped by their embittered scrubbers. Now he, boss Oxted, was similarly vulnerable—but not over petty crimes, by Christ, but over finely-poised whopping big deals dependent on the sharp practices so essential if one was to stay ahead in the jungle of the City.

Sure enough, he discovered there were things missing— nothing in fact from the safe but, in a way more alarming, some of the financial accounts, bank statements and other documents he had kept stored for safety in the house rather than at the Bullring or at Oxted House beside the Barbican. Moreover, there was no way he could report the cow for theft since the missing items were of value only to his City rivals or, worse, to a blackmailer.

Next morning, anxious to check if any of the missing documents were in fact at the office, also to conceal certain other potentially damaging items, he wasted no time getting to the Barbican. Two hours later he headed along to the Chairman's suite at the Bullring to make similar checks. Although not exactly a man on the run, he was eager to conceal possible clues to numerous dodgy deals stretching back over many years.

He had been up in the suite less than an hour and had relaxed enough to pop the day's first bottle of Bollinger '82 when the phone rang.

'Kate Lewis of ITN here, Mr Oxted. After my piece on the news last night, I hoped you might reconsider—'

'You've got a bloody nerve!'

'Thick-skinned by trade, yes. The fact is, some background information I picked up while in Munich and also this morning has thrown up some questions I'd like to put to you.'

What the hell could the woman mean? Could she possibly be referring to Patsy? The previous evening she had been going on about the reporter; could she conceivably have gone scurrying off to ITN to blow the whistle on his secret link with the Jacks?

'Concerning what, Miss Lewis?'

'I honestly don't think you'd welcome an explanation over the telephone.'

'Ah. No more than you'll be expecting to tape anything, then.'

'That may depend on the advice of your lawyer, assuming you have him present again.'

'He'll be here, rest assured.'

'Midday then?'

'In a hurry, aren't you?'

'I have to stay ahead of the Beeb.'

Patsy Craine lay on the bed, revelling in the exquisite sense both of release and anticipation. Not that the whole three

173

years with Ted had been an ordeal. Right at the start, before the novelty of wealth and opulent living had worn off and before familiarity with his moods and appetites, his coarseness and alcoholism, had hardened to hatred—way back, the glitter of it all had been tremendous. A six-month high; a flirtation, not with the man but with his power. Buy this, go there, own that; flying lessons, grouse-shooting, yachting in the Caribbean, Christmas in St Moritz; meet the Prime Minister, entertain the team, pose with the cup . . .

It had been during the many champagne do's at the club and receptions at the Hampstead mansion that she had become increasingly aware of Boss Bryan. Deep and thoughtful by nature, or so he had seemed whenever Ted was around, which he invariably was. Indeed, it had been the very contrast between the two men which had fuelled her fascination with Bryan. The team manager was everything Oxted was not: quiet, considerate, attentive, gentle, and very good-looking. Indeed, he behaved with most unplayer-like decorum towards her. Whereas there seemed to be something of a cryptic challenge among the players to make heavy-handed passes at her, Boss Bryan kept at a respectful distance. So that, on the inevitable occasion when their swaggering mega-host Oxted hopelessly overdid the champagne cocktails and collapsed into the remains of the buffet, it was Patsy rather than Bryan who made the play after he'd helped her clean up the little sot and carry him upstairs.

Naturally, she had long been aware of the contempt in which Oxted held the team manager. Ironically, it had fuelled her own soaring contempt for Oxted—for his coarseness and greed and materialism, his disdain for loyalty and tradition, his consuming egotism, his obsessive cunning and opportunism. Not that there was anything protective in her attraction to Boss Bryan. Quite simply, doubtless heightened by the extreme contrast with Oxted, she hugely fancied him—and the more so, increasingly, once they had become lovers.

Irony, too, in the way she had fuelled Bryan Walton's hatred for Oxted: not through the usual cuckold's guilt-sense, however, so much as the secrets she increasingly shared with him: the man's shady City deals and deviousness, his sharp practices and outright cheating; and worse, gradually emerging over many months, bit by bit like a swamp monster, the appalling realization of his ultimate plan for the fate of the century-old football club.

The club manager, though not one of life's losers, was not a compulsive achiever like his chairman. Straightness and fair play were his criteria—arguably not qualities best suited to the manager of a modern League-status football team. Whereas the impact of Oxted's long-term plan to destroy the club deeply shocked him, the decision to take destructive retaliatory action was initiated by the beautiful woman between the two men. And the galvanic for that action was Judge Hartington's wide-ranging inquiry into the running of the football industry.

Patsy alone could obtain the crucial evidence. She was even the nominee owner of Oxted's secret Chelsea Club shares. During the latter stages of the Judge's inquiry when he was busy refining the mass of collected documents and witness statements into his final report, Vincent Hartington was intrigued to receive the first of several contacts, along with items of supportive photostat evidence, from the covert source he came to refer to as Deep Throat.

CHAPTER 15

It was shortly before midday when Oxted answered the telephone to his tame chief super. He listened in deepening shock as the copper recited the warning and listed off the various items of evidence against him. He might have noticed the somewhat stilted delivery had Ingram not suddenly abandoned his written script to deliver an impassioned rebuke of his own.

'I've got to tell you, Ted, I've known some cheapskate villains in my time. But the gross hypocrisy of what you've done—ruthlessly setting out to destroy that great club, then

175

turning those savages loose on that poor old Judge—I tell you, *mate*, that takes some beating. Fact is, I'm only giving you this tip-off because I don't want any of the shit to stick to me. Otherwise, I tell you straight, far as I'm concerned you could get stuffed and go the distance for it!'

With which, instead of waiting as instructed for any incriminating response from Oxted, he swore bitterly and slammed down the telephone.

The Chairman was also swearing, both in frustration and fear. He felt like a man who, from walking along a secure city street, suddenly finds himself floundering in quicksand. All right, so the source of this damned leak to the Judge, blowing his disposal plans for Balham United, was now clear to him: Patsy! Although why in God's name she should have chosen to piss away a fortune in Chelsea share profits he couldn't begin to fathom.

As for the proof linking him to the Jacks which Ingram had just claimed they'd got from Mervyn George? Unlikely but, yes, possible—especially if the bitch had had a hand in that, too! But *why*? Why should she have taken it into her dumb blonde head to betray him?

Until last night he'd had total confidence in his hold over her—the combined hold of money and his own hypnotic personality . . . unless, for Christ's sake, unless that worm Walton was in some way behind it? Once or twice over the last year or so, catching an unguarded glance or word between them, he'd had a twinge of suspicion. That he had never checked it out was largely because he couldn't conceive of Walton as a possible rival. The man was a no-no, a walking failure who had only held on to the job of manager because, as such, he was ideally fitted to the tycoon's plan of running down the Bulls.

Now, after refilling his glass, he reached for the telephone and dialled down to Walton's office three storeys below. 'You—up here, now.'

'Correction, Mr Oxted.' The manager's voice was unusually assertive. 'You come down here. I've something of very special interest to show you.'

'What you talking about?'

176

'Come down and you'll see.' Then, after a brief hesitation: 'It's to do with the Jacks.'

Bryan Walton braced himself, hands flat on his desk, petrified. The man alone was enough to scare him almost dumb, let alone doing what now had to be done. Yet he would do it—for Patsy and for the club he would do it. He would go through with it for the twin loves in his life, to save them both. But he would succeed less because of love than because of hatred, the consuming, implacable hatred such as he had never believed himself capable of until the little monster had first strutted into his life.

'I'm your new boss. I just bought control of the Bulls. You can expect plenty of changes in the way things are run—both off and on the field. Applying big-business methods: profitability levels, entertainment values, promotional razzamatazz. This is a great club with a great name. That's no reason it can't also be a great success—in terms of cups, gates *and* dividends.'

And sportsmanship? Player skills over and above the professional foul? Game tactics other than attack? And, excuse me, sir, but shouldn't something be done about the kop-end terraces? About curbing the wilder supporter elements and cleaning up the club's image? You call yourself a gamelord, sir, so what about the game?

Well, now the Gamelord would see; today was the day of reckoning.

'Right, then,' the tycoon snapped, striding in to lean his fists on the manager's desk, 'what's this you've got to show me?' Then, glancing mockingly around: 'My woman hidden away down here somewhere, is she?'

He snorted only to rush on. 'Don't think I haven't figured *that* out! You and Pat. Well now, just try and get this into that Geordie skull of yours: whatever your plans, you can forget them, because there's no way I'm letting you sneak what's rightfully mine! You try to take her, I'll break the both of you! I've got the power and the resources. I'll sue you through every court in the land; I'll make sure you never get another job in your life; I'll make it so you can't

177

walk down a street—*anywhere!*—without looking over your shoulder! And Patsy the bloody same, you hear me!'

He had both fists raised now and was shaking them almost as though exhorting the fans at a match, the release of frustration and anger hardening his certainty of the manager's part in his sudden dilemma. Nor was Walton showing any signs of denial. On the contrary, apart from standing in defiance of Oxted's furious tirade, the club manager appeared uncharacteristically calm.

'There's no way I'm letting her go,' Oxted persisted, 'least of all to a sly sod like you! You least of all! Gutless, bungling, pathetic wanker!'

Had he but known it, the tycoon was doing no more than anticipated, his tirade merely fuelling the manager's hatred to the point where he could go through with his own desperate plan.

'What amazes me is how the pair of you figured it out. That cow Patsy must have a few more marbles than I gave her credit for. Worked out just what I was up to with the Jacks and the Chelsea shares, did she? Realized why we were buying in such an ill-matched bag of freaks to try and win our way back up the League ladder? Clocked why the hell I kept on such a worthless idiot duffer to manage them? Did she? *Did she?* Bloody sure it wasn't Boss Bryan's genius at work. Couldn't find the wit to sign yourself on to the dole, much less work out a master plan like that!'

The Chairman, his anger mounting to a frenzy at the lack of response, darted round the desk to prod at Walton, meanwhile yapping terrier-like into his face. 'That poor old man—my friend—he died! Died because of you two idiots, tampering and plotting—'

'*Died?!*'

'Brain dead, if not actually stiff!'

The savage force with which the manager suddenly hit out sent Oxted reeling backwards to smash into a glass cabinet of trophies. Swearing in frenzied rage, the man struggled to extricate himself, regardless of the blood flowing from his lacerated hands. He launched wildly forward, only

178

to check, amazed to find himself staring into the barrel of a service revolver.

'Have you gone totally, bloody insane?'

'On the contrary—' the manager's voice was still oddly calm—'it's probably the most sensible thing I've done since you took over this club.'

'Sensible . . .?'

'Shut up!' The mask of hatred was off at last, his face drawn with loathing as he continued. 'You were right: there's no way you could ever simply let Patsy go. Never. Greed and possession are second nature to you! There's only one way she's ever going to be safe from you.' He motioned with the gun towards the side door. 'Come on.'

'Where . . .?'

'Down to the basement. Come on!' Now that he was committed, the manager felt sharply elated, akin to the pre-match jitters followed by the big high following the kick-off. 'And no clever stuff. If we see anyone, we're doing a tour of inspection.'

The side door led to a passage past toilets, then left along to the main entrance vestibule. In the event, they met no one, duly crossing the vestibule, past the main stairs and across to the small stairway at the far corner which led down to the huge storage area and, at its furthest end, the boiler room.

There were in fact a couple of oil-fired boilers, the second one installed when the top tier of executive boxes were upgraded with glassed-in fronts and heating. Walton motioned the Chairman across to open a tool cupboard in the far corner. Abruptly Oxted swung round, trying to reason with him; but the manager motioned curtly for silence, instead indicating a wrench among other tools on a rack.

'Adjust it for the fuel-inlet valve—to loosen that pipe junction.'

'What . . .' For once Oxted's voice had all but gone. 'What the hell for?'

'It's the way you property sharks do things. The old racket of insure-and-burn.'

*

179

Kate Lewis's presence at the Bullring wasn't a total breach of trust. Had Taff chosen to confide in her and explained his plan to use Ingram to panic the guilty Chairman into an act of self-incrimination, she would have known better than to seek the interview at the Bullring. As it was, her compulsion to be at the centre of the action had prompted her to ring Oxted in the hope of an interview. Much to her surprise, he had agreed.

'Give me ten minutes,' she told Jason Moyle and the sound engineer, 'then go up to the top floor and have your gear ready in the reception area outside the Chairman's suite.' She got out of the car, then leaned back in. 'If you hear any yells or activity, OK kiddies, come in shooting.' Then, unable to contain an excited giggle, she added: 'And if you see any police arriving, tape them as well.'

It was as she was crossing the vestibule to the main stairs that she noticed the blood. There was a lot of it, dripped in a trail from the central door marked toilets across to the smaller stairway in the corner. And, when she checked it with her foot, she found it was still moist. She went through the central door, following the trail down the passage, past the loos, along to the side door into the manager's office and finally to the smashed display cabinet.

Like the old cub-reporter gag about following fire-engines and ambulances, she thought as she hurried back along the trail, across the vestibule and down the stairs. Reaching the basement, she found that the blood led along beside huge racks of stored seating. She was about to nip back up to alert Jason when she heard a shout from an open doorway at the further end of the cavernous storage area.

Go for it, Kate! urged the lunatic voice of ambition, driving her along between the racked plastic seats towards the door: show them who's best! Scoop the buggers!

The pungent smell of fuel oil was in the air now as it seeped from the loosened pipe union.

'Pull it clear,' Walton snapped. 'Let it flow!'

'You're mad!'

'No, just desperate. Desperate to save Pat from you. There's no other way!'

He nodded as the tycoon at last pulled the pipe clear, oil jetting from it to form an ever-widening pool on the floor, then he motioned with the gun towards the other boiler. 'And this one. Hurry!'

'Money! A written guarantee! Name your price! Anything!'

In answer, Walton stepped forward to whack the revolver barrel savagely across his face. 'Hurry, I said!'

He stepped back to watch in grim satisfaction as Oxted, sobbing now with pain and fear, fumbled to unbolt the second pipe junction. Quickly Walton stooped to lift a bottle of petrol from concealment by the door, removing its cork and stuffing a tissue into the neck to fashion a Molotov cocktail.

Already the floor was awash with oil, rivulets streaming out to the storage area to spread under the stored racks of plastic seating, the sickly-sweet fumes heavy in the air.

'Also desperate,' he snapped, 'to stop you destroying this great club. That's why we gave the Judge—your so-called friend—the evidence on what you were up to. No one better, being as he was urging that all League clubs be barred from private ownership. Well, naturally. Since clubs exist for the community, they should be owned by the community, not by evil vandals like you!'

'You're burning it to save it?' Oxted snorted. 'Typical!'

'You, Oxted—*you're* burning it. As part of your damned scheme. Pat and I managed to work in that part of the plan along with the other stuff we leaked to the Judge. A very risky game, though, arson—as your charred corpse will show!'

'And Hartington,' Oxted gasped, pulling the second pipe clear so that fuel gushed from it to add to the deepening pool on the floor, 'why do that to him! Why set the Jacks on him! *Why?!*'

'To nail *you*, Oxted! Motive and means: no one else but you!'

'But—but leaving the poor sod virtually dead!'

'Just *scare* him!' the manager shouted, oppressed by the dreadful guilt of it. 'That was all Pat told Mervyn George to do! That and no more!' At first it had been almost like a fun thing, the elation of gathering the evidence, the pair of them driven with fervent excitement, feeding the Judge piece after piece . . . building to the ultimate ploy of framing the Gamelord with the assault . . . only to have it so tragically misfire: the poor old bloke lying there in a coma, Patsy phoning the hospital desperate for reassurance on his condition . . . 'God's sake, the very last thing either of us wanted was—'

'Murderers! The pair of you!'

'No! NO!'

Walton stepped impulsively forward, the gun levelled at Oxted's head as though about to blow out his brains. Kate, watching from near the entrance to the boiler room, let out an involuntary cry. The manager half turned—and, in so doing, gave Oxted the chance to jump him. Grabbing his wrist, the smaller man heaved wildly round to smash the gun hand down against the boiler, the revolver spinning away to splash into the oil on the floor.

For a moment, the two men staggered around, locked in combat. Then, by chance footwork, Oxted managed to trip Walton, heaving him backwards to sprawl full-length in the pool of oil. The Chairman lunged in feverish search of the gun, while Walton struggled to his feet and headed for the doorway. He snatched up the petrol bottle, then thrust Kate violently away and, backing out, fumbled to light the tissue.

The same second, Oxted found the gun, turning, raising it and pulling the trigger all in the one swift movement. The revolver, in fact a Spanish-made replica, clicked in vain. Twice more Oxted pulled the trigger before flinging the thing as he lunged forward.

He was a split-second too slow to prevent Walton lighting the petrol-soaked tissue and hurling the flaring bottle. Oxted lurched desperately aside, his shoulder deflecting it on to a pile of boxes stored in the corner. Miraculously, the glass failed to break, flaring for several more seconds before finally erupting in a ball of flame. Instantly the fuel oil ignited, a sheet of flame spreading steadily across the surface.

Oxted had escaped from the boiler room well ahead of

the flames, only to be grabbed by the manager. The two men crashed heavily against the nearest rack of stored chairs, their brief struggle culminating in Oxted's flinging his assailant heavily aside.

Walton slithered backwards off balance to whack against the door-post just as the main blaze erupted in the boiler room. A huge mushroom of flame billowed out to engulf him and ignite his oil-soaked clothing. Screaming in terror, he tried to run clear, only to stumble and trip full-length into a pool of burning oil.

Already dense black fumes were starting to billow from the adjacent racks of plastic seats lit by the blazing oil beneath. Kate, edging back in shock from the inferno, was about to turn and run for the stairs when she saw Oxted groping around in the dense fumes. Wrenching off her coat, she wrapped it round her head and, crouching below the layer of fumes, ran forward. She found him and, grabbing his arm with both hands, dragged him clear.

They were barely away from the blaze when Oxted slipped and fell, choking wildly from the fumes. As Kate crawled back, she realized his feet and the lower part of his trouser legs were alight with splashed oil. Frantically, crouching below the black fumes, she managed to cover them with her coat, beating and pounding to smother the flames before heaving the man to his knees. The roar of the inferno behind them was by now so intense she had to shout into his ear, yelling for him to follow her but to stay below the fumes. Whether he heard her through the racket and his choking she wasn't sure, but she could feel him holding on to her ankle as she once again crawled forward.

Kate was no longer sure of the way. Certainly they were moving along an aisle between the rows of stored seating. But was she in fact leading them along a side aisle instead of towards the stairway?

The clouds of choking black fumes were becoming increasingly dense, pressing her ever lower for air, tearing at her throat, sapping her strength. Then Oxted fell again. She only knew because suddenly his grip on her ankle became a dead weight, dragging her to a stop. Worse, in turning, she inhaled a billowing lungful of the deadly fumes. Choking convulsively, she lay flat on the floor in a desperate attempt to escape the thickening black layer.

Kate knew she was finished. Gradually, insidiously, the awful weight of exhaustion rolled over her like the blanket of fumes, dulling her senses, drawing her down a deep, endless swirling hole . . . so that she was barely aware of the figure stumbling into and over her, grabbing hold of her, gasping in dread panic that he was too late to save his lunatic girl as he snatched her up and away from the clutches of death.

CHAPTER 16

Ponse Perry stopped in the entrance to the private ward, shocked by the patient propped in the bed. After hundreds of hours on the terraces, not to mention miles of war videos, he'd thought himself inured to violence. Now he found there was a disturbing contrast between the doing and the result.

Whereas the worser scalp burns were covered with open-meshed dressings, the visible areas of face skin were scorched bright red—a grotesque contrast, weirdly enhanced by the dark glasses, the right-hand lens of which had been replaced with a gauze pad. At the lower end, the bedcovers were raised with a large protective cage to keep pressure off the burned ankles and shins.

He was further startled when the patient spoke, telling him not to stand there gawping and gesturing a bandaged hand towards a seat. 'What's up, Perry?' The blistered lips barely moved, lending an oddly monotonous tone to the voice. 'Never seen a burns patient before?'

'Er—well, no, Guv. I mean, I thought by now—three weeks, like—I thought—'

'Three months, that's the minimum they're reckoning on—and only then if all the grafts take.'

'Cripes.' Ponse smirked, still ill at ease. 'Good job you was insured.'

'If you came here to get smart, you can just shove off again.' The patient paused for a spasm of coughing which, although not extreme, he seemed unable to check. 'Mustn't get excited,' he whispered at last.

'Understood, right.'

'Looking to do a piece for the fanzine, are you?'

'S'right, yeah.' Ponse nodded, focusing on the left-hand side of the dark glasses. 'The future of the club and that.'

'Jack Henderson's the board spokesman . . .'

'I don't want to hear nothing second-hand, Mr Oxted. See, from what Henderson tried to tell me, he didn't hear you right. Spieling on about abandoning the ground and—'

'Not spiel. It's what's happening.' The Chairman checked, breathing steadily for a while to relax his throat. 'The main stand burned out and the club's filing for bankruptcy. As for the players, you want to go ask Ken Bates at Chelsea, not me.'

'The stand was insured as well as you, Mr Oxted.'

'A bloody good job it was, kid, or I'd be a few more million out of pocket than I am already!' He started to cough again, gesturing with the bandaged hand for the editor to leave. 'Now piss off. You're making me ill.'

'Not half as ill as you're making the odd ten thousand Balham supporters, Mr Oxted. Ill and angry, that's what they are. I hope that Hampstead palace of yours is insured and all, 'cos I wouldn't give much for its chances—not if I was to tell 'em what prat Henderson tried to tell me.'

The Chairman was again gesturing for him to go, meanwhile struggling to control his laboured breathing. Ignoring him, the fanzine editor leaned across to move the bell push carefully out of his reach, then turned to beckon a second visitor into the room.

'Like you to meet my editorial assistant. Her name's Patricia Johns. Pat specializes in personal-insight pieces, know what I mean?'

Oxted couldn't recall having seen her in black before; but, as always, she looked stunning. She was wearing less make-up than usual, too, so that the lack of colour in

185

her cheeks lent her a frail, almost ghostlike quality, one unrelieved by the coldness of her eyes.

'Also, Mr Oxted,' she remarked quietly, 'I'm pretty smart at digging up dirt for exposé pieces.'

'You bitch.' Although down, the Chairman was by no means beyond retaliation. 'You vindictive bloody bitch!'

In answer the woman propped a briefcase against the foot cage, opening it with a snap to remove several documents. 'One or two items here which I'm sure you'll recognize.' She held them up one by one before his single functional eye before replacing them in the case. 'No comment? I'm sure a certain senior judge of your acquaintance would find them absolutely fascinating.'

'Which,' Ponse put in with a renewed smirk, 'could turn out a *lot* more expensive than the odd million or two extra investment in the club.'

Oxted was motionless now, the colour of his scorched face a livid puce, his mouth part open for the rapid panting necessary to defer another spasm as the fanzine editor remorselessly continued.

'Right then, before we get down to the exact wording, suppose we go through it in general terms.'

'Huh?' The sound caught like phlegm in the tycoon's throat. 'Go through what?'

'Like I said, Guv, the future of the Balham United Football Club.'

'How's the patient today?'

'He's fine, David.' It was a different hospital, the Balham Infirmary. Since it had no burns unit, Oxted was elsewhere—which was perhaps as well since his status would have been painfully eclipsed by the courageous old Queen's Bench judge. 'That brilliant surgeon. Mind you, the fuss they're all making of him, Vincent's going to be intolerable when I get him home.'

'Is there talk of that already?' It seemed amazing, given the leaden depth of that eternal coma.

'A few weeks—subject, of course, to complications.' There was a renewed vitality about her at the miraculous reprieve from widowhood. 'You didn't bring your fiancée?'

'The usual last-minute story.' He gestured in irony, explaining that TV journalists led even more irregular hours than CID officers, then added lamely that Kate hoped to get to the hospital later on. Isabel Hartington nodded, moving into the ward, only to pause as he asked: 'OK to talk? Any taboos?'

'Would I let you near him if there were?' She strode across to give her husband a quick kiss and hug. 'David's here, so I'll be off home to the dogs. See you tomorrow.'

'Take care, Tibs.'

'Ha—that from you!' To Taff's surprise, he was also graced with a swift kiss on the cheek before she left. Evidently his rating stood high on the Establishment scale.

'Sit you, David.' The Judge's handshake was several times firmer than at his visit the previous week, indeed felt virtually back up to strength. He gave the officer a grin in anticipation, reaching for papers and pen from beside the bed. 'This time I insist on the full, unexpurgated brief.'

Taff nodded and launched in with a sense of rising relief, along the way exorcising the self-imposed demons of guilt and anxiety born of his misconduct over the case.

The Judge remained for the most part expressionless, occasionally motioning for a pause so as to catch up with his notes, sometimes nodding approval or else grunting in surprise, but otherwise silent. Only towards the end, when the copper apologized how it seemed to have turned into a confessional, did he comment, eyeing Taff with an air of wry conspiracy.

'Just as well you're a chancer, David, or you'd likely not have cracked it.'

'But that's just it,' Taff exclaimed, 'I didn't! I let myself be totally blinkered by prejudice!'

'Oh? Against what?'

'City fat cats like Oxted—the Establishment Mafia! Old Chiefie Walsh even tried to warn me, but no, no, no!' With which he let go the full catharsis of how, compulsive Welsh Liberal that he was, he had fixed on Oxted as the villain,

187

had reckoned to panic him into a giveaway via Ingram's warning and instead had forced the man's fatal showdown with Deep Throat.

'If Kate hadn't charged in there like a lunatic, Bryan Walton would likely have left Oxted unconscious at the heart of the fire, the arsonist trapped by his own insurance fraud, and—' he gestured in massive humiliation—'and, damn me, I'd have believed it! Either that or I'd have reckoned Oxted had set up his own suicide in a typically spectacular and extravagant fashion!'

There was a pause, the advocate eyeing the detective with rueful sympathy. 'Well, perhaps you'll feel improved for ventilating it now.'

'Except, don't you see, the bastard's actually better placed now to kill off the club than he was before! The main stand burned to the ground; the entire insurance money going straight into *his* pocket, to pay off prior loans he'd made to the club; a merger the only hope of salvation for the players. Damn it, his deputy chairman, Jack Henderson, virtually spelt all that out earlier this week. The best we can do now is to embarrass the little sod with that appendix to your report.'

'Ah.' The Judge laid aside his pad so as to ease his gaunt frame around under the covers as he muttered about bedsores. Finally he nodded, adding an apology of his own. 'You see, David, I regret to say you've fallen foul of a stray deception of mine. That appendix—there's precious little of it one could ever publish.'

'But—I mean, look, it was all—'

'All sitting there in my safe at home, yes, only needing a final polish before I took it to chambers, aware that the duplicitous Virginia would promptly leak it to her masters—' he gave a dry chuckle—'to Toad Timpson, in fact, who would then have leaked it to Chairman Oxted, who just might have panicked enough to revise his plans for the club. He might. I'm afraid I was indulging in a devious game of bluff, you see, David, sheer bluff.'

'So—er—so you had no intention of publishing the appendix?'

188

'Not with such unsafe corroborative evidence, regretfully no. I'm sorry.'

'So—' Taff sighed in frustration—'so he's laughing all the way to the bank. As usual, the fat cat gets fatter.'

'There's a compensating irony,' the Judge murmured, laying his hand in consolation on Taff's. 'That so-called final draft of my report was also a deception, going in fact far further in its recommendations than I intended. It was a version designed solely for the eyes of Virginia Cohen's masters. I knew it would set the politicians in a frenzy, so I wanted to leave myself room to negotiate a compromise which would in fact achieve precisely what I wanted rather than the overly radical reforms I'd specified in that first draft—what we might call the deception version.'

'Very ironic,' Taff groaned, 'since that version's now been leaked all round and most of it spelt out by the media.'

'Indeed.' He chuckled, shaking his head. 'And since it was my dear Tibs who leaked it to her chum at the Beeb, I fear I shall now have to stand by the recommendations.'

He broke off, his eyes wrinkling round with delight as he noticed the arrival of a second visitor. 'And here, David, is your Tibs. Or rather, your Kate.'

'Kathy,' she corrected, stepping forward to shake his hand but somehow ending up giving him a kiss. 'Kate's just for the screen.'

There was an exchange of mutual appreciation, His Honour exclaiming on the pleasure of meeting a media celebrity, Kate on the privilege of meeting a Queen's Bench judge before then inquiring on his medical progress. Taff could sense her underlying excitement, however, so that eventually he asked what on earth had happened to make her so bright-eyed and bushy-tailed.

'A small visiting present,' she chuckled, taking a cassette from her bag and moving to put it in the video as she switched on the linked TV set. 'You're getting a preview of my piece on tonight's News.'

She pressed the play button, moving back to hug her boy while the tape flickered prior to yielding her image along with her voice.

Mr Oxted telephoned me from his hospital bed where he is recovering from severe burns received during the recent massive blaze at Balham United Football Club of which he is chairman. After first thanking me for saving his life during the fire, Mr Oxted then asked if the following message could be broadcast for the benefit of the many thousands of loyal Balham fans anxious for news regarding the future of their great club and its famous ground, the Bullring.'

A montage of shots showing Oxted, the actual fire, the team and so on, then commenced as backing to the chairman's taped message.

Balham United will go on. The Bulls will survive this present tragic setback just as they have others in the past. Talk of a merger with Chelsea—or for that matter with any other League club—is totally without foundation. The rebuilding, both of the burned-out north stand and also of our once-great League team, will commence with the minimum of delay. Along with all this, the club has plans to invest also in a state-of-the-art cell system grass pitch and to replace both kop-end terraces with all-seater stands.

'Notwithstanding any insurance pay-outs, all this will necessitate a massive injection of fresh capital. To acquire this, the club plans to approach Balham Borough Council with a partnership offer. The offer will include two seats on the board with full voting rights. This move is long overdue: for a club which serves the community should by rights be in partnership with that community.

'One further point: the larger of the new stands will include full premises for the Bulls' official supporters' club; furthermore, a voting seat will be made available on the board to an elected member of the supporters' club.

'Finally, when completed, the new north stand will be dedicated to the memory of one of the great Balham

United troopers of all time, Bryan Walton, and will be known as the Boss Bryan Stand.'

'So there, Taff boyo,' Kate teased with heavy irony as she moved to switch off the video. 'It just shows how easy it is to misjudge these whizzkid property types. Turns out Ted Oxted's really just a gamelord with a heart of gold.'